*Dedicated to Alvina Harris*
*And Kim Jordan*
*Miami Gardens, Florida*
*For your love, support and friendship.*
*Eye love you both dearly.*

*And to the memory of:*
*Jacquessa English*
*And Shaun Ermilus*
*God loves and God never makes a mistake*
*Your life and legacy will live on*
*forever*
*May God give your loved ones*
*Strength to endure another day.*

*Bestselling author Dapharoah69*
*The KING of Erotica*

# Battle

# Plans

BY DAPHAROAH69.
LARRY WILSON, JR
AND THE KING OF EROTICA

INTRODUCING OUR NEW MR. MEAK PRODUCTIONS 2010

## PRESENTATION COMING THIS SPRING

INTRODUCING OUR NEW MR. MEAK PRODUCTIONS 2010

*The King of Erotica*

DAPHAROAH69

PRESENTATION COMING THIS SPRING

# PHAROAH
## THE AUTOBIOGRAPHY
COMING 6.26.20.10
HIS 33RD BDAY

# L / Λ \ Ř ® ¥

Larry Wilson Jr/The King of Erotica
## GOULDS, FLORIDA

ISBN 978-0-578-06551-9

Front and Back Cover Photos by Larry and John Wilson
Photo shopped and text by www.LaFrecnhInk.com
Back Cover by Miko Evans

Published by Larry Wilson Jr.
Dapharah69 and The KING of Erotica™, Goulds, Florida

Meak Productions Flyers
of the KING of Erotica by Miko Evans.

Meak Productions Talent Agency represents Larry Wilson

## Publisher's Note

Damn! This would be the opening of my 8<sup>th</sup> book, The King of Erotica™ 6: B/a\ttle Pl/a\ns. Eyes didn't follow trends and never followed a formula in my life. Eye'm guided by the radiance of my eyes and eye watch my words, so eye use "Eye" instead of "I" in my writing at this point, at least for right now, to elevate my craft to the level EYE see fit! That's a way of me keeping an "eye" on my words and what eye say. *That's* the power of writing. Limitless. So why should eye limit myself when it comes to the ebb and flow of my writing? Eye have *always* been a writer, even before eye knew the cultural impact it'd have on my own life; even before I knew the things eye write would impact and influence thousands upon thousands of people. When other kids were outside playing with toys *eye* was creating characters dignified by the ignorance of my age. Nonetheless, that was the beauty of my writing back then. Eye had an old soul and that soul guided my pen and pad. I scribbled my emotions without a care in the world. Granted, writing saved me from committing murder, espionage and treason against my soul. Writing was therapeutic for me, long before eye understood what being a Pharoah was. Long before eye was a Pharaoh. Eye *loved* a challenge and shunned easy things. Yes, eye have *failed* shunning easy dick and pussy over the years; eye failed the one night stands that had me open wide, blind and well spent when the sun rose and the lover of the moment had packed and left me without another phone call to see how eye'm doing for the rest of my life; often succumbing to the pleasure of busting a GOOD NUT over logic and reason, the weakness of my flesh is a monster of the Creator's design. But hey, that makes me Larry. But as

A

far as my hustle, my drive and the driving force of my intellect, eye never waivered. Even if it appeared that eye have done so. No MATTER what cums or comes my way eye keep going. Eye don't never stop. Even when eye rest, eye don't stop.

Eye Am. Blessed. That the GOD created me, my being, from the combination of opposite sexual seeds. Eye am: blessed. That GOD chose me to do such a marvelous thing with words. The path to greatness was met with quick sand and graveled roads. *Jealous* warriors were out for my blood and only tasted my nut. Eager, green-hearted monsters carefully placed in my family tried to keep my soul at bay. From my body, mind and heart comes my desire to live. A generational curse used to hinder me. But eye broke free. After the scars healed.

This was by far the easiest book eye have ever written. Eye had fun with this. Eye must admit eye was going through some trying times while piecing this together. Still dealing with the aftermath of a somewhat stagnated, procrastinate equation.

Cutting off certain family members was the hardest thing eye ever had to do, but it was a necessary thing to do if eye was to elevate in my craft on my terms. Not theirs. Changed my phone number and didn't give it to my mother at all. Mother hindered my growth as a writer. Larry had to separate himself from Mommie Dearest and build my own way. If eye succeeded or failed depended solely on Larry.

This is my life, my passion and writing breathes in me the way air circulates. Eye know you all thought eye was going to do some sexy book cover, like eye always do, and in this eye played around with a very new concept that beckoned for attention.

Eye knew eye was going to change it up. Eye had to. Eye didn't like folks trying to figure me out, so eye had to do something to keep you scratching your heads.

Eye always focused on the trails and the good times and the things that made me Larry Curtis Wilson Jr.

Eye write as three Alter Egos: Larry. Dapharoah69. And The King of Erotica™.

And that's who presents this conception, procreation chapter to you.

The King of Erotica™.

Yes, bitches. That's me. Eye'm one blunt asshole. The King of Erotica™ was the part of me that didn't care about nothing and no one. This was the part of me that was dark and gruesome.

This was the part of me that will survive no matter the environment. This was the part of me that would walk in your church, get in your Pa$tor'$ face and snatch that robe off his late ass to see what he was really wearing underneath and dare you to get smart. Eye knew a Pa$tor, in the West Kendall area, that wore panties under his dress pants and went on to preach about homosexuals going to Hell. Chile. Jesus never bashed the gays, and he died for us all so kiss my black ass if you didn't like the fact that eye'm bisexual, bitch.

*What would Jesus Do?* he asked the church. Eye raised my hand a few Sundays ago, sexy in a two piece suit minus that itchy ass tie, and said, "Eye know what he won't do. He won't be wearing panties under his pants."

You should have seen his face hit the floor. The place went up in flames, literally. Everybody had something to say and half of them were undercover, slutty ass whores. Three of the men were gay porn stars that wore masks

C

over their faces in their videos. But their tattoos didn't lie, baby.

I sat there, content, eyeing his lying ass. He didn't know whether to run or duck or say boo. I wasn't finished. Faking a yawn I said, "Jesus wouldn't be bashing the gays and bisexuals and lesbians and the *transgenders*. Jesus was a man of love. Show me in the Bible that Jesus hates us. And don't show me no Leviticus chapter bullshit, verse whatever because that Era is over and Jesus wasn't alive in human form yet so miss me with the abomination, the blood-is-on-my-hands bullshit. Try to put me to death bitch eye'll split your head down to the white meat, as my second Mama Jackie would say."

Eye was asked to leave. Eye told his fat ass, "Make me. God said come as eye am. You want me out bitch throw me out. Stop preaching lies. Jesus didn't hate us. So why should you?"

Case. Closed. The King of Erotica™ will make you lose your religion for the greater cause of good. Religion and spirituality are two different things. I am spiritual. Evil assholes hide behind religion, which is a form of conditioning. I could give two shits about The Pope. Yes, the front cover is dark. It shows the dark side of me. And yes we all have a dark side. Most people are in denial about their dark sides, but this volume is preparing you for the arrival of the King of Erotica 7: PHAROAH. My autobiography, which is 97% done and looks to be a 700 page affair. An excerpt of it is on page 325 called "The Pail Man." All praise and thanks for my blessings go to God, that is Jehovah, for those who don't know what eye'm talking about. Not JayHova. Jehovah. Jesus' father.

Eye will leave you now. Eye love you all and thank you so much for your love and support.

D

**The King of Erotica ™**
**The Battle Plans**
**Conception**
**Da.pharoah.6\9**

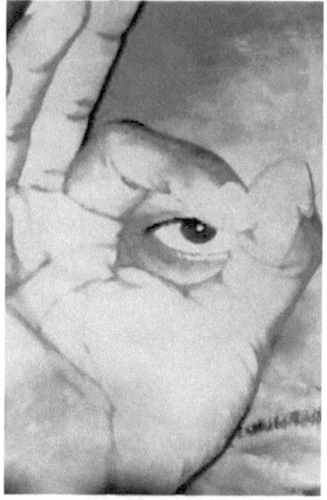

Eye had no sense of direction for the King of Erotica 6, but successfully reaching the 6th installment, eye felt something tugging on my subconscious. And it was painfully strong, something eye had to endure yet wasn't equipped to surpass. Lack of intelligence, maybe. Lack of energy. The fear of the unknown that checkered my past; this notion chased me like *The Blair Witch Project*.

Frantically running through the darkness in a drunken stupor, yet looking back and seeing nothing but fear chasing me and eye wasn't intoxicated.

That Voice in my head called me.

*"Yo! Yo! YOOO KING!* Hey, *you!* Billy bad ass. You sexy muthafuckah," it went on curtly and my mouth fell open while looking into the reflection of my eyes via my iPod screen when eye was shuffling Janet Jackson songs.

E

"Yea you," it continued. "Eye *let* you collaborate with the white little angel on your left shoulder but baby, hey you sexy tall glass of water it's *my* turn. Eye'm on and was always on your RIGHT shoulder. All that innocent shit the Angel of Good Fortune popped to you, all that non-violent bullshit I want you to dismantle it. *Throw* it away. Send it off…and *forget* about it. Let me open your eyes to the secrets of the world.

"Eye love wearing black, *baby*. And eye got some good black dick so you'll have something to pacify while you enjoy your verbal and intellectual stay. Let the devil in you sip some bourbon over herbal tea; pick your brain for a quick second.

"Let's collaborate, *King*. Let's elevate your craft. Make it black; release the demons from your closet. Don't *believe* that man of color bullshit, yo. *You're* black. Shun the way it's been done with books. You're a PHAROAH. Break the norm, raise the bar, set the standard for literary writing. Use your life, put it out there, sacrifice who you used to be by breaking the Cycle, then Writing what kept you so Silent since you were a small abused child."

Eye thought about what It said, and eye didn't know what or how to feel. But something inside me stirred, and It became a metaphor for knowledge. Eye had to find out.

Black was more than a darkened sky, infinity, forever, your cavity-infested heart or battle scars. You wear your feelings under a tough exterior no longer redundant on your familiar shoulders or sleeve.

Eye closed my eyes, in the belly of the midnight hour, and eye felt myself letting go. Mama hated me. Daddy hated me. Nothing was going right. Two of my brothers talked about me more than my enemies, and eye had it up to HERE.

F

So eye listened. Eye had to start living for me.

Gunja smoke vaporized artificially conditioned air. Inhale the earth, become the earth eye fell, as if in a trance, into another part of myself eye never knew existed.

Books open, computer screen continuously glowed in my chiseled face.

Eye fell asleep sitting up, my body leaning to the side of either elbow, my head flat on my arms like a soft pillow.

Eye dreamed instantly, like Satan pressed "pause" and it all came to some sort of surreal afterthought pulsating behind a forgotten yet lingering memory.

And in my *dream* eye was watching myself awaken with a start, grab a pad and jot this shit down before my mind becomes as oblivious as infinity's collective strangulation of death.

Eye received a phone call in this dream. Eye didn't recognize the caller yet eye answered anyway. Eye was King of my erotic Throne, nothing challenged me in my own train of private though.

All that flashed in my glowing cell screen was CELL PHONE, LOUISIANA.

One of my homeboys, and a dear fan (who has all my books, all 7 of them and said he couldn't wait for the KING of Erotica 6), was on the other line.

"Yo, KING!" he enthused energetically.

"Yooo, Niggah!" eye said excitedly. He was my dawg!

"You finally stopped writing long enough to receive a Niggah's call."

"Aw, man sometimes all work and no play equals overrated nuts and a niggah must drain the weasel before a quick nut to receive an *effective* nut."

"*Yooo!* You *always* keepin' a bayou Niggah on game."

G

My eyes were glowing. "Well we rockin' flip flops and tube socks down here in Goulds, Niggah."

"Ha, ha. Goulds. Ain't nobody *heard* of that shit. Who the fuck claiming some shit like Goulds?"

"Have you eva been here fool?"

"Hell, naw! Never heard of it till eye met you and you said you were from there."

"Well shut that shit up niggah and go get some beads courtesy of flashing sagging perky titties, Niggah and get off Goulds jock."

"You be slaughtering a Niggah verbally."

"Man eye ain't anything special. Eye'm my own goddamn Mardis Gras. Talkin' 'bout a bayou, niggah come search the pits of the wreckage aligning the outskirts of my wounded heart."

"You sexy as fuck. Jus' kno' dat, Niggah."

Eye was beaming, grinning then smiling. My halo was dimming above head. Didn't notice it, though; nor did eye notice the fading light across my bleeding heart.

"Thanks, man." My flesh was activated. He took me off my common denominator. The 14 hours a day eye write was unexpectedly compromised. *Intruder Alert! Intruder Alert!* but eye was deaf to the alarming sound and blind to the alarming signs.

The snake made his move disguised as my ally.

He said, "Your heart is draped with the soul of New Orleans."

I chocked on my spit. Where did that come from? Why did he say that? "*Goddamn*. The *soul*? The soul is *deep*, brothah. As deep as blackness. Darkness. Eye don't think eye'm deserving of such a compliment."

"But you *are*! And the way you speak! You make cursing seem so flamboyantly sexy AKA maintaining a

H

level of masculinity. Thugs wanna fuck you. Eye know a few married homeboys who said they want their first in the closet gay experience to be with you."

*Why is he trying to flatter me?* "Well damn!" eye was alarmed, and part of me didn't believe it because eye don't place myself on a pedestal when eye'm the Son of the pedestal maker. The pedestal would have never been made or the object of affection if not for God's programming of the pedestal maker's brain and intelligence. That's the power of the GOD eye serve. His name is JEHOVAH. The King of Kings. Lords of Lords.

Eye was somewhat shell-shocked BKA stunned 'cause, like my friend with his ramblings about never hearing of Goulds and never having been here, eye on the other hand heard of New Orleans, all the bayou, Madis Gras stuff, witch craft, yea, yea, yea bullshit and never been too, drove through or stepped one FOOT in Louisiana, and especially not in New Orleans. Didn't care to, quite honestly. I could Google or You Tube it if eye wanted to experience it that badly.

Eye didn't even read about New Orleans, but this architectural masterpiece was more famous than Goulds and he *knew* more about Goulds than eye knew about New Orleans if you really stopped long enough and averaged it out on an unbiased scale.

At that point it wasn't the Calliope Projects, the Wards or the Cash-Money-back-that-ass-up type Niggahs eye was afraid of, representations of the environments' successes and energetic rap songs keepin' it slow motion for me.

To some of those niggahs Master P was God. To some of those niggahs Juvenile was God. To some of those niggahs Baby was God. To a couple of those niggahs Lil Wayne was their Messiah.

I

Even with the biggest rap star in the world being from New Orleans—drop, drop, drop, drop it like it's hot it's the Carter!—eye *still* wasn't interested in reading up on New Orleans, but eye was a BIG fan of Lil' Wayne.

Eye wasn't afraid of being robbed, meeting people that may or may not like me or afraid of anything common and familiar. Oh, no! Wasn't afraid of ANY OF THAT! Black on black crime has become commonplace and familiar territory for the bucket of crab imitators, instigators and photographers.

Just the thought of Anne Rice living in New Orleans in a castle (eye think, according to the Voices), and the fact that eye'm still shivering and spooked from reading *Interview with a Vampire. The Vampire Lestat and Queen of the Damned* while eye was high on Gunja smoke eye actually tried to stop myself from fainting.

In fact it felt like eye had to vomit, the thought of stepping foot in a place she's from. Such a resilient, beautiful mind warped into the atrocities and monstrosities of blood, fledglings and gay vampires had me about to call out for God early.

Eye said, "Hold on, dawg." Eye barely got the words out. Knocking shit over, eye held the cusp of the epidermis covering my belly with a flat palm and broke the door down falling to my knees.

Before eye could call on God eye puked up everything eye drank, swallowed, chewed, sucked and ate.

Right in the toilet; barely making the toilet. Pinkish/greenish puke was on my clothes, floor, toilet seat and ugh the smell! Now eye had to take a shower.

Glad eye kept a clean bathroom, and eye was like a restaurant, didn't let too many people use my bathroom at *all*.

J

An *Out of Order* sign hangs in the middle of the door. And it was operative as a muthafuckah.

With that out the way eye felt it coming on the breeze of night, through my open bedroom window. It was a cool, *disquieting* breeze. Relaxed my skin yet quickened my heart, accelerating my pulse.

Wide eyed, eye swallowed hard. Eye was receptive to the Voices, like eye was an antenna.

Eye sincerely hoped that satellite sound waves haven't become compatible with my brain, muthafuckahs trying to read the King of Erotica's mind, since eye writes *nothing* but grueling, powerful shit passed off as GHETTO TABOO.

Eye said, "God, something this way comes. Protect me, Lord. You are the tried and true and the driver of my soul. Without you eye wouldn't be able to write a complete sentence, spell *sentence* let alone write a *book* of incarcerated sentences."

Took me a while to clean up the puke and then take a shower to cleanse my burning flesh. Negative thoughts swept my mind with the agitation of forgotten, deceased, raped slaves. Fucked, separated from kids, children, mother and father and abused and still had to go back to the plantation as the employees of the arrogant Caucasian employer.

To clean up the mess, eye used Pine-Sol and Comet the way haters dressed as motivators tried to use me. Once the bathroom was spic and span, drying Mop and Glo on the flo', eye poured two cups of bleach in the toilet and let it sit. *Then* eye cleaned out the tub.

The checkered tiled floor was so damn clean eye could masturbate, nut on floor and lick up my seeds with a smack of the lips. My shit finger lickin' good.

K

After eye put up the cleaning supplies, back into my darkened bedroom eye go, snatching up the phone from the greenish comforter. The cover to the Janet remixed album by my pillow, the songs were ripping to my iPod.

Eye was so deep in cleaning eye forgot he was on hold on the phone.

I put it to my ear. "Eye'm sorry, dawg. Eye'm back…are you still there?"

"It's no sweat. Eye was beating my dick, watching some porn."

There was a flicker of reaction in my flesh, but the flame died out.

The angel on my shoulder kept blowing out the black angel's fire, keeping the flames of hell at bay from my eternal belief window.

"Is that right?" eye found myself asking, intrigued.

I heard his seductive breathing. "Yea, wish that phat ass was here. Eye'd eat your pussy, Pharoah. Let me taste that erotic fruit."

"Niggah keep it G, anyway, dawg," eye said, PHEW, "Eye don't know about coming to New Orleans."

Eye tried to change the subject, but the more his breathing turned me on the more eye was about to go to the point of no return. He was quietly moaning, feeling himself and my dick was hard and eye was a deer caught in the headlights of an 18 wheeler and when that muthafuckah hit me it was *lights out, celibacy!* and eye was butt ass naked on my bed, gyrating to his beautiful, smoky voice. But eye didn't tell his ass that.

"Pharoah eye'm sorry for jacking my dick. Shit feel so goddamn good, niggah. Damn you should see me strokin' this gigantic snake. Hangs so low eye could push the head in my asshole."

L

*Oh my damn! My flesh is so weak!* "Man eye'm just writing," eye said, writing words across my dick with a closed hand as the pen and coconut butter lotion as black stationary paper made of circumcised foreskin.

That's how eye was feeling; finger fucking myself while his moans found the tunnels of my flesh along the crevices of my brain, more activity on the right side.

Eye was cooing and sighing, sounds muffled behind pursed lips, determined to remain meek, mute and quiet so eye didn't give away eye was pimping this Niggah's sweet, sweet thug voice for a quick, much-needed nut.

The instant eye thought it my toes curled, my torso raised, and eye spread my legs. The buildup was so intense I had to bite down on my tongue as eye came all over the sheets and not once did eye breathe hard, said a word or released a moan.

"You getting one, Pharoah?" he could hardly talk.

"Hell naw, niggah you need to stop. Try'na write now, dawg."

"Damn dawg, take off those panties and play in that pussy."

"Naw, dawg. Eye'm good." Eye swallowed my seeds (to burn in the belly of the return-to-normal whore AKA eye'm straight,) now Niggah time to kick you off the phone.

Acknowledging phone play would boost his ego and eye had to keep up my image.

"Pharoah. For real, come to New Orleans. Let a bayou niggah make love to intelligent country King pussy….hold on, hold that thought," he said.

Eye never been to New Orleans, damn it but didn't wanna say it in a mean way. Just never fascinated me.

M

Eye never been to no Mardis Gras, don't have one clue how it looked or what went on there, and STILL EYE Am the KING of Erotica, having become a bestselling author over and over.

Now EYE Am a sex symbol and everyone from select married women with buff husbands were secretly hitting me up, hoping and wishing to eat my boy pussy or give me some good head yet eye respectfully declined.

Said their tongues were so good eye wouldn't want a dick anymore.

*No*, no *girls*. That's what *sheeeeeeee* said. All the E's symbolize all the married Hoes who tried before you, sucking my dick from here to their husband's bedrooms and eye still wound up sucking the husband's dick for the taste. Well, eye used to do that back when eye was a teenager. Eye didn't do that anymore. Eye've matured. Yes, eye am a sinner. Eye confessed that with fear and trembling only to God. Not you select phony ass Catholics.

That's all eye needed sometimes: a quick nut. And eye was cool. Eye loved eating pussy and giving head equally. Didn't really have time to fuck. Books come first. So eye taste to remember the feeling. Eye suck then swallow the taste to remember the images.

Niggah suck, lips bend over my teeth, inhale then stop. *Down*...up, pull the intersections and veins on a dick to make his toes curl. My *throat* moist from rushed breathing impediments; when he cum, bitch eye do the lean back from the rush of nut.

In the air it goes, across his face and chest...navel, abs, and some was running down his balls and asshole and not a DROP got on me. You ain't my Main Squeeze, Niggah. Keep that gushy shit to yourself.

N

Eye'm just a too smooth, sexy, tall ass Niggah from GOULDS that was searching for love for himself.

Mike Lawry. Too real, too blunt, too blood raw with my shit, bitches.

My celebrity was influenced by everything but the Mardis Gras or New Orleans history.

Eye research a lot of things eye write for clarity with a character.

But in my own life eye disregard literature and eye write from my heart, so nothing seemed rehearsed or elegantly studied.

Didn't know about demonic bayous, where dead bodies have rotted to decomposed bones.

Eye never saw the shades lurking along the leaves of whatever trees rooted deep in the muddy sea beneath.

Now the niggahs eating flesh with bread, secret communion drinking blood as wine and eye shook with fear at the very thought. In my dream this was revealed to me emblazoned with gold and fire.

In the dream my skin smelled of cinnamon and ginger and a touch of salt and black pepper.

What made me loose dinner and puke was the inevitable surrender, my own well-thought out conclusion.

After he told me why he felt eye was the soul of New Orleans eye felt enlightened.

He told me when he came back on the phone. But he did this only after *eye* skipped the small talk and got right back to the thrill of the chase.

He said, "You're the soul of New Orleans."

Eye smiled without smiling with my eyes, the true definition of focus. Eye'm stagnant and procrastinate with my studies. Eye study and read things with a Chess mentality.

O

He continued, "You're complacent in architecture (sex symbol), your books are in the hands of all age groups over 18 along the patios and beautiful court yards, you're 32 (33) now and the iron work of your high cheekbones (you look like the Rock!), seductive, exotic eyes, and your flair, preamble and intelligence will be the same wrought iron protecting your casket and grave draped in alabaster and your rise and fall (and rise again, only they don't know this as of yet) is the subject of a few meetings. It's being heavily debated right now with major publishers about leeching your brand and swindling you out of millions in hard earned money. Gays love you. Bi's love you. DL's love you. Transexuals love you. Eye know a lot of straight men now reading your books. Straight women adore you for your candidness and thank you for keeping it real. And you *inspire* others through openly being bi, talking about your past and showing how sexy a man is by embracing his flaws. Eye admire you for talking about *living* with HIV and, best of all, you *still* admit you get on yours knees and give it all to God so faithfully. Your faith in God is moving mountains for you, bruh. *You* are *blessed.* Own your work, Pharoah."

"Appreciate it my friend."

"Listen to me. Eye dreamed this. Never sell The King of Erotica. Your nieces own it. Don't strip them of their inheritance. Those two girls are your *world.* They own all your shit, even your photos and images. Don't sell. No sale. Sharks in publishing are conspiring to take your books. They g'on try to take it like an ATV catalogue. No one has done what you're doing. And by the way don't *ever* come to New Orleans, that's what eye was really building you up to say; now that eye have your undivided attention. Don't come, dawg."

P

Eye was stuck like Chuck. "Why?"

"Because your arch nemesis awaits you here. It was revealed to me in a dream."

Eye hung up quickly and sat on the edge of the bed, rocking back and forth. Mirror in front of me. Truth. Trembling for some reason. He tried calling me back but eye didn't answer. His dream had me spooked.

Eye know what he omitted and what he didn't say. He told me eye was the soul of New Orleans but he *never* talked about, mentioned or brought up the tombs and graves.

Why would he omit that?

Hmm, who knew, but eye didn't like the feeling in my gut.


Eye thought about this in the dream floating on the waves of a deeper blue sea. This blue sea envisions the blackness, blue/black light bounced off my optic nerves.

What eye didn't tell him was that sharks in the publishing industry already came after me.

First, with JL King, author of On the Down Low. He hit me up to write *Some Men Wear Panties*. We came up with the title together. Initially, he wanted it be called *Men Wear Pink Panties* or some bullshit like that and eye hated it so we came up with *Some Men Wear Panties* and eye wrote the book in two days.

Eye paid this man $1,700 TO BE TURNED INTO A BRAND AND ALL THIS OTHER STUFF IN THE EXPIRES-IN-THIRTY-DAYS CONTRACT, shit that never manifested. Eye was a fool and people were warning me not to work with him but eye was star struck. Didn't listen. And my hard head made a soft ass.

Q

He promised a Pink Panties Tour, had me take my own photos and as the months peeled away he focused more on his *play* and fucking niggahs or inviting them to his house to smoke weed.

Then eye flew to Atlanta to meet him at Outwrite Bookstore with my now editor Kevin McNeir. Kevin was a sweet heart, but JL was the opposite. He was cool on the outside, but on the inside was something eye didn't like but eye didn't utter a word. After going over the Some Men Wear Panties edits, JL and eye had a couple beers at a bar around the corner from the bookstore. There, he invited me to his home later that night. Eye knew the play but eye played stupid. "Sure, eye'll come," eye lied, knowing what he was up to. He wanted to invite me back to fuck.

Eye never went, and *Some Men Wear Panties* was pushed back and back and back. He then started sending me text messages. "Eye wanna fuck you. Eye want some ass, lol," he would type. Eye said eye didn't get down like that so he played it off like he never wanted it in the first place.

Then he kept asking for the porn video eye made nearly 6 years ago.

So after writing a ten minute monologue for him for his play and never getting my fucking writing credit he promised, eye realized the game. He wanted me to write 7 monologues for him in a matter of hours and eye said "No." Eye deleted him out my phone and off my social networks, and put out *Some Men Wear Panties* myself. Eye never signed a contract with him to release the book anyway and eye'm *glad* eye didn't.

R

Then, back in September of last year, two thousand years add nine; eye secretly flew to New York behind everyone's back to meet up with a major publisher.

I was on pins and needles the entire time. I mean, the trip could quite possibly change my life and in anticipation of what was to come, I couldn't even sleep.

When eye got there, eye tugged on my carry on bag, maneuvering through all these New York folks at JFK Airport. A driver held up PHAROAH on a huge white index card with MATT finish and my name emblazoned my eyes, provoked a smile and eye approached the driver with the nod of my head.

He had big glossy, glassy watery eyes. "Nice to meet you, Dapharoah69." He shook my hand. His hand trembled, and eye smiled again.

"Please, call me Larry. Eye'm no better than you, bruh. All eye do is write books."

"You are always so humble. Eye follow you on Twitter and Facebook. Your daily updates get me through the day."

He extended an open palm. Eye walked ahead of him, nodding. "Thank you."

"The limo awaits." It was a HUMMER limo.

The rest of what happened is in The King of Erotica 7, PHAROAH, my autobiography. So until then divulge book 6. Remember, I didn't give a shit who liked my books or not. I didn't write for social acceptance or for any damn praise. Quite frankly I didn't give two shits if you praised me or not. But as long as you get something from it then my job was done, give God all the accolades and the praise.

The King of Erotica 6 begins now...

S

# K6

## THΣ BATTLΣ
P
L
A
N
S

Think Like a Niggah      13
Seduction      57
The Rolexx      75
Food Stamp      95
Illusions      107
The Rules      131
Distracting Undies      151
The Perpetrator      163

The Hard On                               183
CHEATERS                                  203
Girl you're Harpin'                       229
Joints, beer and the Cheating Lovers  245
REALITY TV                                279
Acronyms                                  309


Bonus:


The Pail Man                              325
Taken from PHΛ®OΛH
The KING of ∑rotica's Autobiography

# Think like a Niggah
## <u>Earthquake</u>

**Most people fear earthquakes**. It was perhaps one of the *worst* natural disasters in modern history. Considering what has happened to Haiti, my heart truly does go out. But eye had my own problems and eye could hardly afford to take care of myself let alone take care of others. Eye did send about a hundred dollars eye really couldn't afford to send to Haiti. And eye send another $20 through the Yele thingee bring promoted by Wyclef John's late ass.

And the 8.8 measured earthquake that tore through Chile was another shocker. When eye logged onto my Yahoo account on the internet that story was on the front page and as eye read it it said that the earthquake seemed to interrupt earth turning on its axis and that scared the shit out me. Because even eye knew well enough to know earthquakes ain't coming outta nowhere like this. Eye realized that when eye smoked pot and accidentally walked into the wrong movie theatre, thinking eye was about to watch Precious and wound up watching 2012.

Then eye got a link from a friend on Facebook. Her name was Samantha, and it was a video on You tube, about Jay Z and Beyawnsay Knowles being devil worshippers. Eye was shaking my head like oh God, not this shit again. But something in me told me to click it, so, smoking pot eye did so. And let's just say that eye wound up deleting his albums and her music off my goddamn iPod and had my ass in God's church that Wednesday night for bible study, getting over the effects of being high, but eye wound up reading Revelations in the Bible all the way to chapter 14.

And read the rest of Revelations when eye got home, with my mouth hanging half way open, smoking another blunt.

It's amazing what snapped into place when you smoked pot and read some deep shit. Maybe you should try it.

I myself never lived through an earthquake, but I do know a man who survived it. He's *my* man. And he survived the tremors of my pussy.

You know how I do. Being the seasoned professional I am, I shook Retani's young ass up, shook him away from those car keys so a bitch could go to Miami Knights, a happening club in Naranja, Florida, on Fridays and give another Niggah this pussy; eye shook that nut from his dick when I got home to shut his whining where-you-been-at-bitch ass up. Eye shook his wallet right out of his pants pocket to get me another outfit for Miami Knights the next week. Eye never wore the same outfit twice, just how I roll.

He worked for Bellsouth (glad he had an honest job and eye had free phone lines and free internet. *Hey!*), was screwing another bitch on the side (he thought I didn't know. The bitch was my first cousin so of course I was kept in the inner circles like his dick was some secret society), could barely spell "condom," always wanted to fuck me raw and wondered why I made him wear two condoms.

If a man told you he wasn't cheating and you knew he was *why* you would fuck him with no condoms, Ladies and gentleman? Eye'm just saying though. Seemed as easy as 1, 2, 3 to me.

Hell, why wouldn't *you* cancel that check and use your debit card for the purchase in another store?

Goes to show that even bitches that got it together needed to *get* it together.

When he got paid he gave me the money to pay my bills. That's the one thing I can say: the Niggah stayed on his job. He took care of home, mama then my pussy last. No matter how he drank, smoked and partied with the boys he always went to work on time and gave me my cash on time every damn week.

All he wanted was two hundred dollars to keep in his pockets and a few more hundred to pay his own bills, student loans, child support and car note.

And he was going to spend that $200 on his broke ass brothers. Buying booze and weed from Red Rooster Liquor store in Goulds, where eye saw rapper Ludacris promoting that nasty ass liquor a few weeks ago.

And his burnt Kermit the Frog looking ass wouldn't give a bitch an autograph unless eye shelled out thirty dollars for his liquor when my cell phone bill was due the next day. *Bitch*. Talk about stuck up arrogance. *Chile*.

Eye was cute that day, too. Went behind my man's back, hoping to get to him via Groupie status. Took me four hours to turn into a doll.

After he announced what he *wasn't* going to do for his obvious fans, Chile eye dug my panties out my ass, snatched out the weave extensions and pulled my brother's shirt from the fancy bow and let it drop to my knees and eye took my late ass home.

Forget 'ya, forgot 'ya. Never thought about cha, niggah.

I knew my man's heart. He had a big one, especially for his messed up backstabbing family. I couldn't *stand* his brothers Cash and Slash. Two dumb asses who wanted to make children but forfeit fatherly parental rights when they were born, secretly chasing tight male booty holes on those gay chat party lines.

When I started dating Retani, his family hated me. They actually came to my house and said, because he was paying

15 DAPHAROAH69

my bills, the money he gave me cut into the money they used to *swindle* out of him.

Chile, call the Better Business Bureau with that shit. And watch 'em tell you to get a job.

Retani didn't even let me spend my hard-earned money and I worked for DCF (Department of Children and Families, and had my own crib in Hidden Groove, in Naranja).

While most bitches fight their men to get what they wanted I didn't do that.

I had a different approach.

# Questionable shit

**This was what you do.**

And it was quite simple, actually.

Please pay attention, because a bitch wasn't giving you game free of charge for very long.

This was LTO information: Limited Time Only.

Um, Boo! Check it. Keep a Niggah pussy whipped and you're in the money.

Men paid for ass, men tricked with their paychecks, men made strippers feel like they won the lottery, men bought ass behind their wives back. Chile, that ain't no secret. Never think your pussy was golden when your man probably fucking his homeboy in the ass in your bed behind your goddamn back.

Don't act brand new, please.

There ya' go, Ladies and gentleman. I said gentleman because men were sucking dick, too.

Use what a man loves to your advantage while keeping it drama free, cute and your nosey girlfriends at bay.

Half those skanks were miserable, that's why a late bitch was always plotting to take another woman's man.

Never bring a home girl who has nothing around your man because she will use what your man loves to her advantage, smile in your face then WD-40 his dick with hater pussy and serve your dumb ass a sinful dish of backstabbers on ice.

I told Retani if he even sniffed around the New Buildings in Homestead I would cut his ass. Hoes over there had more drama than *Guiding Light*. They had some *this portion is brought to you by!* loose pussy like their ass and tits were commercials.

Get up in that loose hole niggah might walk away touched with that special gift: HIV. Eye saw half those Hoes in the HIV pill line at CHI when eye took my god sister to pick up her HIV medicine.

New Building bitches always in a bitch business. Fucking each other's men. Fucking each other. Some of those bitches got other STD's and passing it off as ABC's and 1-2-3's they're teaching their kids.

Disguising shit, like a bitch was blind. I didn't wear glasses, and I could see my clit when I took a piss.

Women having a secret pussy eating fest up in there and thought a bitch didn't know. I had a Mardis Gras mask on in the last orgy and a fire engine red wig. Eye had dental dams on stand by Chile. Plus eye was drunk and high.

Remember me now, bitches?

Several Niggahs up in the New Building sucked more dick than soap washing their nuts.

Keeping that shit real low while playing Above the Rim on the basketball court like they were reincarnating Tupac Shakur dressing in thug clothes and dirty ass sneakers.

Talking about the next Niggah gay Niggah YOU and YOU and yea YOU, TOO, NIGGAH was gayer than the out-the-closet punks walking around, and half of those Niggahs fucked those very same punks, talking 'bout they were in love and shit.

If all it took was a punk to suck your dick then something was wrong. You've been chopped and screwed, Niggah. One of those punks had AIDS and didn't tell you shit.

But you went home and fucked your girl with no rubbers, like your dick was invincible.

When I needed additional information outta Retani I would suck his dick like a rookie fresh into the NFL and *voila*! I was set! He was an open book. Told me all I wanted to know, just as long as I never gave another man his pussy he really didn't have a problem with me. He knew eye was a go getter bitch. Self-made Hoe.

Swallow his nut and he would tell you he'd swore he'd saw a puddy tat I did I did saw a puddy tat, Sylvester! Just like the cartoons!

He'll work three jobs to keep your ass happy. Let him get the pussy, pull out and then suck your pussy off his dick while shaking your ass to some Young Jeezy and tell him to call you his little dirty, pissy bitch and this man would die for you. Make it rain hundred dollar bills on his main bitch. Niggah would rob a bank just to eat your pussy on top of cash. They used to do it for me all the time.

Men love women who were willing to taste their own pussy without flinching. Cringe one time, game over. He switched to auto pilot and simply spared your feelings.

The minute you rub your twat and suck your fingers in his face and call him "daddy," he will nut instantly because men love a dirty slut. But you better be a lady in public. Or else he will go behind your back and fuck another bitch.

I hope you Hoes and undercover punks were listening, goddamn it!

You fulfill his fantasies he'll fill your bank account, feed your snot-nosed, disrespectful kids and beat their little asses to make them do homework.

I'm telling you, put on a short skirt with no panties and tell him you're his little dirty whore and you're IN THE MONEY!

Retani makes it rain in the clubs but makes it snow at home. And that's the way it should be, because I handles my shit.

I wouldn't care if you made more money than he did. He would fork the bills and let his woman reap the benefits.

The way to my man's heart was not through his stomach, fat bitches, that's some shit he told you because he didn't wanna hurt your feelings. When a man comes to your house to get his dick sucked and leaves with a plate of food then, shit you're the dumb ass.

Let me tell you the real secret.

# His Heart

**Ahem, the way to his heart was by fucking him to sleep,** keeping it on some home boy, home girl shit and when he opened his eyes and realized that you still got off your ass to go to work, still paid your bills, still took care of your kids, didn't need his ass, made him feel like a whore on vacation, told him to have his ass out your crib by the time you snapped the last button on your work shirt he will plead his love, his devotion and do anything for the pussy.

Gentleman, that goes for your asshole, too.

Men ain't using their hearts when they meet you, Hoes! Nine times outta ten his boys told him your pussy was like eggs over easy, good but uncooked like a motherfucker.

So he approaches you knowing he's gonna fuck anyway. So give him what he want, fuck his ass, and flip the script by showing him you got it going on through what you do for a living and send his ass home.

In fact, ladies, when you fuck his ass on the first date (you're grown, life is too short for all that *let's wait awhile before we go too damn far bullshit* when Janet Jackson sucked dick on Damita Jo, Hoes! Listen to "Warmth," of "If" from the *Janet* album) the minute he says, "I gotta nut!" hop off his dick, make him cum all over himself and tell his ass, "Ok, go home. It was ok, had better."

Even if he was "better" than any man you had keep his ego on simmer.

"Damn, Ma. I gotta go?" He'll look hurt, because his plan back fired. Think like a Niggah, bitches to keep a Niggah tamed.

Point at the door and light a cigarette. "Get the fuck out, dude. Thanks, but you didn't even make me nut."

Even if he did make you nut, think like a Niggah and say he didn't make you cum.

"Ma..."

"My Mama never got this pussy so can you go before I call the police. I gotta go to work, I got bills to pay and I gotta pay my car note."

Again, even if you don't have a car and catch the bus you told a Niggah that and if he asked where your car was say it was repossessed.

Send his ass home.

But this rule applied if you had your own crib.

If he picked you up and took you to his house, same thing. Fuck him and the minute he says those magical words, hop up and make him nut on himself and claim you gotta go to work. That shows a Niggah you're a go getter.

I wouldn't care if you bagged grocery, get off your ass when the sun comes up, do your hair, do your make up, look like a queen, read some Bible scripture, go to the bus stop (DON'T LET HIM DRIVE YOU HOME, HOES!) and text message, "Don't call me I'll call you."

DON'T CALL HIS ASS FOR THREE WEEKS.

Why? He's gonna call you in two days.

# When I was 17…

**So the way to his heart, once you get it, was through his** stomach, and then his dick.

My man would turn down a T-bone steak and eggs just to get a shot of pussy. But feed him that T-bone steak and eggs, and ride his dick till he nut and burp then the Niggah will take a bullet for you.

Mama always said "Baby, keep him full and his nuts the reciprocation. Meaning, empty!"

Trust me I know.

I used to be a fat bitch. Just nasty. Wearing my little sister's clothes to the clubs when I was 17 and thought that shit was cute. I was feeding Niggahs and working and giving them my money and was miserable. I was getting a "crazy check." I had the clinics and the hospitals fooled, thinking I was a nut case. Chile. I just wanted my own crib and got out my Mama's house. Guaranteed $1,200 a month. I knew how to get my papers. One Niggah named Mache used to come over to my crib just to eat up my food. When I gave him his plate he turned on the TV then watched cartoons while I sucked his dick.

I'm telling him I wanna be with him, and that I was falling in love, that I needed to lose weight so I could wear that Cindy Crawford shit for him and his eyes sparkling, laughing at Daffy duck, shoving his dick down my throat and by the time he came his plate was empty and he checked his watched and left without even closing my front door or taking his plate to the sink.

When I realized he only called when he needed some food and head I cut him off, got a new attitude, and moved on.

Then I met Dave. He was sweet, sincere and a virgin. He said he loved me but I knew what it was. I was the easy bitch and he never had pussy so he came to me to get easy pussy.

He waxed my ass more than my pussy and dick felt good inside my tight asshole, especially when he tongued it then sucked on it spreading my booty cheeks.

Oh my God. He was slow and so inexperienced but I let him practice because anything was better than nothing.

For the next two years we fucked, fucked, fucked. I was slowly losing weight, the fat falling from my face.

The Niggah had some good dick. The room was steaming, felt like a sauna, and I would do anything to keep him. I didn't know how to suck dick so he called over his second cousin Geisha, who was a gay man, and Geisha sucked his dick and showed me how to do it and my man told me to watch and learn. I did. Geisha could stick a dick down his throat, drop down and get his eagle on and toss it up like Tupac without missing a beat or breaking a nail. Once I learned he canceled Geisha and we fucked for another 6 months.

By the time it dawned on me that he was rehearsing in my pussy for his grand finale with a man behind my back, I canceled his ass, was heartbroken, put up walls, moved on and that's when it occurred to me. I was no longer a fat bitch.

I was one of the finest women in Dade County.

It was on then! Men who dissed me started chasing me. Hoes who called me fat and wrote me off were begging to be in my presence. I didn't feel too special with them, either. Women traveled in packs, not because they liked your ass (so don't flatter yourself, girls), they knew the more good pussy in the bunch the more attractive men were going to sweat them.

Why did you think your home girl brushed your ass off when she got the catch of the day, wrote your ass off when she got the catch of the week and canceled the entire friendship when she married the catch of the century?

Why did you think she had all her girls in her crew in her wedding, had the Hoes who fucked her past men behind her back on the invitation list, and bought a dress that rivaled anything in your closet?

Because she was thanking her home girls she used to boost her stock by letting them be in the wedding and the pictures (I used you Hoes to get my husband, I won!), danced with her husband at the reception in front of jealous Hoes and once she went on her honeymoon she cut all ya'll asses off, moved to another state and didn't send none of ya'll asses a Christmas card.

Gotta know the game. She used your ass to get that man. She got the man by letting all the sexy bitches in her crew talk all loud and fuck all his boys but you were the one who made him wait, never questioned him and told him you better leave all those bitches alone if you want this pussy and you ain't *getting* this pussy till you go to church with me, meet my folks, meet my mean ass brothers and you knew they were from Opa Locka and if my brothers liked you then I love you.

25 DAPHAROAH69

My brothers could spot a secret gay man. How? My brothers got Niggahs high and drunk and fucked them, that's how I knew.

So Hoes wake up. If a female was begging you to go out (or always begging you to come around), that Hoe was using you as bait to lure the lions (fine ass men). Once you get that lion keep him happy. Same way you got him was the same way you kept him. Don't switch it up. Men loved nasty shit in bed. Pussy was an adventure to these Niggahs. Get too emotional or slip up he'll do Survivor: Atlanta in his homeboy's asshole to forget about you.

Men weren't very emotional because half of them were raised to be scavengers; they were cut and dry, either/or. Either you make his dick spit or he gets someone to make it spit behind your back, bitch. Simple. It ain't mathematics. So what you got your Algebra book out for.

You gotta understand when a man was horny and needed that instant nut he would get on the Party Line and get a Niggah to do it. Cut and dry. Hoes came with too much emotional baggage and some grimy Niggahs just didn't have the time or need the drama. Some men loved freaky bitches. If you could swallow his cum in the bedroom and whip his Baby Mama's ass when she get out of line during the custody battle then he'll shoot a Niggah over you.

Men loved women they could made them feel protected without compromising his manhood. A woman that could hold down the fort in the event he was locked up or lost his job put a smile on his face. Sure, he was the man and was the protector but he wanted a gangster bitch who knew when to talk and when to shut the fuck up but when shit hits the fan he wanted a bitch that's gonna get out there and toss those guns up and make those bullets spit at the haters without hesitation.

Hesitate once; he's canceling your ass.

That's why petite Hoes marry Pastors.

# Prima-Donnas

**Men loved women who could hold their own like it was a** pair of nuts. Men love reliable bitches.

Let me tell you what really made a man's dick get hard. I wasn't talking about (or to) the Prima-Donna Niggahs. I wasn't talking about the Tinker belles who fronted with the boys playing 50 Cent and slapping the bitch's booties but when the sun set he put on some high heels, a Freakum Dress and took more dick than the colon could disperse last night's dinner.

This was for the REAL MEN. And this was the potion for getting his dick hard. It wasn't dope. Nah. It wasn't money. Nah. It wasn't his car.

Dope and money was an image. His car was an image. Men loved images.

That's why they watched other Niggahs fucking Hoes in porn videos.

You ever asked yourself why a straight man would watch a pair of nuts slapping pussy.

You ever asked yourself why a straight man would jack his dick to another man on film getting pussy.

"Goddamn that Niggah fucking the shit outta that bitch," my ex boyfriend said before eye met Retani. He was jerking his dick with a smile. I was sucking his nuts, drunk as fuck, weed crumbs mixed with his pubic hairs. My spit trailed his asshole and he took my hand and made me finger his hole, since it was lubricated.

That wasn't what got me. I knew well enough to know that just because a man wanted a finger in his ass didn't mean he was gay. That wasn't always the case. But a dildo, hell no.

What got me confused was when the man on film, porn star Justin Slayer (Niggah always fucked in shades and goddamn boots) made the bitch nut on his dick and my ex boyfriend was smiling like he won the lottery.

I slowed in suction, and looked at his reaction and then my eyes swung to the screen.

Justin Slayer pulled out the pussy and started jerking his dick. It was a camera shot with Justin only.

My ex shook with jubilancy, and couldn't take his eyes off this Niggah and he was humping my face.

"Damn, Justin, get that nut for me Niggah. Nut on that bitch face, damn Niggah I ain't gay but come nut on my face, Niggah. My brother used to nut on my face when I was 13 years old, when Daddy went to work. Hell, yea. I hated that shit but learned to love that shit."

*Questionable* shit, I tell you. Don't be too amazed what a man says when giving him some bomb head. He's liable to tell you his ATM PIN number.

He looked at me with huge tears in his eyes, my heart leaping at him admittedly saying he was abused in the past and gay.

I was devastated.

My ex boyfriend smiled painfully.

"Suck my dick, Trevor. Hell, yea. You look good in Mama's wig, Niggah. You gonna make me nut so you can jerk off and cum on my face. Don't get it in Mama's wig *this* time! Daddy didn't like that shit! Mama found her other wig with your nut on it and thought Daddy was creeping and had other Hoes wearing her wigs. She divorced him, remember but what I didn't tell you was that Daddy raped me and blamed me and beat me till I couldn't move. So be careful."

I bit his dick, made him scream and slammed the Patron bottle over his head.

*Faggot, bitch!*

I loved gay people, but I hated a man I dated or messed around with having thoughts of another man.

Sorry, Mama didn't suck shitty dicks. And I *didn't* date men who were abused.

Sorry, not *my* cup of tea.

But after a few days went by, I went to his house and once he opened the door, his eyes lowering to the floor I took his hand and said, "Mohammed, I understand. I was once raped by my uncle. And I used to hate him. But you know what helped?"

He whispered it, shuddering. I hugged him; I just couldn't blame him for what he went through.

"What did?"

"I gave it to God. Then I called a shrink."

But I battled this eternally. Despite what he went through I just didn't understand why some men were gay or messed around. As a black woman who had a home girl who contracted HIV through her husband cheating with other openly gay men, I had a hard time stomaching men being with men.

That was just me, though. I had my thoughts but I never questioned my gay friends out of respect.

Not all gay men were raped. I knew gay men who said they were born that way.

I remember when I went to college I wrote a paper on this, which I aced. I researched it and read books on it to the best of my knowledge.

There are some theories that show biological differences between heterosexual and homosexual adults. It suggests that people were born with their sexuality already determined.

The American researcher Dean Hamer published research that, once upon a time, seemed to prove that homosexual orientation could be genetically transmitted to men on the x chromosome, which they get from their biological mothers.

More recent research published by George Rice and George Ebers of the University of Western Ontario shed a heavy cloud of doubt on Hamer's theory. And in the end, eye doubted you were born with it.

Rice and Ebers' research also tested the same region of the x chromosome, but failed to come to the same conclusion.

Claims that the part of the brain known as the hypothalamus was influential in determining sexual orientation, have yet to be substantiated.

Biological explanations of sexuality were insufficient, in my opinion, to explain human sexuality.

I also wrote in my paper that science couldn't determine why a person was straight, gay or bisexual.

I wrote that the way they were brought up, their personal experience, being with people, having sex, learning what worked and what didn't, their confidence and their family background, religion and parent's expectations played a part in how they turned out.

I was telling my boy Drake that earlier today.

He was straight, so he said, yet I was always seeing him go to gay clubs.

He also got off on watching men bang chicks on porn videos. I know a lot of gay and bisexual men who watch straight porn.

My gay homeboy, Miss Classy, detests male porn. He said it's baseless and tasteless and would pop a Ron Hightower film in his VCR at the drop of a dime.

Eye talked to a lot of men, and sat back watching how they all acted in different environments like they were lab rats.

Eye noticed a few men were close to their best friends, and those men grew up without fathers. Always had to call the best friend for advice, when they were having bad days and when they needed extra cash.

So I told myself eye would never date a man who called his male best friend more than he called me as his woman.

Women had egos, too.

If he's so straight then why not watch two women fuck and suck each other?

Hell, that's what I was saying.

# Is it the Best?

**Men loved making Niggahs jealous, that's why they** swagger-jacked ideas and bit another man's style. What made a man's soft-shriveled-to-the-left penis a hard dick was when he had a bitch that had her own house, her own car, handled her bills on time, trusted him with her paycheck to flip it three ways then sucked, fucked and put his ass to sleep.

It was when she kept herself up, didn't use much make-up, was close to her family, didn't invite drama over for Hennessy, included him in her transgressions so he felt like he was solving some problems, loved God, cooked a good meal and gave him some good pussy.

That *truly* made a man's dick hard.

Everything else was said from the male mouth just for imaging purposes.

Men loved bitches that got it together like me on a Friday night when my hair, nails, Pop that Pussy Dress and heels were check, good, check, better and check, stunning.

31 DAPHAROAH69

He'll keep your hair and nails done. He'll buy you what the fuck you wanted.

He'll put weave in your hair just to pull that shit out when he fucking you in the ass from the back. Men love to damage shit and make a Hoe sweat out her hair dos.

That's why they spent so much money getting their women's hair done. Imaging purposes, ladies. Come around him looking dirty with a nappy fro and he would call his jump off and fuck her.

Jump offs always stayed readily available, fixed up and cute.

Jump offs had per diem pussy.

Men loved when they felt they devastated the pussy and your lace front wigs with it. Men love tearing shit up. How many men you knew told a woman, "I'll make love to you when you want me to?" Not many.

And you wondered why Boyz to Men were a defunct group with no more hits. Men these days were like, "Where the good pussy at?"

*"Girl, I'ma tear the pussy up!"*

*"Ma, I'ma fuck the shit outta you and I want your home girl to suck my nuts while I make you come."*

Men were beasts in the bed now, but don't read too much into the fireworks display. Don't let a man fool you with his lyrical word play.

All men spat game when they wanted some pussy. Don't believe the hype. He's a MAN, not PUBLIC ENEMY.

Half of them had number 2 pencil dicks; some of them had huge horse dicks and couldn't use it, couldn't stroke the pussy with it or make a bitch skeet, skeet to save her life, secretly wanted it in the ass, probably already had it in the ass and always wanted a bitch to lick his ass.

Um, no, Niggah.

Some of them thought by sucking my pussy really fast meant for dependable pleasure. This wasn't the Boy Scouts!

You weren't rubbing two twigs together to get a spark and some smoke.

You were eating pussy and that required smarts and some damn sense.

You gotta do more than suck my clit to eat from my plate.

Anybody could eat a steak, but goddamn it you don't forget about the vegetables and the yellow rice.

A few of them could fuck really well but they kept asking, AM I GOOD? IS IT THE BEST? all day and you wound up faking an orgasm to get them off you.      If a man couldn't tell when you're faking orgasms then he's a bitch ass Niggah anyways.

Any real man who truly got pussy like he bragged about would know when a bitch faked.

Niggah if you fucked me nice and good I wouldn't have to tell you shit. My pussy farting and my moaning and my nails in your back and me doing My Little Pony Tricks all over your face would *tell* your illiterate ass everything you needed to know.

Men who couldn't read could read a clit in your pussy with aplomb. Make a dumb ass man feel like he's W.E.B. Dubois and he would kill a bitch over you.

And a percentage of these men had breath that was so stank you had to pray for Jesus and get a nut just to get them out your face. And there was an anecdote for *that*.

As a woman keep a little dick man's tongue in your pussy and close your eyes and pretend he's Omar Tyree. You also kept your pussy in a stank breath man's face.

Better he breathe halitosis on your clit instead of your face.

For men who couldn't fuck, get his money.

You stayed in a desperate man's wallet by teasing his ass until he took it. And the last thing I'm going to say was this.

Women.

33 Dapharoah69

If you didn't like it rough or in your stomach get a little dick man.

So when he took it or tried to ram his dick in you it would feel like a finger in your nose trying to get out a bugger.

There would be nothing to worry about.

Boom.

I was done.

# Broke Whores

**I have a friend named Messy Sletty. She's a sexy bitch. She** had nice titties given to her by an underground plastic surgeon, a huge bubble ass that saw more Botox injections than Beyonce's face and dick-sucking lips.

She had it all, but she was a broke whore. How could you have it all as a broke bitch? It took money to get what you got and more money to maintain it. This bitch talked about everybody but her damn self. She had a husband.

All he wanted was for her to be faithful and to suck his dick when he wanted and she could have everything, including the mirror on the wall telling her she's the fairest of 'em all and the keys to his Benz.

But she *didn't* suck dick and when she bitched at him for not eating *her* pussy he dumped a 32 ounce bottle of Old English on her weave and he dropped her like a bad habit and this bitch had the gall to come over to my crib and ask for fifty dollars because she didn't have money for the city bus so she could go job hunting. *Hmm.*

Eye didn't suck dick for free and eye damn sure didn't let a man dig in my pussy free of charge. My pussy wasn't voting for Obama and it damn sure didn't need "Change."

Sorry, baby.

My pussy sometimes made earnest money so if I gave her fifty dollars that would mean I fucked my man for free because I gave Messy Sletty the money I made from taking his big dick. Sucking my teeth, I looked at the ditzy bitch like get a clue, Hoe. Go get your ex husband back and suck his dick for your monthly allowance till you find a J-O-B.

I was tired of these women saying oh I didn't suck dick yet you wanted your man to take a bullet for you. If you couldn't take come from his dick with your lips why should he take a bullet for you dumb Hoes.

You didn't want another woman taking your man then keep his stubborn ass by getting your knees dirty. Suck his dick like you never liked a testicle before. My clue to you was simple. Go find a good man. Give him some good head, some good ass and some good pussy…cook him a good meal, pour Crystal Louisiana Hot sauce on his steak and double fry the onions. Tell him he's a handsome sonofabitch and that he has some good tongue and over-the-top stellar dick skills. Once you do all of the above he will call you his bitch *but* treat you like his Queen. But this is the fine print: make sure he has a career…not a goddamn 7-11 job. You didn't want to be sucking, cooking and fucking for a man who made minimum wage and wasn't guaranteed a definite forty hours a week.

Sorry, baby. That's where I draw the line and when eye draw it eye wasn't standing in line for welfare, food stamps or a WIC coupon for some free milk. I appreciate the man for his goals and for breaking the "white man is holding me down!" mold by getting a job but all work ain't good work and you'll be one pissed bitch if you settle for the bag boy at the supermarket and he gets ten hours next week and he couldn't even buy you a pair of panties from the Kmart Clearance rack.

Got Milk. No, Bitch. Check, Please.

# Pussy and the Gangstah

**His head bobbed and weaved between my sweaty legs** while my twat wrote a song on his slick tongue. And it wasn't Alicia Keys' "Superwoman," either. Yes, I was a Superwoman. Taking a dick in my ass kept the S on my chest enshrined in flames. But this was the song his tongue wrote on my pussy:

*Me and my man were sitting in the tree. F-U-C-K-I-N-G! Eat my pussy! Eat my pussy! Sing along with me. Munch, crunch, munch, crunch…make me cum another song!*

I had some food cooking on the stove. The rice and neck bones were in separate pots. I lowered the temperature to "3" so nothing would burn up. When eye wanted some head the kitchen wasn't a reality.

My baby was 18 years old, fresh out of high school and eye was thirty and yes, I was robbing Aisle Four in Toys R' Us by letting his Gangsta-rapping-ass taste a pussy that pushed out two bad, annoyingly ugly ass children.

I couldn't lie. I didn't have the cutest kids in the world, but they had bubbling personalities. They were always making me laugh.

But right now my kids were the furthest things from my mind. My baby was sucking on my clit and I was about to loose my mind. I wondered if he tasted my husband's cum from behind the left pussy wall. Slurp. Yes, Sir. He just tasted it. My so-called significant other (ahem, my husband Retani) came deep inside me last night and had the nerve to roll over and call me his ex girlfriend's name and they have been separated for nine motherfucking years and he was married to me for the last seven. So that meant anywhere between our Honeymoon and the fucking we did last night, he has gone and fucked the bitch behind my back.

Your ex-bitch's name didn't just pop up out of the clear blue sky unless she was behind my back, kissing your ashy lips, tasting my pussy and fingering your asshole until you came harder than guns.

I remember I got out of bed, holding the sheet to my sweaty titties and eye looked out of the window for the blue moon.

Blue moons didn't exist so there you have it. I felt so betrayed eye gently massaged him until he fell asleep and I boiled some bleach on the stove and threw it on his ass.

Suffice it to say he's still in the emergency wing at Jackson Memorial Hospital and eye didn't lose any sleep.

I didn't call to see if he was alive and when his dumb ass Mama called my phone, telling me that their cousin New New, who spent most of her life in prison getting fucked by broom sticks and plungers, was on her way over to my house to "…teach me a lesson," I told her nosey ass, "Tell her I'll have the Mr. Clean and Mop and Glo' bottles waiting with my broom stick and plunger if she tries me."

She must have told her because nine hours have passed and New-New and her friend Old-Old haven't shown up yet.

To get sweet revenge on my husband, I called over "Chico," a young thug I have wanted to fuck ever since I met his Mama thirteen years ago in high school. She didn't have a son then, but I told her, "Girl, you are so pretty. If you ever have a son in the future and he turns 18, I'm giving him some of this pussy!"

She laughed, key keying all in my ear, like it was funny. When I say someone was "key keying," that meant they were laughing.

"Girl. I am *not* having kids," she had told me, putting books in her locker. "That will never happen."

And now that her son was grown and eating this pussy like some good ole golden fried chicken, I could give a damn what his Mama had to say. Just as long as he made me cum and say "Bon Voyage," then a bitch like me was straight.

The fantasy of fucking an older woman building his ego, he pushed my legs back, his big hands slipping. It was hard to hold this pussy in place, but he handled it with skill. I told him to watch those plates moving in my clit. Earthquakes would be the end result. I could smell my neck bones floating on the air from the kitchen. I should go check on them. Nah. I couldn't. He had me pent up in the bed. Plus he had a rookie spirit. He felt he had something to prove by putting that tongue on my old ass. I didn't care about a Niggah's ego. Just as long as he kept eating my cunt then we wouldn't have any problems.

"Feel that tongue, Ma?" he asked, huffing and puffing on my clit. Tyrone Davis was playing on the stereo.

"Yes, I feel it, Daddy. Michael Phelps that pussy. Swim some world records!"

I heard the munching noises fill my ears. He already got seven gold medals in the Pussy Olympics. He wanted the 8th, and that might be the blank one. A Zane novel didn't have *anything* on this Chico-looking Niggah.

He released my legs, and kissed my lips. Making me taste my good pussy from his tongue. I hated kissing, but the thought of tasting my own clit sent me over the edge into a zone I didn't know existed in the bedroom.

"Hold them up."

"Yes, Sir."

He slapped my pussy with a dick still wet behind the piss hole with powdered Similac. I wanted to cream the atmosphere because it wasn't worth my goddamn panties.

"Put it in…"

"Beg for it."

"PUT IT IN, GODDAMN IT!"

He put his sexy lips to my cunt and he blew inside it, like he's blowing up a balloon. My voice sounded like I was sucking on helium.

"I will put it in when I get good and ready…"

"Well can you open the window? It's hot in here and I can't cut on my AC because my light bill went up a hundred dollars this week."

"Keep those legs pulled back, bitch."

*I got your bitch, Niggah! Why was I fucking a baby anyway? Simple. A youngster kept that dick up like a stick up. As a matter of fact I should dress him as Scarface and make him tell my pussy, "This is a motherfucking Dick Up! Get your clits out, lay your Pussy Walls on my shaft and put the Asshole in the back seat of my Jeep so I could swing an Episode."*

He opened my bedroom window and tied the curtains in a way that would allow the wind to blow fluidly. "Damn! Earth is blowing this pussy right," I said appreciatively, the breeze drying the sweat on my body rapidly.

He stood there, stroking his dick. Narrowing his eyes, he was slowly walking up to me.

"I want you, Daddy…"

"I want you, too."

"You sure you can handle this pussy?"

He was about to tremble out of his skin, his baggy jeans around his ankles, resting on his Jordan sneakers.

"Yes, yea…I can…handle that shit."

I was moaning like a whore. "Take me!"

He hovered above me. I braced myself for his amazing stick. I wanted him to put it in and find the clutch in my pussy.

40 THINK LIKE A NIGGAH

Before he could, the instant the head of his condom-clad dick slid in my pussy he came.

I felt him pulling out, moaning loudly, like somebody shot him and he fell on top of me, shivering.

"That was good," he said, enthused.

*Ok, motherfucker! I know you don't think you just did something!*

I couldn't say anything. I didn't even get a nut. Ok, ok…don't panic, Girl.

Give him a few seconds. He's young! He could get it back up. I was patting his sweaty back.

"Ready for round two? Mama wants her nut…?"

He started snoring.

Oh my God!

He was sleeping!

"Hey!"

He wouldn't answer me. I was shaking him.

"GET YOUR ASS UP!"

He snored louder, rolling over. This wasn't a game. He was really sleeping. Now see.

These men were lame as hell. He got his nut but a bitch had to go to sleep without hers.

# My pussy clamped…

**My asshole throbbing, I picked up the phone and dialed a** series of numbers after I awakened Sleeping Hollow and sent his young ass home to his Mama. My fingers against the glowing green numbers reminded me that a bitch had no self control in her life. *I'm going to divorce my husband. I had to. There's no way I was staying married to a jerk who called me another woman's name.*

When the ringing sounds filled my ears, I felt tingles dancing up and down my spine, but failed to reach my dripping pussy. I dug in my panties with a longing I never felt before and I wanted to chant "Denzel—*Washington* this clit before I eat your bitch!" as loudly as I possibly could!

But I didn't. Because I wasn't in the chanting mood. And being that these tingles were pissing me off, I wanted to throw the phone through my bedroom window. But I decided not to because I just paid the cleaning man, who cleaned my windows once a week, $129 for cleaning all twenty windows on my house the other day. And my money was tighter than my pussy.

Everything was going up. FP&L sent me a letter saying the percentage we paid on power was going up. Motherfuckers! My mortgage company sent me a letter saying my payments were going up by $50. What did they think? That a bitch was rich?

Then to add insult to injury, riding the Metro Bus just went up from $1.50 to $2.00. Two goddamn dollars to ride public transportation.

Could you believe it? I really didn't need to catch the bus, but at the same time eye wasn't about to drive from Homestead to Down Town Miami everyday, either. Traffic was a bitch and you had to pay to park.

So every morning, before going to work, I drove to the Park and Ride on 152nd street and hopped my black ass on the bus. I wanted me a good nut and my dildo wasn't cutting it. I didn't want artificial dick. Ain't nothing like the real thing. I wasn't a big fan of using plastic to get me a nut. Eye didn't want my pussy smelling like a brand new cordless phone when I opened the box.

So hopefully this phone call will give me the best EXPLOSION of my life. Let's see.

"Hello. This is the law offices of Baker and Taylor."

The instant I heard "...law offices..." I came so hard my pussy clamped on my worn-ass panties harder than a fat bitch could say one, two, Twinkie...

# Think like a Niggah — no, really!

**Hello, Letter. I guess I have to give my name and shit. Well,** *why the fuck not? I'm giving everything else. My name was Simonton Clarisse Harriet. I was a five feet 6 Haitian/Jamaican woman with skin so chocolaty I felt like Cocoa Pebbles every time my six year old son fixed them in the mornings, before he went to school.*

*Never mind that he hogged them all up and thought only of himself. Never mind that four people had to eat. But I guess I raised him according to some secret code the Haitians failed to tell me about. The code was, Whip his ass if he didn't clean it right. Kill him if a white bitch came to my door saying she was pregnant with his child. If I calculate it correctly, kids are fucking by the age of twelve and having babies by age 14 so if I added twenty-eight extension cord whippings by the square root of his trying experimental drugs one day in the future I had about, um…6 more years of enjoying watching him grow up before he started fucking.*

*And this is my son we're talking about. My daughter Simone was another matter. She was already eleven years old, looked like her sexy ass Daddy and, just last week, the little bitch snuck my make-up to school.*

43 DAPHAROAH69

She hid it in her Hanna Montana book bag and thought that just because I had over fifty jars of make-up shit that I wouldn't notice it missing. When was she going to realize that the dust spot my Cover Girl blush used to sit remained long after she took my shit? I beat her ass for the old and the new when she got home, while her giggling, I-think-he's-gonna-be-gay brother watched with delight from the table. Eating Cocoa Pebbles.

I had blotchy eyes, just got immunized for the flu (Flu Season was worse than the I.R.S.), and my hair was short, croppy and I hardly got it down because gas prices was a bitch, raising my children were bigger bitches and being alone in love was the fat bitch who was about to fuck my husband to sleep so I could leave his dumb ass.

I don't keep diaries so I will call this Letter number one. Sitting at my dining table, trying to eat eggs and grits didn't cut it right now. Yesteryear, eating when I was stressed would have ballooned my figure to a startling size 9, squeezed my blue jeans to hell quicker than I can make a man come, raised my spending habits past the $200 I spend on groceries and would have made Mama call my phone all day and night with one question in mind, "Are you pregnant, bitch?"

With the way I feel right now I don't know if I will continue this letter or write Letter number 2. Things are not going right and everything from my faith in God to the faith I have in my husband is being tested more than fucking lab rats. Seriously.

A bitch couldn't catch a goddamn break and the breaks I had in life came from punching out for an hour daily at my job and buying the same old Number 1 meal from Wendy's, talking to the same ole loser motherfucking black men who blamed everybody but themselves for their problems and playing with the same ole pussy I been playing with for twenty-one years, the one I happened to have between my legs.

Right now I'm going through something and I don't think I will make it through. I thought about swallowing Tylenol, but killing myself wouldn't make it right and it damn sure wouldn't save me from the hell my life has become. Mama's a nosey bitch and she is so worried about how I situated my living room that she hadn't vacuumed her own in weeks. She was so worried about how I treated my man that she hadn't sucked Daddy's dick in months. I lost my car. It broke down on me right in the middle of I-95. I had to call the Triple A. They came an hour later, after my silk blouse and lace panties started sticking to my titties and pussy like leeches, and the driver of the tow truck had the gall to get an attitude because I didn't give him my phone number. Stupid fuck.

Once my car was towed to my front yard, I closed my eyes and prayed to God that I had enough money to get it fixed. Send me a sign, Lord, I asked him. I need help because I can't do it all by myself.

When I opened my eyes another tow truck had my car chained to some straps.

"What are you doing?" I asked feverishly, about to run inside my home, grab my .22 and blow the fat fuck's head off. I lost my job. Being a paralegal was very rewarding.

I thought I could build a life with a good man who valued promiscuity in the bedroom more than commitment in the board room and when I tried to give him some pussy in the conference room he nearly had a heart attack.

What man you know ran from pussy?

My Daddy always taught me to think like a niggah so I didn't get treated like a bitch. And being that I was a woman with her own moral code and standards, I took this to heart. But not initially. Being that I loved my body, I continuously worked on my well-being, emotional state and emotional state of affairs when it came to talking, dealing and associating with God's Children who were looking more and more like the Devil everyday.

It took me nearly seven years to feel the full impact of the phrase.

Why would Daddy tell me something like that? A man who didn't believe in the word "Niggah" instantly contradicted himself when he uttered the phrase. Why would he use the word in relation *to teaching his only child, his only daughter a little bit of class and decorum?*

It took me through a plethora of emotions before eye arrived in the Plymouth Rock of Understanding. I had umpteen men before eye understood the phrase's power. The phrase could have meant any number of things but eye took it to mean something positive. I remember eye was about eleven years old when he sat me down over burnt eggs and toast at the dining room table.

Mama was crying at the stove, without making it obvious and Daddy was smoking a cigarette.

"Don! You know good and goddamn *well* I don't allow smoking in my house."

"Yet you allow fucking," Daddy snapped, stubbing ashes into the ash tray.

I picked up my fork and started toying with the eggs because I wasn't about to eat them. Plus he put garlic powder in them and that killed it for me.

"I didn't ask you that," Mama quipped sarcastically, wiping tears from her gorgeous eyes.

Turning down the flame, she covered the grits and waited to stir in the cheese.

"Well I told you."

"Why do you always have something smart to say, Don?"

"Why are you crying like a child?"

"I have my reasons."

"What are they?"

They tried to remain civil but I was at the age where simply telling me that Santa Claus slid down the chimney didn't cut it anymore.

"I don't have to tell you." Mama picked up the cigarettes.

"We're married."

"In name, sweetie. Believe you me, in name only." She extracted one, her hands shaking.

"Well file for divorce."

Mama picked up a manila envelope from the counter, by the bowl of margarine and she tossed it on the table in front of Daddy. I was looking at him, my heart cracking. My parents were divorcing. This couldn't be happening.

Daddy looked at the envelope like it was a pile of shit.

"What is this?"

"Open it. Niggahs are nosey motherfuckers anyways." Mama's eyes cleared up, but they were still red.

Daddy fumbled with the envelope. I watched him like a hawk.

"Eat your food," Mama snapped.

"Mama, the eggs are burnt."

"My money is burnt buying that shit. Eat it or get your ass whipped. I'm not playing with you and I don't have the fucking time to go back and forth *with a goddamn child!*"

Lowering my head, I knew not to play with Mama today. Whatever had her in a stupor she was taking it out on me and it wasn't fair.

Daddy pulled out the papers.

"Divorce papers?"

"Yes, sir. When did you figure it out? Just now?"

"But we didn't even talk about this."

"And we're not about to now. For months I tried talking. I tried talking when I cooked your dinner. You ignored me. I tried talking when we dressed for church. You were too busy sneaking a peek of what football game was coming on."

Daddy didn't put up a fight. "So you want me to sign them?"

Mama refused to look at him. This killed Daddy. He loved her more than himself. And maybe that was the problem. You were never supposed to love anybody more than you loved yourself.

"Baby," Daddy went on.

"It would make my life easier," Mama snapped, patting her hair.

"Easier?" he asked, glancing at me.

"Yes. We weren't ready for marriage when we tied the knot and you know it."

Daddy took a pen from his shirt pocket. Grimacing, he looked hurt. He did love Mama. They argued entirely too much. Over dumb, trivial things. Come on. When you argued over which brand of toilet paper to buy then something was wrong.

"How do you know it?"

"When we met you talked to me because eye was the only woman available from the group of girls who came to your Cousin Lloyd's party. So it was almost like you felt *obligated* to talk to me."

"Bull." His temples twitched. Mama was right. But Daddy would never admit it.

"Then on top of that we fucked, fucked and fucked some more. You didn't even know my first and last name but you knew my coochie's name instantly."

"Which was?" Daddy asked with an attitude.

"Pussy."

I chocked. Mama shook her head, ignoring me. I was about to gag.

I stood up and Daddy snatched me back down in the chair.

"Eat your food."

"Daddy. You burnt the eggs and toast. It's blacker than the woman I saw you with last night."

I covered my mouth.

Mama's eyes were so wide trucks could double park in her retinas. I slipped and told her. I promised Daddy I wouldn't say anything and now I had and shit was about to hit the fan.

"You had another woman in my house with my child present?"

"No, Baby." Daddy looked worried.

Mama grabbed the knife and Daddy signed the divorce papers as if he never got married in the first place. The instant the ball point of the pen touched the paper eye died inside. I would no longer trust them. My two loving parents were supposed to remain married forever.

And now they were splitting.

# Your Kids

**So what would my children think when eye filed for divorce?** I really didn't care because eye was the adult and eye wasn't going to stay married to a man who didn't love me. The children would get over it. People put too much emphasis on being married. Do it for the kids. No. You hurt your kids more by *making* them watch two people stay trapped in a loveless marriage. That's like giving children castor oil over a lollipop. And we all know they'll choose a lollipop every time.

Plus my kids didn't pay the fucking bills, put food on the table and bring home the bacon. They hardly wanted to wash the dishes or take out the goddamn trash. So do you think eye give a damn about what they had to say if eye didn't wanna stay married anymore? They weren't the ones married to him. Eye was!

Keep a child in a child's place. I knew they loved their father but *he* called me another woman's name. Unacceptable. And eye didn't want to make the same mistake my Mom made when she didn't talk to Daddy about their problems.

She filed for divorce without rebuttal from Pa. I didn't want to do the same thing. Yet I battled myself internally. I was sleeping with Chico, so eye wasn't any better than my husband. And I only suspected that he cheated on me because he called me his ex girlfriend's name. Maybe I should find out the truth before I decide to do anything.

"Hello, ma'am. Are you there?" the woman asked from the phone.

"Yes." I sat up, the lingering effects of my orgasm subsiding. "I'm Simonton. And I want to file for divorce."

"Then you've called the right place. Do you have an associate in mind to start the process, or do you want me to recommend one?"

I felt the tears stinging my eyes.

*Divorce him, Girl. He shouldn't have called you another woman's name. OK, Chile. Is that a crime? Did you catch him fuckin' her? Did you find lipstick on his shirt collars. Well, no. Did you find another woman's panties under the bed?*

*No.*

*Then what is the...*

"I'm going to recommend..."

My husband walked into the room. He took one look at me and asked, "Who are you on the phone with?"

"Carl. My husband just came home." I faked a smile, standing up, stretching. Playing it cool. "What did you say? Oh, yea. Tell my Aunt to mind her business. I'll call you back."

I hung up.

He sat next to me, turning on the TV. You could feel the tension in the air. I held my breath, wanting to scratch his eyes off. You unfaithful motherfucker. *Ok, girl. But you're fucking an 18 year old. You're no better.*

*Shut up, Conscious. I didn't ask you for your two cents.*

*You threw bleach on him!*

*Chile, you only grazed his big toe. And he went to the hospital and got the big toe patched up.*

He kissed my lips and I welcomed the flattery. He hasn't kissed me in a few months. So it felt good. Even when we have sex we didn't kiss. It felt like the passion was on simmer.

"Why did you call me your ex's name?"

He looked at me. "Is that still *bothering* you?"

"*Yea*, man. Be for real. If I would have called you another man's name you would feel the same way."

"I used to love her, Simonton. *Nothing* more. Why do women want you in their lives then when you get there they want you destroy *every* loving memory you had before she came into the picture?"

"I'm not asking you that."

He glared at me. "*Yes* you are. I had to throw my high school prom pictures away because I was hugging another girl. I can't get those memories back. I had to throw away my letters, my teenage pictures. Why did I have to do that?"

"Because I did that for you."

"Did I ask you to destroy your memories?"

He had me. "Well, no."

"Look. I am sorry. I talked to my ex the day I called you her name. We had a heated discussion."

"About?"

"She wants me back. I don't know how she got my number. My nosey mom probably gave it to her. You know my mom can't *stand* you. But I told my ex that I was in love with you. That I'm *married*. Yes, I'm a man. And I thought things. Shoot me. I'm human."

*He's being honest.*

I appreciate the honesty. "I don't wanna shoot you. But I'm not happy."

"You're not happy?" He turned off the TV and stood up. "What are you trying to tell me?"

"Nothing. I just want us to work. We have kids."

"Who I love very much."

"And my Daddy always taught me to think like a niggah..."

"So you don't get treated like a bitch."

I smiled. "You remembered."

"Yes." He thought about something. "Do me a favor."

"Yes."

"Would you mind going to get me a glass of water? I'm going to take a quick shower."

"Sure."

When Simonton left the room, he sprinted around the bed and picked up the phone. He pressed redial. The phone started to ring and someone answered it.

"...Hello, the law offices of Baker and Taylor."

*The law offices...Why would she call a law office? She didn't work at this one.*

*She worked for Anna and Gillespie.*

"What do you guys specialize in?"

"*Divorces.*"

He hung up the phone.

*She wants a divorce.*

When I came back in the room with my husband's water eye stood in the door way stunned. The TV was off and candles were lit. He sprayed my favorite perfume in the air. He was sitting on the edge of the bed, butt booty naked. His dick looked ripe for the taking. Hell, yea. Give Mama some *Feedback*, strum my guitar like I'm Janet Jackson.

"What is this for?" I asked.

"I love you."

"You do?"

"Yes. You don't believe me?"

"Yes I do."

"If you want her phone number I'll give it to you. So you can ask my ex any question you want. I'm a grown man. I don't lie or hide anything I do."

"Baby..."

"I want my family to work."

"We both have to work on it."

"Bring that pussy over here."

I walked up to him. I sat beside him and we looked at each other. He slowly hugged me, inhaling my scent. It felt good to be in his arms. I was in a Catch 22. I wanted Chico, but at the same time eye loved my husband. I only tip toed with Chico because eye felt my husband was cheating on me.

So I didn't want to look like a damn fool when the shit hit the fan. But now I found out that he really didn't cheat on me. And that was refreshing. I could never tell him about Chico.

It would destroy him.

He stood up and told me to lie down. I did so. He told me to close my eyes. I did so.

He lay something on my tummy.

He pulled something on my hips. Like some shorts or something.

This was freaky!

Yes.

"Open your eyes."

I melted when eye saw the rose on me. Wow.

"Thanks, Baby."

"Do you like your shorts?" he asked with a smile.

I looked down at them and my heart dropped. They weren't shorts at all.

He sat next to me, with the phone in his hand.

"So *whose* boxers are you wearing?"

I stuttered. "*Yours*, baby."

He laughed. "*Come* on now, Simonton. I free ball. I haven't worn underwear in eleven years. Talk to me."

"Um…"

"Was it Carl?"

"Carl?"

"The man you were talking to when I walked in the room. You talked to him on a phone I bought."

"Baby…"

He picked up the rose and trailed it along my neck, torturing me.

I was about to die.

"Come on, Simonton."

He pressed redial.

He put it on speaker and set the phone on the nightstand.

"Hello. This is the law offices of Baker and Taylor."

"What do you specialize in?" my husband asked and my heart dropped. Eye covered my face in shame.

"Divorces," the woman said and my husband looked in my eyes with *Got you, Bitch* dancing in his pupils.

"Thanks, Carl. Tell my auntie I said suck my dick."

He hung up.

"So you want a divorce?"

"I…I…"

"So you were going to do it without talking to me first?"

"Baby, please." I tried to sit up. He held up his hands.

"No. Don't move. Relax. You're wearing your lovers' boxers. Shit, you got it going on."

"Come on, Man."

"What? When I get paid I give you my whole paycheck. I pay for your shit. I fuck you right. I make love to you. And you do this to me?"

"Don't act like you're innocent."

"I am."

"YOU'RE NOT!" I jumped out of bed and started punching him. He stood there, the man he was. My punches didn't hurt him. They were like bugs against the windshield when you're driving on the turnpike. "You called me that bitch's name!"

"Baby…"

"You're *fucking* her! You have to be! You don't just call me another woman's name outta the blue."

He engulfed me until eye calmed down.

"I'm not gonna ask who he is. Let's call it even. I was caught calling you my ex's name. And you were caught when I found another man's undies in my room and the fact that you were about to file for divorce behind my back. I love you and I love my family. Whoever you're seeing please call him and let him know that Daddy's home and Daddy is here to stay."

"Are you serious?"

He was reluctant. "Yes. I thought about cheating on you. But the Bible says that if a man cheats in his heart he has already cheated against the soul. So I'm no better than you."

"I love you."

"I know you do. So I guess you really did do what your father taught you."

"Which was…?"

"Think like a niggah."

"So I don't get treated like a bitch."

We chuckled. But my laugh was a sigh of relief. Chico was out. I would call him and let him know. I knew me and my husband had a lot to work on, but at least we still had our family and our marriage.

"Lay down. I don't wanna make love to you tonight. Can I just hold you?"

"Yes, baby. That'll be fine."

"Let's watch some TV."

"I thought you would never ask."

He fell asleep when Flap Jack, the cartoon, came on the *Cartoon Network*. I loved this show. My husband loved cartoons as well.

I picked up the phone and called Chico. He answered.

"Hey, baby," he said excitedly.

"We can't do this anymore."

"What?"

"See each other. It's *over*."

"I'll never let you go. I will die for you."

"Well die without me."

"Why, Baby? That's my pussy."

"Actually, its mine. Don't call me and stay away from my family."

"I'm coming over."

"I hope you're joking."

"No, I'm not. You can't lay that pussy on a niggah like that and then call him up and dump him cold turkey."

"Don't come over."

"I'm on my way."

"I'm pregnant," I lied.

"What?"

"I'm pregnant with your baby."

"Oh, no, bitch. Good bye."

Click.

I felt a hand on my thigh and I jumped out of my skin. I looked at my husband and he said, "That always make a man run for the hills, doesn't it?"

"Yes, it does."

"Thank you."

"You're welcome."

"You know what this means, right?"

"No..."

"Put your face down and that ass up. I'm fucking the shit out of you. By the time I'm done with you, you're going to run from dick for the next three weeks."

I put my face down on the pillow, and my husband spent the next two hours waxing that ass.

# Seduction

**I didn't care how many times eye told my wife to take the** dog outside; she just never seemed to do so. In fact she never goddamn listened to anything eye said! She always tried to do her own thing, despite being the perfect Proverbs wife. She was a Jehovah's Witness. She went door to door ever day with her fat ass sister Sparkle, trying to invite uncaring black folk in the 'Hood to come to the congregation. And this was her passion, and it became a thorn in my ass when she wouldn't do what eye told her to do when it came to the dog.

I remember when we first met. She tried to pronounce my name and had a hard time with it. Abrams Sicily. She would stutter, spit and choke trying to force the country in her windpipes to correctly enunciate the words. She got better and better. If only she took that attitude with caring for our dog. Maybe because eye was the man in the marriage and men were supposed to take out the trash, slay the scorching sun like dragons just to cut the grass, wash the cars and feed and bathe the dogs.

She wanted a dog for Christmas so eye got her one. And eye reluctantly told her, then, "Baby, when I buy this goddamn dog, it's your responsibility to wash him and feed him. I don't want dogs!"

And she smiled sweetly at me, with her sexy self. "OK, baby."

Yeah right! Men were supposed to fix the toilet, the sink, get up in the middle of the night when you heard unusual sounds in the house while she held the covers up to her tits trying to look concerned. Men were supposed to jump in front of silver bullets to give his woman five more minutes of life. Bullshit. Nowhere in God's *Bible* did it say eye was supposed to take a freaking bullet for my wife, take out trash or tame a fucking dog!

Nowhere. I knew this as fact because I asked my Pa$tor, Reverend Simone's Haitian ass, and eye read the Bible myself.

No reference, unless I overlooked something. Sometimes I wanted to be saved! To my complete dismay (and this put a strain on my wallet), my wife and I had a fearless German Sheppard named "Seduction."

His previous name was "Spot," but after being spotted being naughty a few days ago I changed his name. It's just the dog and I right now.

In a hotel room. Mourning and depressed.

**Appalled, I looked at him with red eyes because I haven't**
really slept and I haven't been to work. I was a construction
worker. I called out for the past five days. Fuck work! Then
to make matters worse, much worse, my nine year old son
has called my cell phone repeatedly.

"Are you and Mom breaking up?" he asked and I'd fake
a smile, stop my heart from doing back flips and lie.

"No, Mama and I are going through it right now."

"Going through it *how*, dad. That sounds so ghetto."

He was too damn smart for his age. Just like Daddy! He
should be playing with his action figures instead of trying to
figure out my goddamn actions. He did as I said not what as
I did.

"Its not Ghetto, son," I corrected him as sternly as I
could without giving too much away with my shaky voice. I
was getting agitated. Every little thing was setting me off.

"And I also know it's a lie."

"Son, watch it." He was pissing me off. I had a bad
temper, I was Jamaican/Cuban. And my father's mother was
Chinese. So that meant I couldn't see straight nor drive right
when I was angry.

59 DAPHAROAH69

"Dad. I asked mom. And she said she doesn't want to see you."

The hell with her!! "And I don't want to say the wrong thing, son."

He giggled. I smiled. "What did Spot do?"

"His name is Seduction. And I got to go, son."

He started sniffling and this tore me up. Hot tears ran down my face. "Dad, my football game is on Goulds Park today. It's Saturday. Are you going to be there?"

"*No, son.*" *Yes, I would be there.*

"I hate you!" Before I could stop my mouth from falling open and my heart from cracking, he bammed the phone in my face.

My hard-headed, trouble-making son, Junior, adored his dog. He was named after my great-great grandfather who died a slave in Alabama. I didn't have any pictures of my great-great grandfather, who lived to be about a hundred and three years old and fathered 39 children from white women and a few black bitches he cared nothing for. Fucking the white girls was his anger towards society for lynching his family.

His mother, sister and youngest brother were all hung from trees and burned to death (while he was lassoed around the neck and forced to watch) for refusing to clean up the plantation, it's a horrifying story that has been passed down generation after generation in my family, which is why we're so damn temperamental.

But Linda won't let me or the dog see my boy. So I gotta sneak to the Park to go to his game. She didn't go to games; she hated sports and football and really didn't want my son playing.

"Baby, he's a boy, he needs to do man things."

She was whole-heartedly stubborn! She'd huff and puff. "He's a boy and needs to do boyish things. Don't force my son—"

"—Our son, *goddamn* it!—"

"—to grow up too soon! I don't want him doing man things. I want him doing boy things, like building Legos, riding his bike and joining the boy scouts and thinking the girls have the Coodies, an imaginary disease.... That's what he needs to be doing! Let him enjoy his childhood. I don't want my son forced into sports, let it be his decision!"

"I don't want my son being a fag!"

She was insulted. I didn't mean to say it like that. "He's a boy!"

Infuriated, I had said, "HE'S MY SON, TOO! And when I'm BEING A FATHER to MY son you stay out of it, got that!"

And I pivoted on my heel and marched to the bedroom, slamming the door closed. I shake my head, present day, thinking to myself I could have handled that better. Despite our outcry, she compassionately understood sometimes. I didn't wanna get a divorce, we have been so happy together. We barely had a bump in the road; our ten year relationship has been super perfect. And that was the problem. She never protested against me, she wouldn't even bet against me.

"Honey, we're partners. *Why* would I pick something opposite you?"

"But baby, it's all in fun," I'd tell her sternly.

"But, no. And *speaking* of which. If you bet against the Dolphins then so will I, we're a team. I hate football, but if my man puts a hundred bucks on the Patriots then goddamn it I do, too. I can't take Miami against you."

"Baby, its competition, Marital Competition."

And she'd start to cry because my words hurt her and I would bow down and do things her way and she seemed happy. I shoulda known better, she's a tough, stubborn woman. I should know she only cried to get her goddamn way! But this time shit has hit the fan. Big Time!

I've had my, well my wife's, German Sheppard for a couple years now. He's grown on me; initially I couldn't stand his ass, cussed his ass out, and hated him because he always took a shit on my side of the room. I guess he got tired of me sticking his nose in his own shit and beating his ass with a rolled-up newspaper until it hurt!

He has all his shots, I keep him well fed with Alpo. Sometimes, when I am in the mood, he will eat KFC and McDonalds with me, but I have to put a halt to that because he dissed the Alpo train and wanted human food and the bitch thinks he's human.

I was rubbing his head; his tongue wagging.

He had sad eyes.

He missed my wife.

I missed her.

**I missed my son. My bed. My house. My Lay Z Boy. ESPN.**
My goddamn weed. My alcohol. My mini bar in the den. My
porno tapes. My *Hustler* magazines. I wanted to log on
Crackspace (Myspace) and check my subscription posts. I
loved reading blogs. I know Audrey Michelle wrote some
passionate shit and Mimi wrote glorious, enlightening stuff.

King James was awesome. I was *hooked* on his dating
blogs…Dean Baker was a very good writer. But enough
about people I didn't even know!

I knew my wife missed me. She'd call my voice mail
and sob and cry and tell me why she was so mad and I was
still in disbelief. She felt betrayed, violated and embarrassed.

I couldn't blame her but it wasn't my fault. If she just
would have taken the dog outside.

She kicked me out a house I bought and paid to be
furnished. Because I didn't put the dog outside.

"Well, Seduction, it's just you and me," I told him. He looked even sadder. I felt like shit. I hadn't shaved. I jacked off three times today. My wife's orgasm has dried up on my dick and I've been inhaling the smell of good pussy for days because I missed her.

I was 6 feet tall with a just-repaired ACL I'd torn in my knee when playing baseball last year. But didn't any of that matter.

I missed Linda.

It all happened so fast...

**A few days before. Horny as hell, Linda put on those lacey** red panties I liked so much. She looked divine. Seductive. Sexy! She had a fat ass!  Not *fat* in an unflattering way but major bounce action that set me off and the fellahs around the 'Hood *always* went crazy. They gave her the nickname Miss Phat Booty.  The type of ass that made me *tote* a pistol in my holster just in case a Niggah got out of line. An ass even the lesbians wanted.

And those fish net stockings clinging to her sexy track runner's legs made my eyes water and my dick go Take It Off!

"Keep the hair piled atop your head," I told her. She listened. I loved an obedient bitch. She wasn't a bitch per say but in the bedroom she was *my* bitch.

I was Daddy! She loved when I told her that. Come here, you sexy bitch!

She'd shudder, about to cream her panties. So I told her she could cream my tongue. My tongue in her pussy was like a tongue dipped into a bowl of sugar.

I looked at her sternly, "Leave the tits bare, baby purr like a cat!"

She purred with a sexy smile. She lay elegantly on our master bed. Her skin perfumed, light lotion. She had the creamy look women had when they had one of those long, hot showers. Her eyes told me she fucked herself with the massager again, the silver nozzle with eight types of massaging speeds.

Huge white throw pillows lined the head of the bed. A huge green comforter was pulled back to the foot of the bed. I had thrown rose petals all over the floor, had a bowl of Fruity Pebbles on the nightstand without the milk, two glasses of Dom.

"I'm hungry," she said, eyeing the cereal. We wanted to try something kinky tonight. She had on furry handcuff bracelets I made from my old handcuffs. My mom was a cop who got shot in the line of duty. I hated authority which was why I loved giving it. It was the Sagittarius in me.

"What do you want to eat?" I asked her seductively, getting on my knees, crawling up to the bed like a cat. I tried to ignore the healed rug burns on them, didn't want to get anymore. But with pussy like she had, those rug burns were so worth it.

I licked my lips, very masculine, and her legs began to shake. Her nipples were *harder* than my dick

With the skill of a stripper, she opened her legs, spread-eagled, and I shuddered...so much moisture and wetness came from her pussy I damn near had a heart attack. She was the epitome of sexy!

"You tell me." She carefully spilled the words. Dripping with innuendo.

I was all open for suggestions. "How about some sausage." I narrowed my eyes, stroking my dick slowly, with light oil on my hands giving myself the jitters.

"Oooh la la, *baby*. I love it when you talk shit to me. I'm glad you took the pants off because a bitch like me loves wearing the panties!"

I was like a general, she was my Private. "Get on your knees!!"

She snapped on her knees in an instant, saluting me. "Oh yes Big Dick Daddy I'll anything for my goddamn husband!"

"But you're a Jehovah's Witness, no cussing, baby."

"God told me to become one with my man and I'm your slutty dirty bitch/whore in the sheets."

*Oh, shit she was driving me crazy!* "Goddamn, baby..." I was at a loss for words, this shit definitely has never happened to me before. Hell my manhood felt compromised. Had to change this shit up, and quick. Before she got ideas of fucking me and I ain't having it.

"Goddamn my pussy to ruins, baby...I want to scream Greece Greece *GREECE*!"

I reached the foot of the bed and stood up, slowly, running my hands over my chest, playing with my nipples, closing my eyes and flowing to punk-ass Eric Bennet singing from my stereo. My wife loved him. I hated him for cheating on Halle Berry. How the fuck do you cheat on Halle Fucking Berry?

I had on my boxers. My dick fell through the hole. I was baby oiled down to the little corn on my big toe. I had pretty feet, or so my wife said. I had ass and my wife loved my ass. I loved my ass. It was a secret fetish of mine to masturbate and finger myself in the bathroom when she was at work. Made me come harder and faster when the prostate turned into All State and let me know I was in good hands. I wasn't bisexual or gay; I wasn't attracted to men. That was the truth. I never kissed a man and sometimes I hated looking at my own dick but I loved masturbating. Finger fucking myself for a powerful nut was my thang and my thang only; I would never tell my wife that shit. Never!

She expertly took my organ into her mouth and I held her head and kept it romantic and sensual. Candles were lit

67 DAPHAROAH69

here and there…I lit strawberry incense, leaning over her while she sucked on my dick, lighting about two of them, juxtaposed next to each other. Smelled good with the weed I took to the head. I semi jacked off in the bathroom ten minutes ago and stopped just as I was about to cum. Stalling the orgasm was powerful. Because when you made love, and you had to cum, it gave you a MORE POWERFUL EXPLOSION, it was like OH SHIT GODDAMN bursting out the head of your organ, making me openly sob in my wife's face.

My lady pulled my dick out her mouth. She *spat* on it a few times.

*Yeeeah, bitch! I loved it real wet. You know how we do baby!*

She massaged it in…Tenderly, a tad bit slutty.  Slutty was good!

She took it back into her hot mouth.  My eyes rolled to the back of my head, my legs open, my nuts bouncing as I felt her tightly squeezing my hardness. She was pulling my shaft like a slot machine handle, taking it to the tonsils…she moaned like a porn star. I loved my wife when she got kinky. "Yea, bitch, pull that handle. I want three cherries to ring up in my goddamn eyes!"

I was squirming, the sensation blinding. With narrowed eyes. "Where you want that nut, baby?"

She looked up at me "Damn, daddy, you bout to cum already?"

A huge build up nearly rendered me speechless. My toes curled, my ass clapped together, my asshole damn near came alive…fire and desire climbed my spine like tiny firecrackers making my legs drum together…"…Yeah, baby, where you want that shit?"

I was slinging dick to her tongue and lips. She jacked it ferociously, her hair falling from the pile atop her head and framing my dick and her face. "Oh shit baby here it come!"

She leaned back, my dick falling from her mouth, and I nearly fell over coming in the bowl of Fruity Pebbles. My dick pulsated ten times while she lay back on the bed, slowly playing with her pretty pussy, cooing and moaning like a slow Janet Jackson song all in front of me.

"Bitch why you playin' wit' me?"

When I got through raining in the cereal she took a spoon, sucking on it and began mixing my nut with the sweet tasting food and she said, "I got some milk now, baby. You still want to see what Mama does with this nut?"

Exhausted as hell, I lay next to her and began diving into her pussy with my tongue.

She spooned some nut and cereal in her mouth and chewed lovingly.

I went crazy.

She dropped the bowl on her stomach and cereal spilled all over her lower body, mixing with her pubic hair and I ate some of my own nutty cereal.

I tongue-kissed her clitoris, pushing her walls back so the clit stuck out like a little dick.

And I sucked and slurped and finger fucked my wife while the titties bounced and she opened her legs wide and I pushed them back.

"I got an idea," I said suddenly.

I opened the nightstand and pulled out the handcuffs.

I handcuffed her to the bed.

"Close your eyes, baby," I told her. She did. "And don't look, whatever you feel don't look baby. Promise?"

"I promise." She said like my little personal slut and my dick jumped.

"If you look you don't get no tongue and no more dick."

"Oh, baby they are closed tightly."

I started putting my plan together...

# Linda

I loved my man. I would do anything for him, so when he told me to close my eyes so he could give my pussy, that was soooo wet, a…tongue lashing, I did so. I was handcuffed, my body on fire, my skin feeling like red ants because I stung for his love, his passion. My husband fucked better than any man I ever had. He wrote so many love letters with his tongue and fingers on my pussy I could release it tomorrow, called Pussy and Me 101. It'd be an instant bestseller!

I felt his tongue. He dove right in, and my legs shook. His tongue was consistent. *Very* hungry. I was about to scream. He has *never* worked his tongue like this before. Covering my entire pussy!

NIGGAH! OMG! What has gotten into you? Goddamn!

I was an explosion in training. "Oh, baby! *Eat* Mama's pussy! Oh, yeah Daddy yes! I will die…for…you my baby…!"

He never ate pussy this good. I mean he was good but goddamn, I wanted to open my eyes but I made a promise, so I kept them closed, biting my inside jaws so hard I tasted blood and I welcomed it because blood was life.

The tongue wet my pussy like my personal water hose…he was munching on my pubic hairs, eating the cereal.

I could barely contain myself. *"Oh baby you freaky!"*

He said nothing.

**He continued eating. I liked men who shut up and got right** on down to business.

Out of nowhere my orgasm slapped me with a force that made me fart. I smelled my own gas but I came with a thunderous yelp. I screamed out in pleasure.

"BABY BABY BABY!"

I shivered everywhere, my legs trembling. I was crying, fuck that I was sobbing.

*"Baby I love you, what would I do without you, baby, yes!"* He kept licking my pussy! *My God!* What has gotten into him? He was a monster!

When I lay, spent, I opened my eyes, deeper in love with my man.

I suddenly tensed up, my body going through a series of knee-jerk reactions. The blood left my face, the room began spinning so fast I reached out for guard rails that weren't anywhere in sight.

I tried to find a ledge to hold, to hang on, anything for balance...I felt a burning in the pit of my stomach, and it exploded up my throat, tingling my larynx and all of a sudden I threw up all over myself when Spot, my damn dog, jumped out the bed with cereal all over his mouth.

And *ran* out the room.

Like a love struck silly fool, my husband came out of the bathroom, confused. His face a twisted mask of anger.

"Did you masturbate, baby? You cheated! You were fucking yourself without me?" He glared at me. "Don't you get enough of that shit fucking yourself with the massager? And that bitch is starting to get bigger and bigger, like you are going to the Home Depot and buying the biggest goddamn shower head massager you can fucking find!"

His eyes were laser beams.

I was disgusted, and he really looked at me, twitching his nose. "Baby," he said cautiously. "I smell vomit."

"Your DOG ATE MY PUSSY! I feel violated! I feel disgusted!"

He was in denial. Smiling sarcastically, he thought I was joking. I wasn't joking at all.

"WHAT?" He was angry. "That's your goddamn dog!"

He thought I was lying.

**I looked at my wife, in denial. She couldn't be serious. Of** all the things to make up, she made up this?

I was boiling with anger. "The dog isn't even in the goddamn room!"

She was a monster. "You BITCH!" Like a lion pouncing on prey, she abruptly jumped out of the bed. I had never seen her so angry, so pissed off. It scared me, and she was only 5 feet 4 inches.

Shit. Maybe she wasn't lying..."Baby, what are you saying? That Spot..."

She was the evil demon! *"Yes!* Spot was eating me out. I didn't open my eyes 'cause I promised you." She threw the lamp at me and it shattered against the wall. "GET OUT GET OUT YOU AND THE GODDAMN DOG OUT!"

"The hell if I leave out my own house! I pay the goddamn mortgage!"

She opened the nightstand and pulled out a huge knife, rushing me with it, swinging it sporadically. I had pushed

73 DAPHAROAH69

her on the floor, the knife flying into the bathroom sink and I grabbed my clothes, confused and told Spot, who I renamed Seduction at that moment, to come on.

I got out of that room as fast as I could!

"And next TIME YOU PUT THAT DOG OUTSIDE!" she screamed as I put on my pants and shirt, and left out the front door, whipping out my cell, calling my best friend Mikki who worked at a hotel. I booked a room.

And I have been here for the next few days.

Wanting my wife back.

Will I get her back?

# The Rolexx

The phone wailed like a drunken sailor. I was snoring, I ain't g'on lie. I wasn't trying to hear that damn phone! I was tired, shit. My body was beat up because I worked out at Gold's Gym last night before eye went to work and my chocolate-coated personal trainer, who was fine as hell, with a dick of gold and lips of fire, worked me into the damn ground. I didn't have a man to massage my muscles back to sanity, so eye could only make do with what I had, which was my goddamn self.

*Ring! Ring!*

Angrily snorting like a pig, I started pounding the pillows with my fists! Now why didn't I turn the ringer off? Who was calling me so goddamn early?

I sat up, reached for the phone and fell slap on my face. Wham! Chin on the carpet. That shit hurt! Now I was deeply upset. "FUCK FUCK FUUUCKKK WHO IS THAT CALLIN' MY GODDAMN HOUSE SO EARLY?" I was a monster. I was not a morning person.

"Could you not do all that yelling?" asked my nosey neighbor, John Hamilton, secret fag, wanna-be-dedicated father of four. "It's too damn early!"

John and I always had problems because eye was a real woman with good pussy and he had a loose asshole. His words falling on deaf ears, I got back in the bed and glared at my thin wall.

"Fuck you, Ho!" I retorted, frowning. "Don't worry about what I do up in mine, Ho! I'll come ova in ya' goddamn face, bitch! Now test me pussy Ho!"

Quiet...utter quietness!

Good. I lay back down, patted my pillow, and rubbed my eyes and lay down, getting back under my cozy covers. Tranquility in its rarest form.

*Ring ring ring!*

Startled, I jumped out of my skin. Pissed, I snatched up the receiver and screamed, "Who the fuck is this—"

"—*Girl*, have you heard the latest?" my friend asked me, cutting me off.

Calming down a bit I yawned and stretched. Felt good to stretch. The first batch of Florida sunshine beaming through my window and lacey curtains, little shapes on my arms.

It would take me a while to fully wake up, if ever.

Before I said anything I looked at my Betty Boop alarm clock.

Goddamn! *This Ho woke me up thirty minutes before the alarm went off.*

Now I was pissed the slap off!

"*Heard* what." *Ew, my damn breath!* Goddamn! Gotta handle that, and fast.

"The rumor about the Club Rolexx."

My brows rose. "What about the Rolexx, girl?" I was having trouble breathing. *Please, girl, don't tell me somebody fuckin' wit' my money! I need my money!*

"The watch company, Rolex Watch U.S.A., those Swiss-bitches are suing your place of business."

Not in the mood for gossip, even though my life thrived on everyone's business but my own, I sat all the way up and leaned against the headboard, hair rollers firmly in place, holding my weave job together. A huge poster of Snoop Dogg's ugly ass hung on the wall behind me, a gift from my son.

"Are you talking about Rolexx, that worn-down-looking club on the corner of UNITY BOULEVARD and NW 119TH STREET? If you are then you got to be shittin' me. You better not be fuckin' wit' me, gurl! You know how overly dramatic your ass can get. I can't have nobody fuckin' wit' my money!"

She guffawed so loud I snatched my head back from the phone in disgust. Goddamn, rhinoceros! "No, *seriously*. Lil Big Head and Big Crunch called and told me."

I sighed, getting out of bed, trying to shake last night into oblivion. It obviously followed me into the next day. I knew one thing; I would never do a gym work out and then go strip off my clothes at work with everything sore. I looked like a stiff block of ice.

"He say/she say bullshit, just like I thought. And anybody who believes Captain Crunch and Lil Big Ho—"

"—Lil Big Head—"

"Has got to be retarded. Those are the same two Niggahs who snitched to the cops and got Big Mack arrested for possession and intent to distribute. Foiled a forty thousand dollar operation.

As many times as Big Mack clothed, fed and looked out for those crummy assholes, they turn him in because he refused to give them a spot."

"Now see don't start that shit, Sonata! And it wasn't over a spot."

"Gurl, Sonata is my stage name. Lashay is my birth name. When I'm off the clock kindly refer to my birth name, ya' feel me?"

"You green, girl. You green."

"I'm not flaking out on you, so don't go there!"

"Don't start!"

"I'm in my own house; I can start whatever I damn well choose." I lit a cigarette and took a huge puff, tossing the lighter back on the nightstand. "Those Niggahs are snitches! They did turn him in because they couldn't get a spot (five dollars). And the streets are buzzing about it."

"The streets are *always* buzzing about something. That's the way the Hood works, the way it'll ever work." She released a large gush of air, sucking her teeth. I heard she sucked dick just as good as she sucked her teeth. That's what I heard. "Girl, get your head out cha ass, let's get back on the lawsuit...I'm bein' fo'real, Chile! They're suing Carl and Reuben LaBrage—"

"—well goddamn, you got first and last names—"

"—because Rolex U.S.A. say Carl and Reuben have been sulking up their image into building the image of the Rolexx Strip Club, Chile. That ain't a rumor. I read it on the internet, too. Plus, according to my sources—"

"—Lord this Ho got sources, do you have 1-800-Crime stoppers on speed dial too, Jaclyn—?"

"—there is a 45 page document carefully listing everything in detail. Everybody's talkin' 'bout it in the 'Hood, gurl. I was up in the Poke-n-Bean projects and even my cousin Bam said it was true, and this Niggah sells weed blind as fuck and can't read to tie his goddamn shoes, so you kno' its true."

OK. She was right about that. Now I was starting to worry. And the more I puffed this cigarette, taking long drags I knew I was starting to get stressed.

If they were talking about it on the internet, maybe they were talking about it on the Channel 7 News. I took the remote from the nightstand drawer and turned on my big screen TV. It hardly ever left Channel 7, and B.E.T. could kiss my ass. I didn't remember Justin Timberpussy, or Justin Timberfake being black. So why was he getting airplay?

The Rolexx was an institution, a cash cow. This place was to Miami what the Twin Towers was to New York, a place identifiable by everyone from the bums and crack heads to the nuns and the evangelists! People from so many states wanted to come to this club. Not everyone could get inside those walls. If those walls could talk happy homes and marriages would be instantly shattered. People talk about the hotness of Atlanta, nah, baby, the Rolexx got more entertainment than Atlanta and the year they hosted the Olympics.

I wasn't much for getting into people's business, but when it pertained to me, and jeopardizing the food that goes into my 11 year old son's mouth, then we got problems.

"Are you absolutely sure about this, Jaclyn?"

Putting the cordless phone on speaker phone, eye was opening and closing drawers, taking off my nightgown, snatching rollers out of my hair, my curls snapping into place; I put on tight blue jeans that rode the crack of my big booty, my titties were a little bit on the sagging side, but they still brought Mama some big money every night.

Last night I made $1,500.

I said, "Do you know how long the club been in existence, with that name. They don't fuck with anybody. All they do is make money; showcase all the Top Notch Hoes in Miami. Niggahs come and spend their entire paychecks on some tits and ass, and maybe get some pussy on the sly."

I put on a decent-looking bra, shifting my tits until they fit snuggly, put on my sling backs, and looked around my Big Lots-decorated room. Everything in here I bought from a store I called the ghetto K-Mart. I was cheap, I had a son who wanted everything on the goddamn TV, and I got it for him.

"Gurl, I don't see the watch company winning this lawsuit. The Rolexx had that name for thirty plus years. After all this time, why would they even *attempt* to sue? Sources say the Swiss bitches have been sending the Club letters for a year, demanding they change the name. Yea, right! Have they ever heard of statue of limitations?"

I scratched my tit and massaged my pussy, a little tingly sensation down there.

"That's what I know. And I don't think the statue of limitations pertains to this matter, I'm black, girl but I ain't stupid by a long shot. What judge is going to grant them compensatory damages?"

"A racist judge, Chile. Crackers are always try'na block a Niggah from making an earnest dollar. Pussy is pussy. And pussy is a business. Pussy is bigger than Hollywood, Chile! You know Niggahs can't catch a break. Bad enough we can't even split a Twix candy bar amongst our own kind, let alone win a lawsuit in a country that made laws for us to fail."

Sensation awakening deep inside my pussy walls. I slowly played with myself, spreading my legs, my eyes rolling to the back of my head. I was so wet I coulda swore a tidal wave washed over me. Bringing my fingers up to my hot mouth I tasted my juices, swallowing myself back into my body, recycling my essence.

My hips twirling, two fingers easily slid into my tight slit-of-an-opening, my pubic hair neatly trimmed...

I attempted to talk, disguising my sexual voice.

"Let's keep this conversation un-political. I'm not...political at all," eye said breathlessly.

Oh, God! My *pussy* was talking to me; I fingered myself for dear life, staring at my reflection in the mirror, my hole sliding up and down two fingers like oiled pistons drilling for oil.

"I don't vote and I could give a damn about George W. Asshole Bush and what that lying, cheating asshole has to goddamn say! I voted for Al Gore, tell me how that lying swine won? He doesn't care about black people, and he doesn't care about the troops either. They're dropping like flies while we pay for these high ass gas prices."

My eyes were stinging as I hold back the tears. My brother died in Iraq when a chopper crashed. I'd hate Bush forever, he needed to send his drunk, slutty goddamn daughters to Iraq and let those out-of-control Hoes pick up a hand grenade and a damn rifle.

All of this added to my sexual outburst. I pinched my clit, sprung my titties free, watching them bounce bounce bounce while I pulled both my legs all the way back, even with my ears, and I shuddered from my fingers…ass cheeks clapped together.

"And an Amen to that and a hallelujah to that one as well, gurl," Jaclyn said.

"Look, I'm about to get outta here. I'll holla."

"Bet."

Before she could hang up I slipped. "I gotta cum, oh God I gotta come I'm coming I'm coming."

"Bitch! Ew!" She was laughing. "Get it, gurl, you so nasty."

"Mommy, are you up for work."

My bedroom door opened and my son, shocked, covering his mouth, pointed at me and started laughing. I was stuck, legs even with my ears, phone pressed to my ear with my shoulder, nut on my fingers and I freaked, doing a somersault off the bed and pushing his ass out of my room, slamming the door closed.

"What did I tell you about coming in my room without knocking?"

"Oooh, Mama planting seeds in the garden."

My home girl and I started laughing.

I gotta be more careful.

I lived on NW 22 Avenue and 33rd Street. Been living in Liberty City all my life. I used to pass the gentlemen's club Rolexx when I was about ten years old. I was naïve and stupid, then. Believed any and everything somebody told me. I heard myths about that place. That behind those huge doors laid a Niggah's paradise, lesbianism, big money, superstars coming through and being thoroughly entertained by all that loose pussy. I heard men spend their entire life savings behind those doors, that big time dope was slung behind those doors, that the bar alone would turn a Kool-Aid drinker into an avid alcoholic. I was pulled by the passion of the place, lured by the rich history. My father called the Rolexx the Black White House. Thug Miami's Garden of Eden. I looked at him like he was crazy, but every Friday night, daddy abandoned me, my sister and Mama, who remained mum about it all, to go to this club with the fellahs.

He said he was a good boy. He never mistreated me or my family. He loved Mama with all his heart. But that club broke up happy homes, and it got to the point that daddy stopped paying bills just to go throw his money away to the "Hoes with the Golden Pussies!" behind those club doors.

I thought about this while sipping Hennessy from a huge red plastic cup, silently cruising NW 22nd Avenue in my 2007 Nissan Maxima, with my son, Melvin, strapped behind the seat belt, nodding his little cute head to some Tupac. Keep your head up, oh Chile. But shit ain't getting' any easier, especially with this lawsuit going on.

It was hard out here for a bitch like me, who liked the Finer Things, despite me shopping at discount stores and thrifty shops for my furniture. But my crib looked like Caesar's Palace.

Nothing was dirty, everything took their respective places. I sucked dick to move into that seedy apartment building. My deep throat skills waived me from paying $1,600 to move in, a security deposit and it also got me some extra cash and a Sugar Daddy on the side I went to see every Thursday night.

When his non-eating-pussy ass got through terrorizing my pussy with too much slob and too many episodes with what I called "loose teeth," just biting me everywhere, and the shit ain't cute, I got my $700 and he went back home to his white woman-of-a-wife, with her air-headed, pop tart ass.

I couldn't wrap my mind around this lawsuit. Why hadn't my boss told me about it? He knew I'd be fuming.

Did this mean we'd be out of a job? I could really use some conch and chicken wings from my job, tasted so good I was smacking my lips now.

I'd been entertaining, not stripping, mind you, for the Rolexx for three years. I loved it there!

On Tuesday nights the club gave free admissions and half-priced drinks to visitors.

You must come there when strippers get center stage, which was a small glass-brick beauty surrounded by the bar, and engage in amateur fights during the hours of the morning my son was in dreamland.

There were four fish tanks, an ancient feel about the place, the music was ravishingly pulsating, jumped right into my body when I did my numbers and made me feel like Jennifer Lopez.

I was well-liked and well-loved; my face was recognizable from here in Liberty City to the Florida Keys. I loved the Rolexx, oh my God where do I begin.

Its not hard work for me, yea I Pop My Pussy, Hey and Look Back At it five nights a goddamn week, but the money is right, and I love the local fame.

I get shit for free, you hear me? The car I'm driving, I gave up a shot of asshole and *voila*, the dealer signed it over to me, with a gracious smile and a lingering hand on my thigh and I was good to go.

No complaints here. I was there when Trina and Trick, club regulars and huge rap recording stars out of Miami, Florida, turned the place into bananas with their prestige. I was there when Jackie-O was so-called pulled out into the streets.

Shit was funny as hell; I ain't g'on lie. I've seen people get shot at, get their asses whipped, I know Uncle Luke Skywalker personally. Young Jeezy has seen the inside of the doors, Lil Wayne, and many others. The Rolexx was Miami Royalty!

83 DAPHAROAH69

I remember when the Florida Division of Alcoholic Beverages and Tobacco (ABT) and the Miami-Dade police raided the club. I remember it like it was yesterday. It was on March 24, 2004. So many people got arrested that it wasn't even funny. Charges of prostitution (big time thing up in there, let's be real, I know I sell pussy), lewdness, unlawful use of weapons, amongst other charges, was the end result. The club lost their liquor license for thirty days. Then to make matters worse on December 26th of the same year, around about 5-5:30 a.m., a dear friend of mine, 22 year old Tavares Gisslander, was shot in the stomach when he was leaving.

That was horrifying. I wanted to quit working at the club then, but I stayed because Tavares lived.

"And now I may be out of a job."

My son looked at me, turning down the radio. My little man. Looked just like his daddy, who was doing twenty-five years to life in prison for murder in the first degree.

"Mama, what are you talking about?"

I was on my way to take him to school. My son didn't catch the school bus; I personally walked him inside, signed him in school, and checked him out. His teachers and I were on first name basis. I was serious about his schooling, didn't want no dumb ass son.

"Nothing, baby."

"Are you gonna get fired?" He had an attitude, and I wasn't in the mood for child's play.

"No, baby."

"You *should* get fired, Mama."

His response shocked me. I looked at him, rubbing his head. "Why do you say that, baby?"

"Because. I don't want my Mama stripping off her clothes."

Darkness befell his face and it made me shudder.

"I don't strip, baby. I entertain," I lied, telling myself this was my reality, lies, despite telling everyone I was a Real

Bitch, that I never lied about anything, that I wasn't scared of anyone when I was indeed scared of how my son viewed me.

He rolled his eyes and turned up the radio. I thought it to be rude, so the black came outta me quick, fast and in a hurry. I turned the music down.

I pointed at him, stopping at the red light. It was hot as hell, so I turned on the AC.

"Don't turn the radio up when I'm talkin', have you lost your fuckin' mind?"

"Sorry Mama, but I don't want you stripping."

My eyes flashed dangerously. "Who's the adult and who's the child?"

He challenged me. "Maybe I should be the adult, at least I wouldn't be stripping."

Impulsively, I slapped him across the face and quickly regretted it. He turned his back on me, arms folded across his chest, staring angrily out of the window. My heart bled, this was my baby! I couldn't take my anger out on my seed.

"Son."

He exploded. "Leave me alone, Mama! I make good grades. I do everything you say. I stay at home by myself while you strip your clothes off." He was huffing and puffing. Broke my heart. I wanted to love him, hold him and squeeze him. "I have no daddy. He's gone forever! How can I respect a man who's locked up for murder and now my friends pick at me in school."

"What do they say?"

"They say I am a bastard child, that my daddy could be one of the thousands of men who pass through that dang club! My friend Kevin said his daddy had sex with you the other night at your private show. He said he hid in the closet and watched you sucking him up until he buss a nut. And my friend Dexter said when he turns 18 he's gonna give you twenty dollars so he can have sex with you!"

My world was spinning; never had I known my son was getting the brut of my decisions in his school. He didn't deserve that.

"I can't believe my son is talking to me about my indiscretions. What am I doing wrong?"

"Well I'm not talking to you, until you quit taking off your clothes. I hate you so much."

And he closed his eyes really tight and I died inside, I couldn't lose my son. Eye already lost his daddy to the prison system. He'll be fucking men in the ass soon.

"Son." I reached over to touch him and he jumped away from me, took off his seat belt, opened the door, jumped out and ran off.

I died, what was I to do?

I parked at the corner store and ran behind my child, these shoes killing my feet. I was starting to sweat my hair do out my head, and this pissed me off because I took pride in my hair.

My son ran fast and hard, not looking back, turning the corner.

I was right behind him. Mama did run track in high school and got some first place medals.

When he tried to hop the wooden fence I grabbed his little ass, turned him into my face and grabbed both his arms, shaking him.

"Are you crazy? Are you try'na give me a heart attack?"

"Fuck you, Mama! *Let* me go!"

I couldn't believe this! He never cursed me, never disrespected me.

Why now?

"Take it back! *Take* back that word."

"No!" He spat in my face.

I was shocked into silence.

I stood up, taking a few steps back. He looked at me maliciously.

"I'm running away, I don't want you to be my Mama anymore."

Before I could grab my son a tall, handsome man in a pair of blue coveralls snatched my son up, and pulled him to his stern face.

"Did you just spit in your Mama's face young man?"

"Fuck you, Niggah who you supposed to be?"

The sexy specimen turned my son upside down and started spanking his ass.

Why did I smile?

"I am 29 years old. I was raised to respect my elders and goddamn it, I ain't your daddy. I don't know you. But. You. Will. Respect. Me."

He dropped my son on the floor.

He lay there, crying and putting, looking at me and eye turned my head.

For some reason I didn't do anything. I just covered my mouth in shock, wide-eyed.

"Stand up young man, now!" the Stranger demanded, authority coming to him like a sixth sense.

My son flipped him the middle finger. "Fuck you I ain't—"

"—NOW!—"

The house seemed to shake. I was startled.
My son snapped to attention. "You ain't my daddy! Fuck niggah step the fuck back mah niggah!"

"You're right, but that's your goddamn mother. My Mama is dead young man. I can *never* have her back and I'll be damned if I let you disrespect her, now apologize before I whip your little ass up and down 79th street."

Reluctantly, he walked up to me and hesitated.
My Chocolate Angel whisked him off the ground.

"Do I sense hesitation?" he asked my son. My son was scared shitless. "I tell you what. I was about to cut my grass and fix my goddamn toilet."

He looked at me, holding my son in mid-air with one hand and he took my hand and kissed it. My pussy started crying tears I didn't know it had. "I'm Kevin. Can I borrow him for a couple hours?"

I smiled. "Sure, as long as his Mama can stay and watch."

"I got a 62 inch plasma TV mounted in the wall, my fridge is stocked to the roof, and got thousands of movies, and you can go and lounge inside while me and your bad ass son get some yard work done."

"What about your wife. *Man* you're too fine to be single."

He was silent. "My wife died last year in car accident."

I gave him a quick hug; he was still holding my son in mid air. My son was scared of him.

Kevin's sleeves were rolled up. His muscles flexed.

"I'm sorry for your loss."

He nodded towards the door.

"Go inside. We're gonna be a while."

Inside I went!  Paradise!  This Niggah was loaded.  He had the best of everything!  I started comparing his house to my crib.  I was Miss Big Lots and Miss Super Wal-Mart.  He was Burdines, Bloomindales, and JCPenny.  The best fabrics on the beds.

I went through a few drawers, neatly folded clothing. Ceramic clay pots were here and there…in the master bedroom his ties were out of this world.

His walk-in-closet looked like a living-room-closet, shoes, shoes and more shoes.

I got dizzy when I got to pair number eighty.

On to the living room. Beige and black. Entertainment shelf to die for, a huge plasma TV that made mine look like a tic tac. The high tech kitchen was the show stopper.

My pussy was wet from the sight of all this.

Oriental carpeting. A picture of a beautiful woman and her son on the end table.

I suspected it was his son.

I got a little upset.

Why didn't he say all this when I was outside?

He had to be a player.

A polished Jag was in the driveway.  The back yard was so big I counted about eleven huge trees.

Well-cut grass, a pool, the whole nine. The man lived like a dream.

"Admiring the back yard?" he asked and I spun to face him. He was behind me, handing me an opened Heineken. I usually didn't drink this beer but what the hell. It was free and ice cold. We looked each other deep in the eyes.

"Yes. I am."

"You admired mine, and I was admiring yours. Not to sound crass but you have a phat ass."

I smiled. "Thank you."

"What do you do for a living?"

"I entertain."

"Really?" He smiled easily. "Where do you sing?"

I laughed, patting his shoulder. "I dance. I have a dance troupe," I lied.

"Really, when can I come show my support?" He leaned up to my lips and I panicked.

Damn it, the man was fine fine FINE and he wanted to kiss me but the instant I leaned up to his lips to complete the transaction he averted them and kissed my cheek.

"Anytime you wanna come."

"Just give me the directions," he said.

Did he not know who I was? Sonata. The Stripper? I was a bit impervious.

Despite my angst, I was horny. Extremely horny. Still embarrassed my son walked in on me. But I wanted this man deep inside me.

"Where's my son?"

He pointed behind me. I saw my boy. Driving the lawn mower, looked like a little four wheeler. I was smiling, opening his back door, saying, "I didn't know my baby could drive one of those things."

"Gurl you are in the City! Every little niggah know how to drive those things. Your son has great potential, but he is also hurting. He told me about his father while I was taking the lawn mower from the shed."

I wouldn't look at him. We were getting too personal. Too fast. We just met. Now was not the time to tie strings together.

"Yea, he's locked up for life."

"I could mentor him."

I faced him. "I love my son."

"He said he doesn't wanna go home with you."

I was quiet for a moment, my heart beating so fast I felt like a hurricane. I looked at the floor, wringing my hands.

"Nonsense." I looked at him. "He's going home. In fact he's going now."

"Let him at least finish cutting the grass."

"How much are you paying him?"

"I am giving him a book on Andrew Young and another on Martin Luther King. And if he does an extremely good job, I am giving him Harriet Tubman's autobiography."

My eyes flashed dangerously. "Fuck them! How much are you paying—"

"He's getting books *filled* with knowledge. Without it, how do you expect to go into the world and make money, let alone become a man?"

"Listen Mr. Book Keeper." Now I was getting an attitude. He remained calm, observing me, and that even drove me crazy. "Fuck Harriet, Martin and his Mama, too. This is the '*Hood*! We're *stressed* around these parts. Now I don't know what planet you fell from, but you need to go back. I'ma real bitch, a gangster bitch! I get my money!"

I saw something in his eyes snap. He got defensive.

"*Look*. You can take your ass home. Don't anybody disrespect me in my house. I was just showing you some love because your son shows signs of disaster. He needs a man in his life, a black man, someone like me who is doing the right thing, been to jail, even did five years in prison but turned my life around, got a B.A. degree in business, my Masters from U.C.L.A., and I'm still young: 29 years old to be exact."

"You just want your yard cut for free. My son doesn't need your Oxford-colored ass. Why do you gregarious Niggahs think you're God's Gift?"

He got snappy. "I guess he made you a Present."

"He did!"

"A stripper. A stripper, Miss Realness? I guess you *are* a real bitch!"

I slapped him and bit my bottom lip, wide-eyed. I was offended. He put his hands on his hips, averted his face, his temples twitching wildly. I got a little scared. This man was well into the 6 feet tall arena and I was five-four, five-five.

"Look. Go home. I tried to be civil."

"No you tried to get in my panties. This is all about pussy; all that you got a phat ass bullshit. It didn't flatter me. My son doesn't need you. He needs me."

"Even though he *doesn't* wanna go home with you."

I was thrown through a damn loop. "He's a child, Kevin! He doesn't know what he wants."

"I know what you need."

*Bullshit! Drop dead, punk!* "What would that be?" I stormed past him, pausing by the island counter, pots dangling from the ceiling.

"Your ass kicked."

I snapped. "Bitch you don't..." I was throwing punches at him and he caught both my hands, yanking me into his face.

He said through clinched teeth. "You know they lock women up for masturbating in front of their kids."

I got really quiet.

I measured my words. "What are you talking about?" I played really stupid. I was gonna kick my son's ass for telling my business; it ain't my fucking fault he just waltzed into my damn room without knocking.

"Your son told me what he walked in on. Are you aware I am a Miami-Dade Police Officer, I could have you arrested right now, charged and booked before your head could spin?"

"*Whatever*. You do that I'll tell your wife and son you're trying to fuck me."

He laughed. "Wife? *Son*?" He let me go and I walked over, snatched up the huge photo and held it up. "These two, your family. All you men are fucking dogs!"

"I'm...not."

"Your voice just betrayed you. I guess this ain't your son, 'ey?"

He got chocked up. "No, it's not."

"You deny your own son! Look at him, spitting image of you. He got your eyes, your chin, and your nose. If you were Austin Powers this would be Mini-me."

"That is not my son."

I put the picture back and said, "I guess Billy Jean is not your lover as well, 'ey Michael Jackson. I'm going to get my son. We'll be leaving; you can arrest me all you want. Kids lie all the goddamn time. Can you prove I masturbated in front of my son?"

He was quiet.

I smiled in victory.

"Figures. Nice meeting you. Have a good day."

I sashayed out into his back yard and when I grabbed my son's arm, telling him to "Get off this lawn mower and bring your ass on. He ain't paying you, he trying to give you books," I heard Kevin say, "The woman in the picture is my mother, and she's holding me, over nineteen years ago."

I lowered my head.

For some reason I turned around, walked up to him, wrapped my arms around him and gave him the slowest, most passionate tongue kiss known to man.

At that moment I knew I was no longer a single woman, or a single mother.

I finally had a good man.

But would it last?

# F[o]O[d]
# St[am]p

I meet men just to get their money. Um, that's about it. Nothing more nothing less. And with the way things were going, I was about to bring my pussy out of hibernation. Depressed, I sat in my home (I got through Section 8) on NW 37th Avenue and 183rd Street for about two weeks, pondering how I was going to pay my $90 dollar rent. And over in these apartments across from the Walgreen's people were nosier and lied worse than Pinocchio.

What set it off was the letter I got in the mail from the Department of Children and Families. I was so upset at the contents I went to the food stamp office.

Upset, I was in the food stamp line and I was having a bad goddamn time. I got $345 a month for three kids and they just cut my stamps because of some faulty paperwork glitch which wasn't my fault.

I gave them all the information they needed so what was the fucking problem? How was my kids gonna eat? I went there in an ankle-length floral skirt and my hair pulled into a tight Chinese bun that made my eyes look *sa ca dah ah dong wong*. That's Chinese for *bitch I need these stamps*.

A few ladies said I smelled good and I said thanks, I used my pussy spray. Feminine Deodorant Spray.

I FDS'ed this damn dress because it smelled like Black and Milds.

Yea, I smoked 'gars (cigars).

I asked for my social worker or case worker, whichever it's called. Walked right past everybody in the line because I didn't have time to wait. And the place was so jam packed people were waiting outside in that hot ass sun.

I was told, with an attitude, to have a seat. So I found a seat by the restroom. Must have been fate a seat was empty.

After waiting tirelessly for three hours, my case manager came out with a chip on her shoulder. I didn't give a damn. She tried to avoid my eyes and I got up and walked right in her face.

"Why did they cancel my stamps?" I asked angrily. I could hardly breathe.

I got rowdy, showing my ass and she took me by the hand and pulled me inside her small ass office. I snatched my arm free. "Don't grab me like that, are you crazy"

I didn't care about the tons of pictures of her kids all over the place and her Miami Dade Community College degrees.

Anybody can get a degree from that damn college. All they want is your fucking money. She said, "We had to cancel your stamps."

"But my kids need to eat."

"Then get a job. Get on your grind."

"Do you have a heart? Are your kids starving?"

"No. I have gainful employment."

"And you're going to be a bald headed bitch if my kids don't eat."

"Calm down Miss Thing. You broke one of the rules."

"Yet you haven't told me why my stamps are canceled."

"With your attitude I just want you to get out of this office. You have been denied."

I looked at this bitch sideways. Oh, no! "What?"

"Denied, lady."

"Well you don't have to get an attitude about it."

"You got one first."

"Ya'll gonna give me my goddamn stamps! I gotta feed my fucking children."

"You need to stop cursing."

"BITCH!" I stood up and pushed her files and shit on the floor and she sat there looking at me, frowning.

"So ghetto."

"At least I know I'm ghetto bitch clearly you forgot where you come from."

"I come from my Mama's womb."

"Chile, fuck off."

"Go to hell."

"What, Hoe?" I said, getting in her face and she placed her palms flat on the desk, eyeing me as she stood up.

"Who are you calling a Hoe?"

"You, bitch!"

"Get out my office."

"With pleasure you pussy munching dyke!"

When they told me, "No" and turned me down, saying someone else used my name and identity and got some stamps, eye snatched the lower part of my dress off until it was a you-can-see-my-pussy skirt, my ass cheeks were like peek a boo I see you and eye grabbed my knock off Chanel purse and left her office, my heels clicking against the cheap marble.

I entered the lobby, my titties jiggling and I shook this ass to the door. I didn't know how I was going to feed my children this month and Lord knows I didn't feeling like putting my pussy on the market.

I dropped out of school when I was 15 when I had my first child, my baby daddy, who promised to marry me, left me high and dry, went to college and never checked on us. I was alone, vulnerable and very bitter.

I tried going back to school. I really did. But trying wasn't doing and I gave the hell up. Especially with my mother telling me I couldn't do it (she didn't even do it, bitch could barely spell her name). My Daddy didn't care. I didn't like his ass and he knew it. He had 5 daughters and fucked all five, including me, one night when I was drunk last year.

When I found out what he did I tried to cut the bitch but he pulled a gun on me and threatened to kill me so I left and never called him again.

And now I had to do something to feed my kids.

I wasn't doing right by my stamps anyway and this was why God probably took them away. I would cash them in for money. What I meant was I'd go to the store being as cute as I could be. When I saw someone about to pay for groceries with cash I would walk up to them, tell them to give me that money and I would pay for it with my EBT card, that way they paid in food stamps and left with their food and I left with their money. But I charged a fee. For $50 worth of food on my card they had to give me $80, and these Cubans were so goddamn dumb I made a killing and could still pay rent on time.

Now my hustle was fucked off.

With my dress ripped into a pussy popping skirt, somebody was going to bite. And the first man I walked by, who was applying for Medicaid and stamps, pulled me out the door.

Muthafuckah eye don't know you! I snatched my hand back. I hated when off brand, lame ass Niggahs grabbed on me like he knew me. I don't *know* where your *hands* been. I looked him up and down. He smelled good. He had on name brand this and that. He licked his lips and I rolled my eyes, smelling garlic bread on his breath.

Scratching my pussy eye told him eye didn't want a broke Niggah.

He said he wasn't broke. Yea, okay kay kay. But you're applying for stamps and Medicare. Only broke niggahs do that, I said. But I got a big dick, he retaliated childishly.

Big dicks don't pay the bills, and coming in my pussy adds another child to my inventory.

He said he applied for stamps because thugs and dope boys needed to eat.

Well, he had a point.

Never looked at it like that.

He then said "Dope dealers get sick too, pretty thang... I make money under the table and sometimes bitches and Niggahs suck my dick when they cant afford the coke, and we're not talking about canned sodas."

"How much you make in a week?" I asked.

"None of your business."

"Damn, why you're so secretive?"

"I don't know you."

"Your dick doesn't know me but I want to know it, Niggah."

"Damn you blunt."

I licked my lips. "I'm a whore, too."

I stuck my finger in my pussy till my asshole got jealous and my tits sent out APB's and I quickly rubbed it on his thick, dark lips, making him suck it off my fingers.

I was kind of turned off. I had threesomes before, when men sucked a dick and fucked me in the ass in the process. And the way his tongue ran up and down my pussy further let me know he sucked a few…pipes in his life time. Real men didn't suck a finger they licked a finger.

They didn't want anything but food and gold grills in their mouths. But he moaned, closing his eyes sucking my fingers like my thumbs were testicles. Opening his eyes, he took my finger out of his mouth and said he made about $14,000 a MONTH.

Ok.

I gave him my number and told him to text me because my phone was off and Metro PCS only allowed incoming texts to your phone.

He text me and his number came up and I stored it. He text me again when I hopped in my brother's beat up Mazda.

He said come over to his girl's crib. I couldn't text him back so he text her address. He said she was out of town. Your girl or your wife.

My wife when she's home but she's my girl when she's out of town.

Yawn. So I came over. What a jazzy house. I wasn't Martha Stewart Living, I was a bad bitch trying to make a living so I ignored the fancy couches and throw pillows. I ignored the eyes following me in the hanging pictures and I stripped off my clothes and let him get a visual of the pussy.

He gave me four hundred to put on a purple mask and suck his dick while humping his fingers.

My pussy was so wet it was like someone poured a Coors light on my head and the beer ran down my face like misplaced tears.

That paid my rent.

I needed grocery.

I had kids.

It was all about them.

He bought me a ton of food. At the grocery store. We actually shopped together. He walked a few feet behind me the entire time, putting his phone on silent and pretending to be talking to his wife.

"Yea baby I love you. When are you coming in from out of town. Yea I fed the dogs. I miss you."

A few of his wife's friends passed by and he spoke and they asked about her and he said she's fine.

My pussy ate up these tight ass jeans and it was irritating my pink walls and I had to keep digging them out of there. I pretended like I didn't know him. When I got home he helped me put up the food and he then said he wanted to fuck my ass.

I said that was risky, so give me some whiskey. He got me drunk and fucked me so good I woke up with a hang over and full of cum.

If money makes the world go around then his paycheck stands the motherfucker still. I have bills to pay.

I am not going to bullshit.

Mama always taught me that a kept man is the best man to keep because when he wines and dines you in your home bringing shit his wife bought then it's as easy as a b c.

You don't have possession of the marriage license and it's not in your goddamn name.

He's a visitor in your home, not a house guest or a name on your lease.

I will suck his dick, drumming my fingers along the shaft.

Before he has to cum its all good because if he cums in two minutes I will get his money in thirty seconds.

Don't ask me am I ok, don't ask are my kids good, don't ask about my daughter's recital and don't fluff my goddamn pillow.

Get your nut, save your Hallmark moments, drop company funds on the dresser and get the fuck out.

# *Illusions*

At a low volume, Barry White softly coos into the moist bedroom from the Infinity speakers. Damien, a 56 year old professional male, turned over and kissed his beautiful wife, India, a 50 year old Caucasian/African American. She stared into his loving eyes the way she had for 32 years, rubbing his low-fade. She felt safe and secure with her husband, a man she met one rainy, muggy day so many years ago when she was shopping with her grandparents at the local Goodwill. She was a mere 18 years old then, still figuring out the world.

The stud-of-a-black man, who was a college hopeful and a well sought after football player with dreams of making it big, seemed to drop from the sky.

Presently, she kissed his lips, remembering how passionate he was back then about the NFL Draft. He stroked her backside, remembering himself.

After she introduced him to her grandmother, who didn't like him very well (because she *knew* his type), he told her she was the most beautiful woman he'd ever seen.

Grandma nodded her disapproval, mumbling that he was trying to move in, screw her and move out. But he turned out to be a doll.

They exchanged phone numbers and he'd given her a necklace his dad had once given him. It was a promise to call him. He'd never let anyone hold the necklace, yet he gave it to India.

He knew then he'd love her forever because she wasn't like the other whores he'd screwed without a conscious.

She was innocent and pure. She dressed so beautifully. She was very curvaceous, but she had every ounce covered up.

She wore her hair in a loose ponytail and thin glasses rested on the tip of her pointy nose. She had a little attitude, sticking her nose up at certain points like he was the ugliest man alive.

He loved it.

She kept her promise. She'd called him around 4 p.m. and he offered to take her out to eat. She said, "Sure," but he had to have her home by twelve a.m. because she didn't stay out late with guys she just met.

Plus her grandmother had a Midnight Rule: *If you knocked on the door at 12:01 a.m. you were "Shit out of luck."*

He respected that.

After his father helped him pick out something nice to wear, he was heading out the door with pep in his step. He then promised his father he'd bring her by so they could meet.

His father, a military man more decorated than any American living room, said, "You never brought anyone over for me to meet." He smiled at his son, patting his shoulder. "I would love to meet her, Son. But I'm going fishing by my lonesome. Your mother upset me, but I just need to fish, set up a pole, drink a couple Coors Light and I'll be fine."

*You may not meet her. I'm going to bone her. I know she'll give it up to me. They always give it up to me.*

"OK, Pa. Just don't be out there too late."

James was pleased. "Love you, Son," he told Damien.

Damien said, "I love you, too,"

He was all set for Virginia Tech when disaster struck.

While Damien and India were out eating and laughing the hours away, his father drank too many beers. When they were dancing on the dance floor, wowing restaurant patrons, his father fell over the small boat and into the water.

He couldn't swim. When Damien lured her to the male bathroom and tried kissing her, his father was screaming out to God for help, with no one around.

When Damien hugged India, squeezing her buttocks with a warm kiss, his father's body was growing weaker and weaker.

His life was slowly transitioning back to God.

When India pushed Damien into the stall and said, "I am a virgin! I am not ready! And you bring me in the bathroom, Creep?" his father was so out of it he began to sink in the salt water.

When Damien bought India a dozen roses, apologizing—Yes! She's the One! I want to marry her— walking her out to his mother's stuffer car, his father's body took one final jerk, tiny ripples forming in the water, and he floated up to the shore.

With his little boom box playing Otis Redding, nine beer cans opened and empty and his pick up truck sitting there, fading into the sunset.

A wallet-sized picture of Damien and his father floated up to the rocky ledge, bouncing on the tiny waves.

James was Damien's life.

When Damien parked in his parent's drive way, his mother was sitting on the porch in tears.

She rocked back and forth, rubbing her arms.

Damien opened India's door and took her hand as they slowly approached her.

She said, "He hasn't come home yet. I upset him. He's probably with another woman."

Deeply hurt, Damien offered to take India home but she didn't feel good and she said she'd come along.

He squeezed her upper leg and said, "Thank you."

She knew then he'd be her husband.

When Damien saw his father's truck he told India, "He's probably wasted. He always comes to this spot to fish when things bother him. I love that about him. He'd rather walk away and think about it then come back with a rational mind and talk about it."

"I can't wait to meet him."

He parked the car by the truck and got out. India got out and closed her door, noticing all the beer cans.

"Dad, wake up," said Damien, looking inside the truck. "He isn't in there…"

Into the night, with a huge full moon beaming over the earth below, the rustle of the waters arrested his attention.

India walked ahead of him and said, "It looks beautiful out here tonight…"

He paused beside her, taking her hand and cupping it. "I want you to be my girl."

She looked into his eyes. "Really. And why should I, after the stunt you pulled."

*I love her! She talks to me like she means what she says. She didn't open her legs, she actually kept them closed.*

"I apologized."

"But I haven't forgotten. Sex scares me. People say it feels good and all this stuff but I heard it hurts and women aren't appreciated or respected once a man deflowers her."

"I won't do that to you."

They embraced and she closed her eyes, loving his arms. She rubbed his back and he didn't want to let her go.

He wanted to pour into her body, become one and make it official.

He had an erection that pulsated in his slacks, ready to burst.

India opened her eyes and stared a moment at the floating body.

A photograph was stuck on one of the rocks on the ledge.

She backed away from Damien, shaking her head, huge tears falling from her eyes.

She covered her face and he was alarmed.

"What, baby! What did I do wrong?" he asked desperately.

Fright colored his face and she was about to run.

She walked towards the truck and said, "I have to go. I have to go *NOW!*"

"Why?" He grabbed her by the arms and shook from her sudden pain.

He saw the fright in her eyes.

He hugged her tight. "What is it?"

She waited a moment, her arms limp.

She inhaled, taking his hand.

"You're not going to like this. In fact, it's going to destroy you."

She pointed towards the lake and he looked back.

He didn't see anything.

They slowly approached the waters.

He was serene and full of solitude.

The moon in perfect position, the glow turning shapes and trees into black silhouettes.

She paused at the ledge.

He looked down and he lost sensation in his entire body. He could barely form the words in his mind.

"*DADDY!*" He got in the water and India helped pull James out.

"*DADDY! WAKE UP! I TOLD YOU TO BE CAREFUL!*"

He shook with revulsion, vomiting by the ledge.

He felt faint. "HOW WILL I TELL MOM?"

India said, "Damien. He's gone."

He hugged his father close and sobbed.

India hugged Damien from behind, and vowed to love him, always.

His mother, Dee, took it harder than Damien. She lost the love of her life and felt guilty for accusing him of cheating when he hadn't.

Damien became a shell and would only talk to India.

He was there for his mother, still cut the grass like she expected and he dropped college.

He wasn't pursuing any football dreams when his dad wasn't there to see it.

Damien didn't believe in ghosts so all that "He's there in spirit" bullshit was just that: a load of bullshit.

Dee blamed herself. She was sitting in the living room with James's photographs spread about her from different stages of his life.

She guardedly sipped some coffee with liquor.

Damien sat on the sofa with his head low, dead inside.

India sat next to his mother.

Depressed, Dee said that if she hadn't upset him over something so small he'd be alive.

India looked at her and said, "That's not true."

Damien and Dee looked up slowly.

"There are no mistakes with human life," India said. "*Everyone* who dies, gets killed, drowns, well...it was their time to go. God called them home. A stray bullet through a child's temple isn't a mistake. It wasn't meant for someone else, no matter what the public says. It was her time to go. That means the purpose was served. It is finished. We all have to go. There's only two ways humans will die: tragically or peacefully."

Impulsively, Damien jumped up to his feet and said, "So you're telling me that it was his time to go?"

She wasn't intimidated. She looked him deep in the eyes. "Yes. It was, Damien."

"I think you should go home," he said, stomping to the door.

Dee said, "Damien, calm down."

"Its bad enough my dad is gone but I won't have a girl I just met justifying anything."

She stood up and grabbed her purse. "What did I justify?"

"That crap. Innocent people dying."

"We all have to go."

Dee reached up and cupped India's hand and Damien said, "Well, you have to go."

"I have no way home. You brought me here."

"Walk."

Dee said, "DAMIEN!"

He stuck out his bottom lip. "She can walk."

"Well you won't be driving my car anywhere," his mother said. "You can walk. *Period.*" She stood up and told India, "I'll take you home. Come on, Sweetie."

"Thanks, Dee."

India walked up to Damien and he turned his head. He wanted her to leave. He didn't know how he felt about her anymore.

Maybe she wasn't the one.

How dare she butt in and say bullshit that wasn't true.

"You are selfish. But that's ok. I'll go home. Do you think you're the only one with problems?"

Dee said, "My husband just drowned, young lady. Don't badger my son."

"Yea," said Damien, acting like a child, turning India off. Defensively, India shook her head.

"Well let me tell you a story."

Damien said, "No, thanks. Let Mama take you home."

India spat, "…My mother died after giving birth to me."

Damien looked deep into her eyes and Dee took a few steps back, sitting on the couch in shock.

"Ever wonder *why* I live with my grandparents? I never touched or smelled my mother. I never got to play with dolls or comb her hair. My father…I never met him. He came into her life and they got married. He then left town when she wound up pregnant. He would later get murdered by the mafia because he stole money from them. Both of my parents are gone. So don't you goddamn dare tell me no one has it worst?"

Dee said, "Baby..."

India snapped so fast Dee fell into silence.

"Don't baby me. You and your son need to get your heads out of your asses. Yea, your husband died. But you enjoyed him. Damien got to know his father, tell him I love you and all that. I didn't have the opportunity. I miss my mother and I don't even remember her. That's the greatest crime. To see the sunset and hope it's the sunrise and it turns out to be nine planets, one more mysterious than the other. That's what it feels like."

India walked past Damien and opened the door. She stamped down the porch.

Dee said, "Baby, *please* wait. I'll drive you."

"I'll walk," said India. "For every yard I walk I'll say a prayer to the mother I never met. Damien has his mother."

And she didn't look back.

India didn't walk half a mile when Dee's car paused beside her and Damien hopped out.

"That was strike two and three," she told him. "I don't want to ever see you again."

His heart dropped. Bad enough he had to cope with his father's death. It was all still fresh. "Get in the car."

She glared into his eyes. "Screw you. I don't want you anymore. My grandmother was right. You are a self-serving sex maniac who took me into the male bathroom in a public restaurant hoping I'd have sex with you."

He took her hands and she snatched them away. Felt like blades slammed through his heart. He couldn't breathe.

"Please, I love you. Don't leave."

*Please, I love you. Don't leave.*

"The damage has been done," she said, weakening. "It's over. We will never be."

"I said I was sorry."

"And that makes it right? Just because you said I'm sorry? You said a lot of shit, man."

"I need you."

"You need me? I don't think you even believe that."

"I do."

"Listen. Leave me alone."

121 DAPHAROAH69

She walked off, leaving him to take out his anger on his mom's car.

*Time to show him what love is.* She put him through eight months of hell. She dated other guys. She maintained *class* while doing so. Everywhere she went Damien popped up.

He brutally beat her dates to a pulp. She lost her virginity with a church boy who loved God and appreciated the female body. He was slow and tender, explosive and magnetic.

But he wasn't Damien. In fact she called out Damien's name when he made her cum for the very first time in her natural life.

She would later leave the church boy because he tried to manipulate and control her; tell her what she could and couldn't do. She talked to Damien about that. He whipped the boy's ass so badly he and his parents packed up and left town.

"Take me back," he told India.

She studied him. *He hasn't learned yet.* "Earn it."

She kept dating and having relationships with *hot* guys. Damien stalked her, following her everywhere.

She didn't care.

She once told him, "You put your goddamn hands on me I will put you in jail and fuck up your life."

Boom. That was the end of his stalking in a nutshell.

She went through the highs and lows of love, finding out that a handsome face didn't equal brains and manners.

She found out men could be assholes.

They wanted what they wanted when they wanted and it didn't work like that.

In fact she used to cry herself to sleep at night trying to make her boyfriends love her.

She got a job and tried to buy their love and she wound up broke, got a yeast infection and had to have an abortion because she really didn't know who the father was. Part of her was becoming bitter.

She moved out of her grandma's house and got an apartment in Opa Locka.

She thought about Damien.

*Nah. He still hasn't learned.*

*He thinks its all about him.*

India got a phone call from one of the guys who liked her.

He said that he had something to tell her.

"What is it?"

"It's about your boy, Damien."

"What about him?"

"You should talk to him. He's *miserable* without you. I didn't know you two had a thing for each other. If I'd known, I wouldn't have pursued you."

"He's a prick who thinks its all about him."

"Listen. He's letting go. Its like that smooth guy he used to be is turning into a thug. He's starting to sell drugs and he gave up football."

She sat up in her bed, wide-eyed.

*He hasn't learned yet, though.*

"Not my problem."

"He loves you."

"How do you know?"

"He goes downtown everyday singing to the public, anybody that'll listen. I love India, he chants, and he means it. Everyone thinks he's on crack but he's not. He quit his job and he stopped talking to his mom."

*So what. He still hasn't learned.*

"I'm tired. I'm going back to bed. You should come over so we can talk."

"Ok, but I leave you with this. Pay his father's grave site a visit."

"Why."

"You'll see."

Click.

She waited up for homeboy but he never showed. She put on a dress and some sandals, grabbed her purse and was out the door.

She took the county bus to Richmond Heights and got off by Bethel Baptist Church. She had to walk a ways, the sun bearable, thank God.

She saw a few people she knew but she didn't speak.

She put on her shades and walked towards the grave yard.

To see Damien's father.

She slowly approached the inconspicuous-looking tomb. It had one inscription on the headstone.

## JAMES

That's it. No year of birth nor the year he died.

She got on her knees and lowered her head. There was a cherry bush behind it. And it was decorated. With "I love India!" on construction paper. She smiled so hard she started to cry. On one of the pictures, Damien had drawn, was of them eating out for the first time.

The other was of her receiving roses. The third drawing was of them hugging by his father's pick up truck.

Very detailed pictures, like he'd sat out there all day and night and created his heart's memories.

*He's finally learned.*

She looked up and said, "*Well*, James. Your son's a good man. And he's starting to look more and more like you when you were his age."

She took off her shades. She looked into the sunlight and let it warm up her gorgeous face.

"I will love and honor your son from here on out. He had to learn that not all women want to screw him. He had to learn responsibility and I had the experience of playing the field. Hell, he got to do the same thing before we met. We're opposite of each other. He was experienced and immature and I was inexperienced and mature. Now life has balanced us out."

She stood up and grabbed her shades.

For a while I thought you were my father, James. Military man, you came into town and I remember once seeing you sneak into my Mom's room. You never saw me, of course, but I used to read the letters you wrote her, saying, 'Make sure my daughter is ok,' and all that. But it turned out that you weren't my Dad. I knew this even when Damien first approached me in the Good will."

She took a few steps back.

"But I did lie to your family about my mother dying when she gave birth to me. No. She didn't die. She's very much alive. In fact when she gave birth to me I was savagely taken and switched with another child. I was then put up for adoption. An elderly woman adopted me. I would call her my grandmother. Even when I looked Dee in the eyes when Damien introduced me to her I *knew* she was my mother. But tell me something, James. Why didn't you tell her the truth about Damien? That you had a child out of wedlock? That

Damien isn't her biological son? That he's the son of her best friend."

India sat on the grass and played around with the blades.

She sighed.

"...Dee's best friend, Mindy, is now on drugs. I know it all. Dee and Mindy got pregnant around the same time. Mindy had been having sex with you, James, behind Dee's back. Mindy and Dee had a scheduled C-section at the same time. They wanted to have babies together. Dee was pregnant with me and her best friend was pregnant with Damien. I guess you all lied. Dee had slept with someone else and got pregnant and she made you think you were the father. Since you were one of the doctors at the hospital, you helped her switch Damien at birth. Dee wound up with Mindy's son and Mindy wound up with me. But Mindy didn't *want* me. So she gave me up. Dee kissed Damien's little head and thought it was her child. He looks nothing like Dee and I look *exactly* like her. We have the same eyes and nose and chin. Why did you keep the secret?"

India stood up and decided she wanted to leave.

She inhaled and said, "Adults always talk the good talk. That young people don't know anything. Yet there are grown people fucking each other and don't even know they are brother and sister because adult men lie and adult women have other kids and they fall into orphanages and go through a second slavery, being stripped of their names and identities and once they are 18 they are unleashed to a cold world and they meet people and they have become their adoptive names and adoptive lives and they sleep with cousins and uncles and brothers and have no clue that they are family. Brainwashing I call it."

She started to leave.

"I will never tell Damien that Dee isn't his mother, that she is *mine*. I will never tell Dee that my grandmother isn't really my grandmother, but she's my adoptive mother. I will never tell Damien I was raised in an orphanage at one point in my life, stripped of who I used to be. My birth name was Desha Phillips. My adoptive mother named me India Tomlinson."

Damien and India would marry eight months later. Damien was a changed man. He wasn't persuaded by females trying to use his body for carnal pleasure and his life was solely focused on his mother and his bride.

They had a very small affair. A few friends and family came from all over and showed their support. Her grandmother read a nice poem and Dee took a million pictures.

Now. Thirty plus years later. They were still in love. Still making it work. Still keeping it simple. *Sometimes* simple was better. They still argued and made up. They still paid bills and supported each other.

Damien smiled.

The warmth of her breasts invigoratingly lapping at his nipples. He closed his eyes and reached under the covers, massaging her wet opening just the way she loved.

He gave her clit some action with his huge index finger. She bumped against him with urgency.

Into the wee hours goes the Earth and they were oblivious to the sun rising.

Trapped in the darkness of their bedroom, each blind and curtain closed. They *loved* the peace of making love every morning.

They even set the alarm for 3 a.m. just so his amazing dick would never miss the curtain call of her velvet room.

They have been doing this every day for thirty years. Whether she was on her period or not she didn't deny her husband.

If Aunt Flow came to town she gave him head and pleasured him with a massage and warm kisses on his thighs and face.

She helped him masturbate. But she never used PMS as an excuse to turn him away. He was too good at what he did. Every time she made love to him she felt the bloom of a new rose deep in her pussy.

They started to kiss again. The heat rose in his loins and he tenderly glided into the confines of her soul, rummaging around…*looking* for the light at the end of a seemingly never-ending tunnel.

Where was the soil, for the bloom of a new rose? Her warmth sufficiently engulfed him, taking his breath away.

There was nothing sweeter or more loving than being inside his wife and her loving every second of it.

Deciding that he wanted to do something else, he buried his face between her breasts and rolled atop her like a great water fall and dug deeper.

Her sides were slippery and invitingly sensational. She gasped, digging her nails into his back.

He was well into his fifties, and he still bucked the bulls into retirement.

He wanted oil this time.

His loving was too amazing for her body.

She hadn't had many lovers in her lifetime and the ones she did manage to start relationships with always built her up for the great fall.

Couldn't last in the sack.

Made it seem like it was *her* fault.

He looked deep into her eyes and shifted his 267 pound body through her frail 156 pounds.

She loved every ounce of his loving.

When she felt the build up she held his face and told him how much she loved him.

"Make me cum," he said. "I want to throb inside you."

She braced herself for the eruption. She felt like a little girl, walking the streets with her adoptive father to the candy store.

He would buy her candy apples, get on his knee after he paid for them and kiss her forehead.

He would say he loved her and would always love her. She believed him.

India told herself, *I will never tell you that Dee isn't your mother. Some things are better left unsaid.*

*Am I any better than the adults who cheat and lie and have children and separate and destroy everybody's lives in the process?*

*Either way.*

*Not my problem!*

# The R.u.l.e.s.

I was a pompous, sexy Mexican/black woman with ample breasts, a moderate ass and all the trappings of a freak-a-lic. I loved it long, strong and hard in my pussy. I wanted it three times a day, no ifs ands or buts. But sex wasn't on my mind. Nor was my best friend: my husband's dick. I didn't feel right in my heart. In fact for the last few days I have been staring into a pill bottle, trying to stop myself from swallowing them all. I didn't want to live anymore. I didn't have the passion for life that I used to have. When problems arose I withdrew from all signs of strength because, deep down, I didn't think I was mature enough to execute my thoughts.

I loved my beautiful home. I'd rather be home then in the streets. I got this home before I met my husband at a club in Vegas.

He was just getting out of a relationship at the time and he was on the verge of giving up on all black women, saying we're all whores.

I told him, over a game of poker, that all women weren't sluts and that he'd pass up on a good thing holding on to all that anger.

He wasn't hearing me.

The more defiant he became the more I was interested in him. He won the game and to celebrate he bought me dinner.

I had gone there by myself because I was tired of boring ass Georgia and I needed a new scene.

We talked almost all night about what we'd gone through in our individual lives leading up to us meeting accidentally.

The more he spoke the more he pulled me in and by the time one a.m. hit I was in his hotel room looking at the stars while he spread my booty cheeks and ate my asshole with those thick lips.

Naked with stilettos on, he turned me on my stomach and stroked my pussy from the back, telling me I taste just like candy.

I shivered with delight, my clitoris getting a burst of excitement.

He opened a small squeeze bottle of honey and squirted it all over my booty cheeks. I felt the cold stuff trailing down my hole and my hairy lips.

He dove for cover, low crawling to the anus and high crawling to the coochie, my eyes fluttering closed.

I was moaning so loud he slapped my ass and my booty cheeks jiggled with fierce abandon. He was cautiously and expertly stroking my pussy with his tongue and making me come on it and when my sweaty body arched like McDonald's was building a new location on my titties he held me and fell asleep.

He just wanted to give me the beauty of an orgasm. I knew then I wanted to be his woman, considering I had never given up the pussy on a first, second or fifth date.

We had never been out of each other's sight again. Two weeks later, after patiently getting to know one another and shunning sex, trying to balance a long distance relationship (he was from Vegas), he asked to be my husband and I said *Yes* because I was tired of being alone and he was the best thing I had going in my life at that particular moment.

This seemed something ripped out of a fairy tale book.

He was my Prince Charming the hell out of my mind, soul and body.

He loved God and went to church when he could. His parents lived in Jamaica and they adored me. His brothers were hoodlums and they tried to fuck me the instant my husband turned his back. After the tongue lashing I gave them they never tried to scratch and sniff this pussy anymore. To date we've been married eight and a half years.

But tonight I didn't care where I went but I had to leave my sanctuary. I had to get some fresh air. I could hardly think. I didn't feed the dog. I didn't put the bills and written checks in the mail and I let my husband's dinner burn in the oven. I left him frantically opening windows and doors in his boxers, thigh-high socks and flip flops, turning on every ceiling fan and swinging a huge wet towel, trying to get the smoke out.

"Woman, have you lost your mind?" he asked, that beer belly jiggling for my eyes to see and it sickened me that a once fine, sexy tyrant he used to be fluctuated into an obese walrus. Watching walk pained me because those huge ass cheeks rubbed together like a bitch scrubbing floors. Despite his weight he still had the most gorgeous eyes known to man and I avoided them because he knew I was a sucker for them.

I grabbed my purse and smacked my lips.

"No, I didn't lose my mind. I think I *lost* it when I decided to be your wife."

He walked over to me and I rushed to the other side of the table.

"I do have 9-1-1 on speed dial; don't push your luck today."

He was still fanning smoke. "That food cost money and you fucked it off."

"Maybe if you try cooking sometimes then I won't forget the food is on the stove when I'm trying to spend some quality time with myself."

He looked helpless.

So you regret marrying me?"

I rolled my eyes. He wasn't getting any pussy for a while. He just didn't know it. "Is that a trick question?"

"Are you going to answer it?" he asked, clearly hurt. I didn't marry a fag so I didn't care about his feelings.

"Maybe."

"Don't make me beat your ass," he threatened. "Don't fuck with me. Do you regret marrying me?"

"No, man. I don't. I'm just saying you haven't progressed. I have a degree and a stable job and you lost your job because you wanted to smoke weed in the bathroom. You're too old to act like a thug."

The smoke detector sounded and he took the broom and beat it off the wall.

"I'm not a thug."

"Well act like you aren't one. You are trying to hold onto your youth. What grown man you know fancy throwback jerseys, still wear his pants under his fat ass and curse every other word? Surely this is not the man I married."

He sat on the chair, smoke still lingering in the air.

"Your problem is that you always set these standards for my life and its mine. I'm a black man and you're a black woman, stay in your place."

I walked past him and opened the fridge. "I'm Mexican/black. Don't deny my other race goddamnit I love both sides equally! And what's my place?"

He gave me an ugly look. "The place of a wife. Be nurturing and compassionate."

"In Laymen terms: be a dumb bitch that jump when you say jump and stay home barefooted and pregnant…"

He sighed. "I didn't say that."

"You didn't have to." His cell phone vibrated on the counter and he jumped up, snatching it up. He smiled, answering it.

"Excuse me, why did you have to leave the room to talk on the phone?" This infuriated me. I followed him, determined to find out who was on the phone.

He was in the living room, propped on the sofa, his hand on his crotch. Despite being 267 pounds he did have his sexy side. The way he smiled, the softness of his eyes. He had pretty feet and a huge dick. I couldn't get enough of his loving in the sheets. But tonight I didn't want it.

He was saying, "Hey, girl. I'm fine. How's your Mama? She's good. What, you're stranded? I know you're my cousin..."

*Oh, his cousin. I didn't mean to be so jealous.*

"I'll come get you," he said. "But it will be a little later. Can you hang in there for another hour? I got matters at home to take care of. Love you." He kissed through the phone. "Bye."

Turning off the phone, he jumped up to his feet, gave me an evil glare and walked past me back into the kitchen as if I wasn't standing there. This irked me.

I turned to face him. "Anyway dinner is blackened in the oven. Have it with a side of burnt rice and a cold beer. I'm going out."

He said, "You are not. You're a married woman. You can't just go out when you feel like it. What about me? I have needs…"

"Watch me go out. You are lazy, baby. Be for real. You only want me to stay home so we can have sex."

He had the gall to smile and nod his head, pointing at the dinner table.

So you knew what a sister had to do.

I left his fat ass standing right at the table.

In a myriad of negative thoughts, I slowly drove past the Big City Club, thinking about my husband. I knew marriage came with its own hard work but no one told me it'd be that damn hard. For real. Felt like I was studying for a Physics test.

The nightclub was thick. Crawling with festive black people. I loved to see blacks in one spot having a good time and spreading some love. It was one of the most beautiful things in the world. But these days you rarely (if ever) seen it no matter where you went.

I saw so many fine men I had to slow down a bit, my eyes about to pop out of my head. Wow.

*I'm married but I'm not dead! I can look, shit.*

*Men stare us down day in and day out.*

A few gay ones pranced by with their tight jeans dangerously riding their ass cracks and I wanted to puke. If I had half a brain I'd admit that I was a scorned woman right now. I was really contemplating calling my lawyer and filing for divorce. The feeling was so strong I couldn't breathe. I dug in my need-to-throw-some-of-this-shit-away purse and pulled out a cigarette. Pushing in the car lighter, I parked by a row of trees and cut the engine. *God, give me a reason to stay with my husband. He isn't what I married. I had married a confident, reassuring Pisces who had his shit together. Then after we married Greece slowly turned into ancient ruins.*

The one thing that's stopping me from getting a divorce was my children. They loved their father. They breathed him. And I didn't want to look like the bad guy. I saw this all the time with my friends who had gotten divorced. They pit the children against the parent. Its Daddy's fault. And then Daddy tells the child, "It's your Mama's fault," putting kids in a very unnatural and heartbreaking situation. Then they felt they had to choose: Mama's Story or Daddy's Lies. And I didn't want to put my kids through that. If my husband and I fought we kept it away from our kids. That's the one thing I respected about him.

*But he doesn't respect me. I swear men think women are born yesterday. I know he's cheating on me. I just know it and I can't shake it or put it out of my mind. A woman knows these things.* If you wanted to cheat on your lover there were some rules you had to follow. After all this was my opinion so you could either take it or leave it and quite frankly I didn't give a shit if you did one or the other. I was a blunt woman. I told it like it was without apology. This has been both a gift and a burden.

A gift because some people will respect you for being candidly real. And it has been my curse because I have lost some good friends in the process because I believe in what I believe.

You see, I've been married to a man who has been cheating on me left and right. But you know me, I played stupid. My husband fulfilled my desires with aplomb. But he was a womanizer, couldn't leave the ladies alone.

And I wasn't about to fuck him when I know he's testing new pussy behind my back.

The goddamn rules were clear.

- Goddamn Rule #1: If you were going to cheat please don't let it be with my best friend. Because if she started using your mirror and make-up more than you do, made her dresses into skirts every time your husband came around and changed her once defunct hairstyle into a thing of art then honey she's getting your man's dick.

- Goddamn Rule #2: if you're going to cheat, make sure you erase your online activity and please make sure I don't know any of your passwords. Black Planet was filled with whores just waiting to pounce on your man.

- Goddamn rule #3: *Try* to find a woman who was *also* married so she could go back home to hubby. Never fuck an unattached bitch who was dick sick because sooner or later she was gonna get jealous and envious of the wife, Ring the Alarm, and show up at her job or at her home trying to claim the lost and found prize.

143 DAPHAROAH69

- Goddamn Rule 4: *Don't* involve your children in your schemes. I can't stress this enough, Dumb Ass Men! The *younger* they are the *more* they will snitch on your ass. I don't care if you buy your daughter Hanna Montana and tell her to be quiet. The instant she steps in the house and sees her Mama it's over. SOUND OFF! "We went to the Mall, Mama, and he bought me Hanna Montana, and he told me not to tell you about the woman who sucked his dick in the back seat with the visors up." Nuff said.

- Goddamn Rule # 5: *Don't* use your KIDS to bait or get Ho's.

- Goddamn Rule #6: Um, of course use condoms when you cheat. It's not rocket Science, Men. Secretly boning other Ho's behind your wife's back then coming home and sliding it inside her raw puts her in danger of contracting something Tylenol isn't *powerful* enough to fix.

Now that all the goddamn rules were out of the way, it was time to face reality.

I had to confront him I knew this much. I really didn't feel up to it, though.

I did love him.

Or did I?

Honestly, I don't even think I love myself.

I do have to leave the asshole, though.

But with children involved it complicated everything. I was confused. If I didn't leave he would do it again and again and estimate that I was a weak bitch. But if I did leave then my kids might blame me and I didn't need that.

Sometimes I wished I would have waited to have kids.

Sure, I love them to death, but at the same time there were things that I wanted to do and accomplish in life.

Why couldn't I have kept my legs closed?

In fact I should have super glued my pussy and my legs shut.

I walked into my doctor's office for my Pap Smear test. I took the day off work. My boss didn't mind. She couldn't stand my ass anyway so anything involving, "Can I take the day off…"

She cut me off instantly. "SURE, GO AHEAD!"

And she meant it.

"Hi, Girl. You look nice," Frankie, the receptionist told me. She knew me for five years. I met her here at the doctor's office.

"Thank you. I learned from you."

She smiled gorgeously, her hair pulled into a tight making-your-eyes-look-Korean bun. "You always flatter me…" She looked at the log books. "Are you here for your Pap Smear?"

"Yes."

"While you're at it you should have your three month psychical done."

"Nah, I'm good. Just had one not too long ago."

She looked at me with friendly eyes. "Take the physical."

Something in her voice alarmed me and I didn't know what it was.

"Sure. Schedule me."

"Ok, girl. See you soon."

I was called in by the doctor. He was a young-looking, youthful 39 year old with ocean blue eyes, blonde hair and a gorgeous smile. Hard to believe this sack of beauty actually had brains.

"Hello, Miss Alice McCrary."

I stifled a yawn. "Hey, man. How's life been treating you?"

I closed the door behind us and led me down a very crafty-decorated hallway laced with fake plants and fancy cheap-looking framed art.

He held a folder. "I've been good. Just got back from Aspen."

"You love the snow."

"Yes, ma'am." He opened the examining room door. "Right in here. You can change into that medical gown over on the chair. And tap the door when you're ready."

Why was I nervous? It crept along my spine. "Ok."

"I understand you're having a physical?"

"Yea. Why not."

"I'm gonna have some blood drawn also. Check and make sure you're healthy."

"I understand."

"A nurse will be in shortly to draw your blood."

I cringed. "I hate needles."

"Tell me about it. I do, too."

We shared a smile.

When the nurse came into the room I looked at him. He was a very handsome man with the whitest teeth. He looked good in a light blue medial uniform and his black, glossy shoes looked a little worn out. Greeting me, I shook his hand.

"How are you?" he asked, barely looking at me.

I stared at his butt. *Girl, you're married! Stop looking at other men. But shit I'm not dead. I am still attracted to other men. So what! I won't cheat on my husband. I will never do that to him. Then behave, Bitch! OK, conscious.*

"I'm ok." I felt uneasy. My legs were trembling.

He took out a medium-sized white package. He explained to me that it was an HIV antibody test. He said he would swab my mouth and I said "Sure." I knew I wasn't positive. I always kept myself up.

He told me to open my mouth and I did. He swabbed a few times on my right cheek, behind my gums and on my left cheek. Once he was done he put the swab in a little small plastic device and said, "We should know the results in about fifteen minutes."

"That fast?"

He smiled again. "Yes." He grabbed a chart. "If you would excuse me…"

Twelve whole minutes had gone by. I couldn't stop looking at the device. The minutes felt like years and it was tugging horribly at my stomach. It felt like I had to throw up.

Something beckoned me to look at it but I was glued to the chair. Before I could stand up the door opened again and he returned. Again, he smiled. He seemed a little shy. I didn't really care. He looked at the instrument and I looked at his face. He closed his eyes and looked at me.

"Is the verdict in?" I asked.

He said, "Yes. I will be back shortly."

I was bugging out. "But what is the result?"

He smiled again. "I will be right back."

And he was gone.

I had my face in my hands. All this waiting was killing me. The door opened and I didn't look up. The young doctor returned. He said, "Are you ok?"

I looked at him, my eyes red. "Yes." Wrong! I was nervous as hell. Really nervous. No one wanted to be faced with something so hideous. I just knew I was negative. The last time I got tested I was negative so I didn't have anything to worry about.

He looked at my results and he sighed, sitting next to me. He put his hand on my lap and looked into my eyes.

"Are you ready to know the results?"

"Yes…"

He lowered his head and breathed in deeply. I was gripping his hands, squeezing, sucking in my cheeks.

He looked up into my eyes. "The test is retroactive. It shows that you are H.I.V. positive."

"WHAT?" I jumped up to my feet, opening the door.

"ALICE! Wait! Don't leave! Please…"

I was running up the hallway, out towards the EXIT door. The EXIT was where I needed to be. That test had to be wrong! It just had to be. I couldn't be H.I.V. positive, he had to be lying. That test had to be wrong!

I got to my car and unlocked the door. Getting inside, I locked the door and closed it, punching the steering wheel.

*I don't have H.I.V. I'm sure of it. He doesn't know what he's talking about.*

I put the key in the ignition and I left the parking lot.

149 Dapharoah69

With one thing on my mind.

*How many people can I infect before I die? No one protected me. No one saw to it that I was safe. I am a married woman. I was H.I.V. negative when I married my husband. So I know he gave it to me. So I know he has been cheating and creeping. How could he go out behind y back, fuck somebody else and bring something home to me that will destroy me? Men were dogs so I might as well be a goddamn Pit bull. God didn't watch over me. So God help the first dumb man who wants to eat my pussy.*

*If I was going to die…I was taking some people with me.*

*Starting with my husband…*

# Distracting Undies

Francesca and I were happily dining at Dick's— a small, bustling restaurant on South Beach that catered to snotty, arrogant motherfuckers such as me. The place was jumpin', jumpin' and I enjoyed the parade of eye candy that walked by my table.

There was an African, chocolate man who strutted his stuff, giving me the eye and kissing at me when he sat at the table behind me.

He was with a chubby woman with three chins and more bling, bling than Elizabeth Taylor. Chile, flossing with costume jewelry wasn't cute.

I would have turned and engaged in polite conversation, but eye had to keep tugging on my expensive sequined gown so I didn't suffer a wardrobe malfunction. And with these big ass titties, eye didn't need the unwanted attention.

Especially not from a man.

Of course, I had the middle table. I *had* to be the center of attention, considering the center of this booty was tingling and wanted a tongue to lick it all up before crunching the Tootsie Pop.

I paid a good three hundred dollars for my dish; and another ninety dollars for Francesca's meat loaf and glass of

Patron. I was a bit pissed because, before I scooped her up in my Mazda Miata, looking grand I might add, she told me she had just got paid on this Friday night and her body was shaking and she felt like getting down like her name was Mr. Kemp, an '80's one hit wonder.

But when she walked out of her apartment, located in Sea Pines, a rental community in Leisure City, looking a mess in pumps I gagged.

Wearing a pink dress and green shoes wasn't my idea of your body shaking.

That long, curly wig looked like God sliced a possum on her scalp and said, "Let thy lie dead!"

But I didn't say anything because I could be nice when I wanted to be.

When she got in my car she slammed the door closed, with no respect for my shit, kissed my cheek (can you say "*Ew!*") and asked could she drive.

Ah, *no*, bitch.

When we got on the turnpike, she turned off Bach and put in some TuPac.

Um, *Ew*! I didn't *jam* to dead men, sorry. There were too many seamen in the Navy and I wanted to float on the waters of diversion.

When we got to the beach, she slammed my door again, flirting with every man who walked up Ocean Drive like she was a cute bitch and every man she spoke to tried to run away. And she was my company. My stock value dropped just because of my association with her late ass.

I was so embarrassed I had to pinch her arm and say, "Bitch, act grand, not whorish."

When we got to Dick's, and ordered our food, it was time to pay. We had to pay *before* we were served the food.

She gave me the puppy dog, I'm-a-broke-bitch look and my wig nearly disintegrated from my scalp because I was one pissed bitch.

If she knew she didn't *have* any money she should have stayed her broke ass home. Eye could barely take care of myself and eye wasn't into taking are of grown bitches.

There was only room for one pussy in my panties and bitch that was mine.

Eye should have known better. She was being evicted, had a leaky roof, wore the same pumps to work, jogging and sowing and always asked a bitch for five dollars.

She either had a habit or a goddamn problem because I didn't know too many women who went jogging in high heels begging for crack head money ($5).

Phew. With that out of the way, I should introduce myself.

*Hi*, I'm Heartbroken. I'm the son of She Can't Buy Some Sense, and my Daddy, maybe you heard of him, Mr. Street Pharmacist with a Knack for Tongues in his Ass, just calls my cell phone and tells me I am banned from the family home in Liberty City (just off N.W. 22nd Avenue) if I don't trade in my long, flowing wigs for a low-cut bald fade and baggy jeans.

I guess he didn't understand that I'm gay right now because I showed my ass wearing baggy jeans as a teen, making all the boys come to the yard (my asshole and mouth)to bury their bones; but now as an adult who sometimes cross dressed, my *yard* had property taxes and a fee of two hundred dollars.

This separated the broke bitches from the more, you know, prevalent customers and patrons.

"Chile, when are we going home?" Francesca asked with an attitude. She was stuffing a bread roll down her throat.

I pulled on my cigarillo, eyeing her. "When I'm done eating my sautéed fish."

She frowned. "But you don't *do* fish."

I was shaking my head. "I do it today."

She rolled her eyes. "That's what I'm saying. You don't even *eat* fish."

"*Ew*! Ok. You can leave with the visuals."

She squeezed a tall man's ass when he walked by and he looked disgusted. "I'm just saying, man."

"Where do you see a man?"

She pointed at me.

"Don't disrespect me, Fran. I have on a gown that cost more than your rent (have you paid it by the way) and my pumps cost enough to pay your car note for six months. I have on a lace front wig, flawless make-up and I put estrogen in my alcohol every time a bitch gets tipsy so, again, where do you see a man?"

"You know what I mean. You were born a man."

"OK, and you were born a moose, but just because you don't have any antlers doesn't mean your titties mean any less."

She frowned. Getting in her feelings. "You don't have to diss me."

*Chile, sit.* "Yet you've dissed me, Chile. I know we're not going to argue about something so trivial."

"But you're eating fish, I don't get it."

My brows rose. "I do fish today, Francesca, because I'm horny, lonely and I want to pout for a while."

She smiled then. "We can pout at home."

Eye tucked my chin back. "At home?"

"*Yes.*"

"But we don't live together, are you mad?"

"No. But when I move in with you next week we will have a blast."

I chocked off the smoke, picking up the wine. "You're not living with me, OK. I don't need house guests or couch warmers."

"But..."

"Is this the real reason why you came out with me tonight? To indirectly move in with me?"

She looked sad. The sad trick didn't work on me, bitch. "Why yes."

"Well the answer is *no.*"

She was so angry she slammed her hand down on the table.

Chile, boo. Yawn.

"You're cold hearted."

"Bitch I just paid over ninety dollars for that food you're sucking down your throat and I'm cold hearted."

"I'm sorry."

"Sorry about what? A bitch ain't never thankful for what somebody do for her."

"It's not that. I just need some place to stay."

"And you think you're living with me."

"We're friends."

"We're friends when you got money and you can pay for your own shit. We're associates when eye gotta spend money on your broke ass, bitch."

Quietly I sipped the red wine. Doesn't taste as good as it normally does, but it'll do because love didn't want to do me and it *damn* sure didn't live here anymore.

Love and friends I cut out of my life has treated me so badly I couldn't even *shit* right because my colon has a vacancy worthy of Oprah Winfrey's couch.

Tell the world, bitch, because I didn't love men and they could kiss my natural black ass.

And this was why Francesca, or whatever her name was, couldn't live with me.

Because, like Sunshine Anderson:
Bitch, I heard it all before.
And I wasn't about to hear it from my home.

I'M NOT TRYING TO BE FUNNY (EVEN THOUGH I CAN BE QUITE THE COMEDIAN—shit, didn't realize I was yelling at you), but I am very self-conscious about my petite body.

Being that I was a man, a man of decorum, a man who lives by his own Code of Ethics, I was known to be a bit blunt.

I spoke my mind and eye didn't hold back what I wanted to say.

Imagine the number of ass whippings I went through because Mama told me to "SHUT UP!" one too many times.

I guess she didn't understand something. Why should I shut up when she a) provoked me every damn day to do this and that and b) Daddy whipped her ass when she didn't give him pussy?

I never shut up for a weak-minded bitch. I'm not saying she's a bitch, but she has bitch tendencies. Mama had this notion, OK, that she could say and do what she wanted just because I came kicking and screaming out of her pussy back in 1979. When the doctor spanked my ass and I wailed I have been wailing ever since.

If I hate it I hate it and if I love it I love it. At least that's what Mama used to tell me.

As far as my father, he always had something indecent to tell me. I think we hated each other the day I threw down the foot ball and sucked on my best friend James' balls while he was jacking off and inevitably came all over my face, lips, wiping it up and making me suck it off his fingers. Then we kissed.

Oh, well. I'm gay. I have been gay since I wore my mother's pink panties under my football pants when I was eleven years old. When all the boys saw me in panties they were trying to fuck me or get me to give them head and they succeeded. I let eight of them buss my asshole.

To make a statement, after practice I took off all the football gear and pranced to my rendition of Madonna's *Like a Prayer* in those very same pink panties, my booty cheeks jiggling.

My football team mates were so shocked they chased my ass up and down the park because they didn't want me out the closet. They wanted me to keep playing football so they could fuck me and eye couldn't be silenced.

I didn't care. At least they knew why I never scored any touch downs.

They chased me all over the park, trying to beat my ass and fight me. They were yelling all sorts of things. Saying eye better not tell anybody we all fucked.

Chile.

Once I got to my daddy's truck and pulled his Gat from the glove box, they ran for the hill and never bothered me again.

I never talked about my sexuality and I never spoke on it, until I stood up to my intimidating father and told him the deal. We fought. He punched me all over the living room and eye picked up the vacuum cleaner and beat his late ass under the low table. Its my business if eye wanted to get fucked and suck dick, bitch!

Eye threw the vacuum on the floor, tossed the holy Bible and packed my shit and moved the fuck out.

160 DISTRACTING UNDIES

Eye lived in a shelter for a while, working on myself, my self esteem and turning my back on anybody that talked shit about me. Didn't have any time for moose-looking bitches.

When the smoke cleared and the dust settled on my amazing curves, I felt like a new person.

I have a deep fetish for small panties. The smaller the draws the fatter my ass looks. For real. If women could wear those four-sizes-too-small bras then I could wear those two-sizes-too-small draws.

My ass looked good enough to eat and fuck. Why was I so obsessed with my booty?

I treated my booty like a mother treated and nurtured a child. I worked out six days a week at the 24 Hour Shaq gym by the Cutler Ridge Mall.

I did squats three times a day for fifteen minutes. As a result, I had a very well-together ass. Straight men had to look when I walked past them.

I ate apples and oranges and strawberries. I stayed away from red meats. I ate a lot of salads. I had a high fiber diet. I drank prune juice and I douched my hole the way a woman douched her pussy.

When I met a man he had to a) treat my hole as equally as I treated it, b) had to play in it more than I did and c) must use my toys in my hole at least four times a week. I wanted toys before I wanted his tongue or dick.

My dude came over and he was mad about my size *too* small draws. I really didn't care because eye paid my own bills and eye had my own mortgage and the last time eye checked eye was Miss Bitch.

"Why do you wear those gay ass drawls?"

"They're not drawls. They are undies" I said. "And I am gay, hello. Didn't you get the memo?"

"Whatever."

He kicked off his Timbs and then pulled off his pants and he had on panties, yet he was talking about my undies?

I said, "It's turning me off. Those panties you got on. I am in shock! I like *gutter* niggahs. Not fem boys and you are a gutter niggah but when you took off your pants and show off those little panties I was turned off."

"I have to wear these small, designer panties."

He props down on the couch and lights his joint. "Take 'em off."

"No. Take off those panties. I'm a transvestite. I'm the only stone cold bitch in here wearing female underwear."

"NOW!" he shouted, pulling on his blunt.

"No," eye said sternly, eyeing him. I was about to send him home.

"Why?" he asked.

"Because I gotta wear something to distract me from your can't fuck can't suck the booty hole-right ass."

I covered my mouth when I said it.

I didn't mean to hurt his feelings.

But he has been slacking. My asshole was a pussy, not the dope hole.

I already

My didn't do love or the bullshit that came with it and if he wasn't going to leave his wife and come stay with me then he can grab his shit and get outta my house.

Until then, I'll keep on my distracting undies.

# The Perpetrator

I froze where I stood when I entered my home on Wiltshire Street, Miami-Dade County, Florida.

"Keep 'em off."

Scared out of my mind, eye kept the lights off.

"Come inside the goddamn house. Nonchalantly..."

Reluctantly, bile rising in my throat, I did what eye was told.

Why was he whispering?

"Close the door."

Fright nearly coloring me blind, my hands trembling uncontrollably, I flinchingly closed the door, getting more eerie and nervous as the hand on my grandfather clock by the start of the foyer steadily turned.

"Lock it."

I locked it. The sound of the lock jumped like angry monkeys from every wall down to the start of the hallway in the form of an echo. I barely had any furniture in my home, just a simple love seat, low-table, black and white TV eye bought from the Good Will and bedroom furniture. I didn't even have a refrigerator or stove because I still used my homeboy's resources at his crib. Kept my light bill down fifty percent.

Scared and tired from a grueling day at work (and my throat parched 'cause I cussed out the Bank of America bitch at the Teller for giving me back two hundred dollars out my account when I asked for twenty) I sat down on the ottoman by the front door.

I was trying to fathom the idea of accepting this farce in my beautiful home in all black, ski-mask, black laced tightly boots and black silky gloves that shined with a certain zeal I never saw in diamonds.

"Stand up."

Hesitantly, I stood up. The Niggah said it so silently I felt feathers turn to Medusa's eyes in my blood stream transforming every vein, every artery and every pulse of my heart to stone.

And now inside my soul there was suddenly the new Era of the Ice Age meets the Stone Age.

I shoulda felt like that when I hurt all those people...

The Perpetrator smiled. Smiled big, Cheshire cat smile.

The eyes glittered dangerously close to diamonds. I could see the rays of the Sahara Desert sand oozing from his wicked voice.

He stood there so meticulously. So immaculately, the way he stood shot images of my ex-wife into my mind.

She used to stand like that. With the head slightly slanted to the left. But this wasn't my wife, this Niggah was try'na rob me. How long had he been in here?

Why wasn't anything moved? Ravaged?

I surveyed my room so fast he didn't notice: six hundred dollars on my low-table, on the side of him, hadn't been touched, hadn't been moved, the crisp-feeling and smelling bills were just the way I left them. Three Rolex's on the TV, behind him, hadn't been moved.

It was then I realized he wasn't try'na rob me.

He just wanted me.

The Perpetrator kept the Beretta aimed at my chest, while I stood here, bloody and naked.

My legs drummed together like a cracked out marching band sent to the wrong parade and now everything was

165 DAPHAROAH69

drenched from a very unwanted summer rain in the fall of my life at the moment and now I prayed for solitude.

And I continued to turn into winter. I could build Inca pyramids with the stone of my heart alone.

"Unzip my pants." Another harsh whisper. The words were rushed like a great, much-needed wind through my front door when I opened every morning, like I usually do, taking my 6 feet, 210 pound ass to work.

"*Unzip*..." I couldn't talk. I swallowed hard, frightened at the sight of that shiny pistol.

That scary, life-threatening pistol.

It was kinda dark in this room and kinda dark in my life; the glow of the moon shining through the open window housed with termite-infested wainscoting and absolutely no curtains added to the autonomy of my soul.

Eye didn't have curtains put up because when my wife left me two years ago—I was 24 years old, then—catching me in bed with a man I told her was my Daddy's son, my brother, and he was anything but blood to me—she took our two sons, Dexter and Hector, who were Lil' Hot Boys in the making, and every piece of furniture and every article of clothing there was to take; she even took my clothes so eye was left with nothing.

And I never saw her again.

She never called.

She jumped the state of Florida and went to California where, over the next two years she got married and had two daughters, concreting her status as the Woman who Left the One Alfred Symons.

One of the sexiest, arrogantly-dressed Niggahs in Florida.

All the Hoes wanted this dick. All the Niggahs wanted this dick.

Straight Niggahs begged to fuck me or be my first.

167 DAPHAROAH69

Confused Niggahs just wanted to suck my dick and eye never turned down free money or free head. Never.

Stupid Niggahs let me dick 'em down and leave 'em.

Rich Niggahs spent doe on me when I wanted cheddar.

Crazy Niggahs became fatal attractions.

Like the Perpetrator standing before me.

My so-called brother, James Black Love, was my secret lover who I wanted to be mine for a life time; I met him when I was thirteen. I fucked him when he turned fourteen. I claimed the asshole when eye was fifteen, around the time I met Fran, who was to have both my sons and be my faithful wife.

She had nine brothers and two sisters and I fucked EVERY LAST ONE OF THEM, even her delusional mother Maria. Maria with the Killer Pussy.

I see why her late husband kept those babies coming: the bitch had good pussy.

Goddamn. Make you yodel like Chester the Cheetah when you nut up in that shit, for real.

But this ain't about Maria. This is about her son. James. Who loved being Black. And was *filled* with Love.

I was jealous of anybody that came around this niggah.

I shot Niggahs over him. I never let a bitch or a man touch him. If he told me he gave up the ass to a Niggah I found the Niggah and beat his ass so badly I didn't think the Coroner's wanted to be bothered.

And then eye took James to bed at a fuck Motel and fucked him so long, so hard, so fast, that he screamed out he would never give it up.

I had the little bitch scared of dick after I was done.

I came all over his ass, face, stomach and all down his throat. He swallowed my load eight times that night 'til I shot blanks. That's why the Niggah got all that pretty dark chocolate Taye Diggs skin.

He was a Niggah I fucked from here and all through his Mama's house, Brother's condo, and grandma's trailer.

His grandma was deaf, dumb and blind and to secretly mock her handicap I fucked him down right in front of her while she sat there trying to watch the *Golden Girls* by moving her old, elegant-swinging, shaking fingers over the Braille on her lap.

Thirteen states in three years I fucked James while we were in college having the biggest freaky sex of our young lives (like we were supposed to).

And now my life was in danger.

I zipped down the Perpetrators pants.

"Pull it out," said the stone-cold freak.

Nervously, eye look up at him. Breathing hard. I didn't know I was pissing all over my rug. Expensive carpeting at that: $12 per yard. And that could feed the homeless.

Reluctantly, eye pulled out his dick. It was hard. Rubber. Mocking. It was a dildo. Thick. Filled with jelly.

And when the whisper filled my clammy ears, telling me to wipe my piss all over it and suck it off I jumped up and the butt of the Beretta came crashing down on my head and I wound up back on my knees.

Face to face with a five foot eight perpetrator with a dildo as a dick all in my face.

"If you think I'm just gonna let you jump up in my face then *no, no, NO, NO, NO!* I won't have it, *bitch*," he whispered to me.

And eye withered like a fat bitch falling down four flights of stairs.

I put my hand in the warm, clear-looking piss.

The Perpetrator smiled.

"Rub it on all the plastic!"

The Perpetrator laughed at me, silently, a hearty chuckle. I was filled with fear.

I started thinking of all the people I hurt in my life; who could this person be who was in my home doing this to me?

I hesitantly wiped piss on this dildo, about to puke; eye was staring at it like it was the one holding the Beretta.

I hurt so many people in my life because I was selfish. It was all about my dick and making it spit pleasure back then.

"Suck it," said the Perpetrator, with that goddamn whispering tone of voice that drove me crazy; and not in a good way.

I had a thought and I hoped I was right.

What if the gun wasn't loaded?
What if he was just scaring me?
What if...

"No," I shouted, my voice filling my house at breakneck speed.

I hopped up to my feet so fast the Perpetrator took a step back and shot at my feet, sparks flying from the nozzle and impulsively eye hit a perfect back flip over the low-table and landed on the couch, shaking like a great snow storm was terrorizing my living room.

"Get down."

I got down.

"Get on your knees."

I got on my knees, tears falling down my face, hands trembling, legs cramping, palms sweaty, scalp itching so terribly I was too afraid to flinch, too afraid to scratch it.

"Come closer to the dick."

Reluctantly, I did.

"Suck the dildo, *bitch*! Suck the piss off it. Like you love it."

*Fuck that! Hell to the nah! Not me!* "Goddamn! Why are you doing this?"

I looked up and the smile returned, the glittering eyes, the danger.

This was unnecessary.

Uncalled for.
Ridiculous.
Crazy.
Sheer lunacy.

And yet there was something.
Something about...
Something about that smile!
He put the Beretta on my nose.
"Suck the dick or Coroners will decipher your brain cells from your buggers on the fucking wall behind you."
Whisper, whisper, WHISPER!
Talk, bitch! my mind screamed.
I was crazed. I had a feeling if the Perpetrator started using his regular voice I would recognize it.
I hesitantly sucked the pissy dildo, my stomach, heart and bowels moving towards my asshole for one quick release and all that came out was gas. I farted so loud I nearly passed out.
The Perpetrator didn't care.

"Dick...dick is a powerful thing, isn't it? Dick causes men to cheat, steal, rob, kill, yearn, satisfy, pleasure, commit suicide...all that."

Tears ran from my eyes, my hands shaking uncontrollably.

"Dick...will bring about your ruin. You hurt me really, really bad..." the Niggah whispered, like a nursery rhyme.

I shook with fear. The hair stood up on my body. For one quick second the Beretta dropped to his side and I jumped up and took a swing at him, for dear life, it was now or never.

And he ducked, fell to his knees and raised the back of his head into my nuts, sending me to the floor and he stomped my chest.

I have never known so much pain in my life, and this reaffirmed in my mind that old saying about Karma. About it coming back to haunt you. About it coming back to hurt you. And for me the time has come.

"Bitch," came the angrily harsh whisper. "Get up, bend over the arm of the chair. Its time to show you who do the fucking up in this house. And it ain't your Mama!"

I was in so much pain.

"Alfred Symons, get the fuck up. Or my little friend will show you how big of a man he is."

I struggled to get up.

He took me by the arm, gently, and helped me up, the gun aimed at my ass. I couldn't believe this. And yet there was something about his touch.

Familiar. So recognizable.

But from who, and where?

I started thinking about all the people I hurt in my life. All my brothers, sisters, parents, friends, family, foes...I was a selfish prick back in the day, drop-dead good looks, a die-hard body I worked on like Picasso on the regular. I got a lot of pussy.

All the Niggahs I fucked and left, left, left. Like Howard, a Niggah with sickle cell (but fine as a bitch) that was my best friend since first grade.

We were closer than close; we knew everything about each other.

One day the Selfish side of me, when we were in the 12th grade, made me fuck the Niggah.

I wanted his sexy ass, 'cause all the bitches wanted him; bitches *eye* wanted at that and he was cock blocking so I unblocked my cock and did what I had to do.

I drugged his soda when we went out to eat, lured him to my Ford pick-up truck I bought for three hundred dollars from a cluck, drove him out into the wilderness, fucked the Niggah in every which way, making him moan and scream.

He was fine like that. He begged me to stop, telling me some sob story that he trusted me, he was drunk anyway, and I said, "Naw, Niggah you gotta let me get that ass! I want it! Every Niggah in school wanna fuck you, you pretty bitch!"

And the crickets heard him when I tore through him without no lube and left him bleeding to death.

I changed schools, moved out of the state with a relative and never heard from him again.

And now karma was in my house as I bent over the arm of the chair.

"Spread that beautiful ass, bitch. I remember this ass. How sweet it looked from the reflection of the mirror. I won't say what mirror, but I watch that ass wiggle when you fucked me..."

My face was pressed on the cold, sweet-smelling leather.

I spread my ass and he traced it with the Beretta. I felt like a WHORE!

177 DAPHAROAH69

He slid the dildo inside me without any lube. I'd never been fucked before and this killed me, it was so big I squirmed.

"Take this dick, bitch! Take all of it; take all fourteen inches of this dildo! I'ma show you you can't hurt me and get away with it."

He pounded my asshole, making my legs buckle, my body was on fire. This shit hurt! All the pain abashedly killed me, and then pleasure came.

All this pleasure and my torso started to move against the dildo, opening me up.

This shit felt good and I started to smell shit and I remember I had to shit when I came into my house and I froze 'cause I felt shit all over me.

Stinking the goddamn room and he kept fucking me and fucking me, grabbing my ass and spreading it, sticking all that dildo in me and it hurt and I started screaming.

"Scream!" came the harsh whisper.

And then it was over.


I fell to the floor, covered in shit, sweat and I wanted to die. This must be hell. I was unnaturally hot, I wanted to die.

The Perpetrator looked over me.

This had to be Howard. Getting his revenge, though I didn't see him for over ten, maybe eleven or twelve years.

How did he find me? There's *no* way he coulda found me. Payback was a bitch.

The Perpetrator began stripping. Oh God! It wasn't over.

My tired eyes widened. I felt wetness oozing from my ass.

I then realized I was bleeding, blood was all over the carpet, I seen it.

I rolled over and pleaded. "Please let me get to a doctor."

Off came the Perpetrator's boots. He was sitting next to me.

I kept my narrowed eyes on him; I was in so much pain.

Now I know how my wife felt when she found me in our bed fucking James.

I met and fucked James before I raped Howard Hoe ass and Howard was in my home returning the favor.

He fucked me senseless.

But why did he use a dildo? Was his dick too good to issue out to me?

Did he think I had AIDS? A rubber woulda been just fine.

179 DAPHAROAH69

He set the gun on the chair. I was too tired and drained to move. Plus pain shot through my body.

He stood up.

Off came the pants and I realized he had on a strap-on dildo.

Nice ass.

Pubic hair sprouting from around the base of the dildo wildly.

Off came the black coat. There was a fake stomach and chest on him.

Why was that? What was this? Hide the body parts? Off came the ski mask. He had on a hairnet.

He was looking at the floor.

Off came the extra padding and the hair net and when my ex-wife Fran's titties popped from the silicon tape and her beautiful hair fell all around her face she shook it like Barbie, dropped the padding on the floor and stroked the shit off the dildo, wiping it all over my face, squatting by me so evilly.

"Surprise, surprise."

I was too stunned to say anything.

A woman did this to me?

She laughed. "You think you can hurt me, screw some Niggah in my bed and I let you just get away with it."

She used her normal voice now, but it was different, full of darkness and evil.

She looked really psycho right now: the wide eyes, the plain-looking expression on her face...

"No, no, no, no, no, no..." She was shaking her head feverishly. "Naw, playah. You've just been served but this ain't a summons to court. There's no jury, no bailiff and no judge. How this shit taste?"

She forced it in my mouth and slapped me across the face, repeatedly, with the flapping dildo after she snatched it off her hip.

That thing sting. Badly.

I spit repeatedly, I didn't wanna taste shit!

She said, "My husband, my loyal husband, who is the father of my daughters, told me his life story. He opened up to me. He thought if he told me about some significant part of his life I would leave him, but he told me to get revenge on you because you hurt me, you used me, you married me knowing full and goddamn well you loved men!"

She bit my dick so hard, gnawing her teeth into my skin and I screamed so loud, grabbing her head and trying to choke the crazy bitch but she bit harder.

I felt the blood gushing out. She pushed my hands off her and slapped me. Hard.

"I gotta call my husband and tell him what I've done."

"Why, who..., why are you doing this?"

She stood up, the woman who used to love watching my ass when we fucked, she loved the mirrors in our old bedroom...and all I remembered before I passed out was, "'cause, honey love, Howard, my husband, told me to do so. The way you brutally raped him in an open field surrounded by bushes but honey, ain't no crickets in here to witness the hysteria of your downfall, playah. After all, what are...best friends for?"

I fainted...

# The Hard On

I had to do something, since eye was bored out of my mind. I hated feeling like this, being that I was a hyper-active woman.

Maybe being bored was a good thing considering Mama had high blood pressure and was taking medicine for it daily. I didn't want to go through that so eye started watching what eye ate.

But as of late I have been having mood swings and eating to replace whatever it was that was missing from my 27 year old life. I was always worrying about this and that. Did I pay all the bills?

Had I kept up all my appointments? When was the last time I saw my doctor?

When should I schedule my next Pap Smear test? Why was Mama getting on my nerves?

When was she going to get back with Daddy (who was in a relationship with a white woman, pretending to be happy when he missed Mama and wanted her back) and stop breathing fire down my back?

Questions I may never get answers to simply depressed me.

Mama has been on my mind lately. When Daddy left her she hadn't been the same.

Sure, he was the one who cheated in the next room behind Mama's back, and actually hid it for months.

Until he developed feelings for the white woman who would suck and kiss any part of his body his heart desired (Mama never kissed below the belt, and that was the problem in their marriage).

After he fell in love he timed his sexual discretions perfectly with Mama's work schedule one Monday morning after Easter.

On her way home Daddy was undressing the lady, whose name was Gene. When Mama got on the turnpike battling traffic Daddy was performing foreplay. Heartlessly he destroyed my mother before she ever found out. And even when *eye* found out eye had to question his love and faithfulness to a woman he married. This would change how I viewed men for the rest of my natural life.

When Mama got off the Turnpike in Perrine, Daddy was putting on a condom.

When Mama turned in the driveway, Daddy was fucking the woman so good, long and deep he swore he was 20 years old again.

When Mama came in the house and heard the moaning she thought her brother Yearns Gregory was watching a porno tape.

She smiled and thought nothing of it.

When she got to her room, her feet aching, she saw her husband making out with the woman and she damn near went blind.

She grabbed her chest and Daddy was nearing his orgasm.

When he came he pulled out, pulled off the condom and moaned…

Mama quietly walked out the house.

Leaving the door open.

Today was Sunday and this week I was thinking about attending the Jazz in the Garden Concert being held at Dolphin Stadium, even though the Dolphins haven't been winning any games. And let's not think of last season. I wound up burning my jersey.

Smiling to myself, I parked my Chevy truck by a row of trees, cutting the engine.

Grabbing my purse, I looked over my make-up in the rear view mirror, my titties sweating from all this heat.

Getting out the truck, my cell phone rang and it was Mama.

Closing the truck door, I said, "Yes, Darling."

"Where are you?" she asked huskily.

"Where Daddy ain't," I joked, walking towards the Plaza at Dolphin Stadium to see how much those concert tickets were.

I heard Chaka Khan was going to be one of the performers. Or was it Mary J. Blige screaming ass?

The wind was blowing my hair do, and I was mad because I spent an hour blow drying it.

"Now why did you have to bring up the white girl lover?"

I was laughing, stopping by the median to let a woman driving a Hyundai pass by.

"You know you love him."

"I was married to him for twenty-eight years, of course I love him."

*Yea, right!* I crossed the street. "If you love him go get him back."

"I have been chasing my marriage for twenty years, girl. Ever since you were a lad. When is he gonna chase me?"

I was approaching the glass doors. "When you show him that you love him."

187 DAPHAROAH69

"I showed him by having his kids, being loyal and faithful."

"Sometimes that's not enough, Mama."

"What would you know?" she shot acidly, and I cringed. "You can't even keep a man."

"Right." I entered the Plaza and looked around at all the Dolphin and Marlins display racks. A short, stocky black woman was talking on her cell phone.

"Hold on Mama…" I stopped at the cashier. I smiled. She ignored me. "Excuse me…"

She rolled her eyes and looked at me, covering the phone. "Yes."

*All right bitch, watch your tone.* "Where are they selling the Jazz in the Garden—"

—She pointed to a back plexus-glass window, where I saw about eight people in line.

"Well you could have let me finish…"

She put the phone back to her ear. "Yea, girl….so we went to the club and…"

I shook my head at the rude bitch and made my way to the back.

"I'm back, Mama."

"Did I hear you correctly? You're going to the Jazz in the Garden Concert? I know you're buying me a ticket. I went last year by myself, I don't know who that white male artist was but he turned the place out!"

"I don't know either," I said, and didn't really care.

"And I heard Kem is performing." She was chuckling like something was funny. I was still fuming that she said I can't keep a man and I have been married for a couple years. Happily.

"I don't know." I stopped at a Marlins jersey, looking it over with my mouth hanging open. A hundred and twenty dollars? I think not.

"Are you paying for me?"

"I don't even know if I'm going, woman."

"Watch your tone. And I am 'Mama,' not woman. You're sounding like your father."

"He's my Daddy and right now were not talking because his head is so far up that white bitch's ass he can't see the shit from the green pastures."

Mama sucked her teeth. "You're a mess, Chile. So, are you…um, gonna get…"

"Yea, Ma."

I paused behind a short white woman, my heart racing. Mama had her own money, yet *loved* spending mine and I loved and respected her too much to tell her *"No"* because when I was growing up any and everything I wanted I got; and what I *needed* I got.

She hardly said the word "No," so I would feel guilty telling her "no" right now when my heart wanted to say HELL NO!

I stood in my bathroom, admiring my taut body. Endless hours at the gym and secret Botox shots fulfilled my agenda. A more gorgeous face and thick, gorgeous lips. Sometimes going to seasoned professionals brought about results. Maybe I should enlarge my breasts. Have some liposuction, even though my stomach makes Halle Berry's look like a chopping board. My thighs are definitely a little on the thick size. Maybe I should get my husband's name tattooed on my pussy walls. Nah. Too painful. Let's be real. My husband said I was getting old and that threw me past the loops, not through them. It actually hurt to the core of my soul that a man who said he had eyes for me and only me would say such degrading things. No, I wasn't a spring chicken but I was still the springs in the chicken. I wanted love right now and I wasn't getting it at home. Husband wanted to drink and hang out with friends more than be with his loving wife.

He would rather tell THE BOYS how he truly felt about the ways of the world and keep me guessing and when I do swallow my pride and ask him it's always the same thing, "What do you think? How do you think I feel about you? You KNOW I love you."

Blah blah blah dah dah dah dah.

Same song.

Yet I couldn't walk past a shirt in the department store and not buy t for him, or get him those Timberland boots because he looks utterly sexy in them.

He never seemed surprised when I showered him with clothes and gifts. He'd suck his teeth, toss the gift and just hug me.

He'd kiss me on the forehead and say, "I'm going out with The Boys. I'll be in before ten p.m., though. Just need to get out."

It's easy to forget why I loved him so much by looking in his dreamy eyes. Those eyes I could give pillows and lay on the base of his brain while he talked and talked and talked. Didn't he understand that?

"can I come?" I asked.

He said, "You gotta watch the kids."

"But I need a break from them. They are driving me up the wall. Four sons isn't easy, that's your job."

"I always have them."

"And you know why!" And he'd look at his attaché case and resumes, his face getting dark.

"I'll talk to you later."  He'd storm out the room like a hurricane.

No, he didn't curse me or talk down to me. He actually treated me with respect, but he was the type of Jamaican/Cuban man that, when he didn't get his way, he messed up everyone's mood.

I tried to smile, tracing my lips with my fingertips. I got these lips so when I gave him head he'd feel the heightened pleasure. But its almost as if he didn't notice. This was another problem. I was a Gemini and I tended to let the Evil Twin surface during the most critical times in my life and this has cost me some good people.

I rest my hands on the sink and lowered my head, my hair swinging in my face. My heart felt the weight of the world. I called Mama but she always said the same thing and I got tired of hearing it over and over:

"There are people worse off than you."

"OK, fuck those people!" I told her. "Do they know me? Do they pay my bills? Are they fuckin my husband and feeding my children? Am I supposed to push to the side my problems because God gave the theirs? Its their cross to bare, not mine so I'd appreciate it if you left STRANGERS out of my conversation."

"You're a disrespectful pop tart. And I won't stand for it."

"Your lazy ass, standing? All you do is sit and knit, sit and shit, sit and eat, sit and talk, sit and blaspheme, sit and drink. Did I mention you sit on your tail?"

"You have your nerves..."

"I get them from you."

"I won't take this disrespect from you young lady."

"Well, let me do the honors," I said.

"What would that…"

CLICK.

I said something to my husband, who was watching ESPN, threw a scarf around my neck and snatched up my keys. He grunted, eyeing me suspiciously and I didn't care.

"What time are you coming back?"

"Don't wait up for me. And my watch doesn't work."

"I just bought you that watch."

"It doesn't work."

I slammed the door behind me, hopped in my car and smiled instead of cry.

I had something to do and see.

$$\Sigma$$

Inhaling, I rest my hands on the door. I knew I shouldn't be here, I knew I was wrong. Or was I? I knew if I crossed the threshold there was no TURNINGBACK.

U-turns were made for the highways and regular roads, not a room.

Gathering my nerves, I walked into the dark room and immediately frowned. As much as I didn't want to admit it, it would be the same ole thing for the umpteenth time. Bending, squatting and…um, yea: lifting.

Yet I needed this, whatever it was. The air stale, I could smell the oldness of the room and I turned on the light and I saw it just sitting there.

I couldn't help but smile at it, this beautiful thing. eye loved a challenge which was why I married my husband. Marriage was the most heart-wrenching, challenging thing in the world. But right now he wasn't challenging and making me flex those brain muscles. No. He was whining, bitching and moaning like he suddenly had a pair, and eye wasn't talking about his testicles, either. Breasts were more like it.

Such the immaculate slut, I got on my knees, getting them dirty and tried to make it react to my touch but the soul of my opponent wouldn't admonish. I pushed a little but no reaction.

"I came back. I know you think I wasn't. You think I'm a scared girl who can't handle a little…pressure but as you can see I'm here."

Nothing. Just silence.

I touched it and said, "No need to talk. Mama will take care of you."

I stood up and did a little booty shake taking off the scarf and turning around in circles like a ballerina laughing to myself.

I wanted to be appeased, have the dust knocked off my bones because it had been a while since I had any type of action. I work too much, some say, which was why I push and pull yet it won't move.

Panting, I take a deep breath and I sit there, looking at it.

Smiling occasionally because my so-called husband was at home, looking after the children and I was here trying to get my knees dirty.

*Hmm*, I had the inspiration. Would he get upset if he found out my attention was focused elsewhere, on a place different from the bedroom we shared for fifteen years?

His temper was his biggest problem. Pair that with his ego and his pride and you got the next episode of The Wire on *HBO*.

The fact of the matter was that he hasn't touched me in about ten months and I was a touchy-feely woman. He lost his job at the airport and hasn't been able to find another one. His family are always telling me to do this and that, that he should be wearing the pants. I had to tell his nagging-think-her-son-doesn't-do-any-wrong mother (with her horse-lipped ass) where to get off.

Initially, he was wearing them but when he got fired (for saying Niggah on the clock), there was no excuse that I had to jump on the horse of employment and pull the reigns, readjust the IRS forms so I could put all four kids as the dependents while he searched for employment.

Sometimes I'd get upset to come home and see him watching ESPN instead of tweaking his resume. He did this yesterday.

His excuse was simple: I job hunt all day, now I need to rest. I'm sorry, when you're jobless with four kids and a wife you can't afford to rest.

That led to an argument and I felt guilty because, when we met (on South Beach, I was going through a divorce) I told him I was the type of woman who fought his fight and held up her man when he was down yet he was down on this couch and doing extracurricular activities that didn't spell PAY CHECK in the end.

Now I was on my knees, running my hands all over the hardness…I could tell it hadn't been touched or caressed in a while.

I smiled, tears falling down my face, shuddering because the world seemed cold being on the opposite end of my husband.

He doesn't want to make love to me, and every time we tried he started talking about his problems like he's the only one in the world with them. We all have them.

Like now. I closed my eyes and inhaled, the scent turning me on. I got a burst of energy knowing my husband didn't know I was here. He was probably drinking beer after beer.

I guess I had to do all the work so I stood up, the adrenaline going to my head, making me tingle.

I felt it in my pussy, my nipples and it activated some kind of spirit in my eyes because I blinked a few times, my heart hammering and I touched it again. Jesus, it was so hard, so stern…so…hard to please. My feet were slipping.

So I stood up, grabbed the ladder and wanted to try something new, something daring. I turned on some music.

Jill Scott coos through the speaker. I felt good then. I turned, brushing my hair from my face with my bejeweled right hand, my knees shaking. I wanted to be handled on the ladder. Yea, why not? I was scared of them.

What better way then to get on it, and try to touch it then.

Slowly, cautiously I put my foot on the start of the ladder and held both sides, my ass sticking out as I looked up at it.

I giggled, moving my hips to the music. My husband thought I was out getting ice cream. I knew he never listened to me, because after we got married and he licked ice cream off my breasts, I told him THEN that I couldn't EAT ice cream because of the milk in it.

Oh, well. Devastated, I shook the thoughts away. I love my husband, but I love this more. It fulfills me, like now. I'm at the top of the latter. A hard one below me and a hard one in my face. I kiss it for effect. OF course I have to touch it, rub it, feel all on it.

Jill was sounding good singing Whenever, Whatever.

My skin seemed to crawl with fear yet a little pleasure seeped through. Butterflies in my stomach, I stuck out my ass and tried to pick it up.

Gently at first, because it was…so big and I loved huge packages.

I always loved size.

The smaller the more alienated I'd become.

198 THE HARD ON

My cell phone vibrates in my pocket.

Then Flo-Rida's "Low" started to chime from it. My husband.

I answered it with a silent, "Yes."

He was silent. "I can't believe you. You haven't come home yet. It's late. I don't like my wife out dolo by herself."

"I'm busy. What do you want? And please, don't start using Ebonics. It's 'solo,' not 'dolo.'"

"I'm grown, and like I said I don't want my woman out dolo. What if something happens to you?"

"I'm a big girl." I closed my eyes, forcing the lump in my throat to go down.

"Where are you?"

I snapped, "Getting ice cream."

He was breathing hard. "Right, why are you lying?"

I looked around the room, ignoring my friend with the hard on. "I'm not."

He gets quiet again. "What grocery store plays Jill Scott after 11 p.m.?"

I smiled bitterly. "Dairy Queen."

"They close at 9 p.m. I think."

"What does it matter to you? Have you found a job yet?"

He was quiet. "Who is he?"

My eyes wide. "What?"

"The man you're seeing. I hear the music in the background."

I sat down on the ladder, my hand on the hard thing. I was tracing my name on it gently with a fingernail.

J-E-N-N-I-F-E-R.

Then I pet it. I loved to pet it before handling it. A real bitch did it that way.

I told him, "I'm at Dairy Queen."

He wasn't having it.

"Have you given him my pussy?"

I couldn't lie. "Yes, I have. I gave it to him. As a matter of fact I'm touching it now."

He was quiet. "Damn, I can't believe this shit!" he exploded. "I lost my job and you go to someone else? I didn't know I married a whore!"

"Well, shit, what do you expect! He has a hefty 401 (k) plan, medical and dental and stock options. He is NEVER without a job, and he always supports me and my kids." I quivered at the thought of him calling me a whore. His last wife cheated on him with his brother, had his kid and named him "George." That's my husband's name as well. Talk about three slaps in the face.

He was stunned. "You took him around my kids? Are you CRAZY? Bitch, I'll kill you."

I smiled through my tears. I didn't mean to hurt him.

I got down off the ladder and said, "I have to go. He's here. Bye."

I hung up, got on my knees in this warehouse, put my hand on the hard box and said, "Well, my job is my man, so let's try to push this goddamn box to the back so I can, somehow get the box of shirts down from the top shelf"

My ass sticking out, I whispered, "Somebody gotta work, and no honey I'm not getting ice cream. I came back to work and asked my fat ass boss could I get a few extra hours. And she said 'sure.'"

I tried to push the box, but it was just so goddamn heavy.

And then I'll call my jealous husband and let him know my Job was the man I brought around my kids, not a real man. Jeez.

Men and their egos.

I smiled, jamming to Erykah Badu's "Honey," my mind on buying Janet's *Discipline* album early tomorrow morning from Best Buy because *"Honey"* wasn't hitting on shit!

# Cheaters

I love him. Yes I do. I got a good man and I knew better than to let rumors break us up. Bitter faggots were jealous that I had an unelectable man. Meaning one couldn't tell he was bisexual just by looking and talking to him. His name was Sampson Dames and he was from Portland, Oregon. The City of Roses.

I met him when I was visiting Michigan. I had gone back to see mama, because her house went into foreclosure and I remember Sampson approached me on the street. I was on my way to the grocery store because I had a headache and Mama didn't have any more Tylenol.

"Wanna buy some bud?" he asked and my mouth fell open. He was one of the most gorgeous men I had ever seen. I didn't smoke bud but I bought four dime bags. He had asked for my number and I gave it to him.

"Thanks," he said, shaking my hand. I was intrigued because he was clad in a business suit, selling dope. He had a book bag strap across his right shoulder, fresh gators and long, flowing hair with huge Snoop Dog curls that made him look ultra sophisticated.

I had walked off, thinking I would never see him again. I knew in my heart he wouldn't call. I bought the Tylenol, thinking about him. His smile and the way he spoke blew my mind.

When I got home I swallowed two pills, opened the gallon of orange juice mama told me to leave closed and poured a glass.

I then watched the tube, wondering why I didn't stay an additional week with Mama. She was widowed and lonely and I hated her being alone in Flint, Michigan. I guess the guilt ate away at me because I convinced her to move with me, and wound up forking over $3,500 to make that happen. So far so good. She stayed mostly to herself, ordering shit from the Home Shopping Network, and the few friends she met, neighbors, seemed to bring some joy back into her life.

I was channel surfing when my cell rang. I looked at the screen and it said Sampson Dames. Who was that? I answered with an attitude because I hated strange people calling me.

"Hello."

"Hey, how are you? It's the weed man."

I died right there. I flipped off the TV, hopped up to my feet and swung a fist in the air.

"I'm, I'm good," I said, my voice going through a Mariah Carey phase. I should sing Opera.

"Are you free? I know you don't know me but I am going to a party and I don't wanna go alone. I'm visiting from P-Town and my homeboy who was supposed to go with me called me and said he had to work."

"Sure. I'll go. Where are you?"

"Next door. My Mom's stay next door to yours."

I dropped the phone, smiling.

Small world.

We linked up and he looked as good as ever in a Calvin Klein outfit. Really classy. He was so masculine he made me feel feminine and I wasn't a fem at all. We shook hands and looked each other over. I didn't tell him that I went through twenty outfits until I settled for red suede pants, a red sweater with hearts on it and a white T-shirt with glittering sapphires on the chest.

"You look good, Fam," he said, looking me over. He licked his lips and I licked mine. We couldn't look away from each other. People were walking by, chatting and living life. Cars zoomed to and fro. I looked to the side and I saw a rented BMW. At least he rode in style.

He walked up to me and looked in my eyes.

"Are you on the low?" he asked.

"Yes."

"Are you a top or bottom?"

"What are you?"

"A Top."

I was a Top. But I wanted him. "I'm a bottom, I haven't let a guy smash yet but I will.'

He wrapped his arms around me and gave me some tongue. In public! For some reason I kissed him back and he pulled away from me and said, "I never kissed a man in public. But you are so fine. How could I not? Let's go," he went on, opening the passenger side door. I got in and he closed it.

I reached over and unlocked his door. He got inside, snapped his seat belt across his body and closed the door.

"Let's roll."

That was a year and a half ago. We have been inseparable since. We knew everything about each other I didn't trust men because I was always getting cheated on but I loved Sampson. We lived together in Miami, Florida. He traded in the Pacific Northwest for the mean streets of Dade County.

We had a gorgeous house in Pinecrest, complete with security guard and all. The neighbors were rich and we were living it up. He sold drugs but he maintained gainful employment. He was a stock broker and he knew his shit. I was a modeling consultant/model. I brought in $4,500 a week after taxes.

I loved his swagger. Quick tempered, but I tolerated it. He didn't smoke cigarettes but he smoked blunts and was an alcoholic. Every Friday he liked to take me out to Bayside and fuck me when I got home. At first it hurt because I had never been penetrated but once I got used to his foreplay, his alertness and his sense of calm I relaxed and became a full-fledged bottom. I did and said anything to keep him.

One day he was at work and I was washing his clothes. Because I wanted to. I had gone into the bedroom and noticed the computer was logged onto his account. I sat down and decided to snoop. I trusted him and he never did anything questionable but I still had major trust issues with men.

I opened his emails and I read. Totally harmless. I smiled. I knew I could trust...

I read one email from a Lloyd Baxter.

*When are you coming back to get this ass? I know you have a man now and ya'll live together and you claim you love him but be for real. Were you thinking of that love when you were riding my dick the other night?*

I couldn't move. Riding his dick? Sampson was a Top. A complete Top. He told me he had never been a Bottom for anybody. He didn't even like me messing with his ass. I saw that the guy was logged on Yahoo Instant Messenger.

I hit him up.

Hey, Fam, I typed, my heard cringing...

Sup, baby. When are you going to let me get the booty again?

[I cringed again!] Tonight.

Word?

Yes, word.

What about your man?

He's out of town.

And your other man?

*Other man? Oh, God! He had two men?* He's gone, too.

You're a pimp. You are dating three niggahs and one doesn't know about the other.

Tears fell down my face. He lied to me. My heart was torn in two. I couldn't breathe and I had to stand up suck in air and hold the table. I was shaking my head, in denial.

He was my baby. We lived together and paid bills together. Every time I put my guard down. EVERY TIME! Boom, bitch. It blew up in my face.

Who needed a face lift with things always blowing up on me?

I heard the door bell and I decided to ignore it. Who ever it was they could come back. I wasn't up for company. Not right now. I wouldn't be the best host.

Are you there Pimp Sampson? Mr. Portland.

[Eye wanted to blow my cover] Yes.

Can we fuck again? Maybe you can do that thing with your tongue when you suck my dick and swallow my come.

[Oh, God!] *He sucks dick? He swallows? He told me he doesn't give head and that he never swallowed. Oh my God!*

[Eye kept my composure] Yes. I would *love* to suck on your dick, Fam. I'll make you come in 5 minutes.

Word. That's what's up. But how do you juggle all those men without getting caught?

[Oh, he's caught now. He just doesn't know it yet. And you don't either, bitch!] I do what I can. Come over. I have instructions, though. Wanna play a game?

Yes.

[The evil side of my began plotting...] Here's what I want you to do...

I heard the door bell again. I rubbed my arms, tears stinging my eyes.

I slowly walked down the stairs, wanting to get the gun from my closet and kill myself.

I loved Sampson with my soul.

He was my soul mate.

The things I shared with him. Secrets I never told a soul.

I paused at the front door and looked through the peep hole. A pretty lady and a little boy stood on my porch.

Neighbors.

And I don't have food or money to give them.

I answered with a curt, "Yes."

She smiled, extending her hand. *God! Jehovah's Witnesses!*

"Hi. I'm Gail. And this here is my son, Sam."

I shook his little hand. "How do you do?"

The breath caught in my throat.

"Does Sampson live here?"

"Yes. Yes, he does. And you are?"

She smiled. "His wife. I came all the way from Portland to ask him to come home and be with me and his son."

I had to sit down.

My stomach was in knots. How much of a fool was I?

"And you are?" she asked.

"His room mate," I said, my voice cracking. "Come in."

"No, thanks. If he isn't here then I shouldn't stay. I don't wanna intrude. Just give him my new cell number and tell him to call me."

"I wanna see Daddy," Sam said, disappointed.

"You will…" She shook my hand. "Nice to meet you." She opened her purse and pulled out a piece of paper and pen. She scribbled down her number and handed it to me.

"I'll make sure he gets it."

"Thanks."

When I closed the door I flushed the number down the toilet. I fell to my knees and sobbed into my hands. Why were black men such cheaters? Why do they do what they do?

And he was married.

The doorbell rang again and I walked to it, answering. A fine man with chocolate skin and gorgeous eyes blinked back at me.

"*You're* not Sampson."

I faked a smile. "I *know*."

He started to back up. I walked up to him and said, "Come in."

"Are you going to *kill* me?"

"No. I'm his *room* mate."

He was relieved. "Oh. Is he here?"

"He went to the store. He said you were coming. Damn you're fine."

He smiled. "And you got a phat ass."

"Damn. Are you and Sampson dating? I'm single and I wanna wallow in your swagger."

He came inside and closed my door. He gripped his dick and looked me in the eyes.

*What a goddamn whore. He doesn't know me from a can of paint,* I thought miserably.

"I got enough dick to go around."

I kissed his lips and let go. My relationship was over so I didn't care. I want to find out what made his ass so special. He kissed like a pro, rubbing my big booty like he was crazy.

His huge dick pressed against my thigh and I dug in his pants.

"Can I eat that ass, Shawty?"

*Hell, yeah. You can eat it.* I was going to let him fuck and send his ass home. I knew that was the game plan. And I was gonna stick to it.

I was stroking his manhood and he reached into my Calvin Klein briefs and played around with my hole. His fingers were warm and invitingly courageous.

Exploring and Imploring.

I was dying for some head. I got on my knees and started to give *him* head.

I didn't know this man from Adam but I wanted to taste a dick that fucked my man, a dick that had him sprung, a dick that had him sucking and swallowing and maybe spitting and gargling.

I sucked for dear life, my lips the autopsy and my tongue the dissector. I wanted to see if I could taste the DNA and see if it matched Sampson Dames.

Ole boy was grinding in my mouth, putting a Timberland boot-clad foot on my pricey low-table and throat stroking my tonsils. I took it like a trooper.

He moaned so sensually. Not like a gun shot victim. The hairs on my arms stood up.

He told me he had to come and I took him out of my mouth and let him come on my shirt.

After it was over he asked could he fuck and I told him one simple thing.

"Time is up. Go home. Please."

"But…"

"Please go. Just shut up. Go. Get the fuck out. Now. Please. Goddamn. Don't make it complicated."

"But."

"Don't make me go get my pit bulls."

My heart was an ice box.

I called my boo, Sampson. Hating him and wanting him dead. All I could see was red. I opened my closet and took something down from the top shelf. Holding it, I sat on the sofa while the phone continued to ring.

"Yes, Boo."

"Where are you?" I asked, wanting to scream.

"On the way home."

"I miss you. Hurry."

I hung up, rubbing the Berretta.

About forty minutes later, he walked through the door and I had candles lit. He smiled at me and gave me a hug. I gave him a kiss and he rubbed my booty the way he always did.

"You miss Daddy?" this secret bottom asked.

"Yes." I was looking spiffy and jazzy. Nothing but a thong on. *Nothing* else.

"Damn you are fine, baby."

What does your wife and son think. You have been committing adultery times three. The nerve of you!

I wanted to shoot him. I eyed the Berretta under the low-table. Had to plan it just right.

"Sit down," I told him, the artist of persuasion.

He was taking off his Goose Down jacket. I helped him, went over to the closet and hung it up.

He gave me some tongue. He dug in my draws and finger fucked me real good, twitching his finger in my hole and making me quiver.

This was our last Dance. Our Donna Summer good bye. I told him to sit down and he did. I pulled out his dick and begin sucking him. I sucked so fast his head spun. He gripped my head and gyrated in my mouth. There was no need for words. My head screamed SHOOT HIM NOW!

He was pumping me faster and harder. Sweat was starting to form on his forehead.

"Damn, baby… I hadn't come all day. It's starting to come."

I pulled it out my mouth and said, "You love me?"

He was about to pop. "Yes?"

"You do?" I asked, teasing him.

He slapped my booty. Whack. "Yes, put it back in your mouth! Suck it!"

"Are you faithful to me, Daddy?"

"YES!"

I put it back in my mouth and begin to suck it. His eyes were closed and I told him to keep them closed. I had my cell in my hand and I had pressed "send." Two text messages went to two different phones.

I felt him jerk and tense up. His dick started to pulsate in my mouth.

His eyes were wide. "I'M ABOUT TO COME!"

The front door opened and my guests entered. They were shocked, standing there watching him come in my mouth. The third guest came from my bedroom, clad in a pair of boxers, with his dick out. When he saw the other two guests he lost his hard on.

"Open your eyes, baby."

When he did he covered his face.

His wife and son stood there, in tears.

"Daddy's gay?"

His dear wife didn't know what to do. She was so hurt she had to shake her head and sneer. She tried to cover her son's eyes but he slapped her hands away, both offended and crushed. I didn't care. I refused to care.

"Come on, Son. Time to go. We'll see you in court. I want a divorce!"

I stood up, and said, "Baby, your *man* is here."

He slowly looked to the right and saw ole boy.

I shot my cuffs. "You *secret* Bottom you can stay for the night. But when you awaken tomorrow, I want you gone."

He tried to talk to me but I wasn't having it.

I was turned off that he would try to save our relationship and not run after his wife and child. Come on, Man. Love your son more than you love me. He just got the news of his life. He's hurt beyond comprehension and you were trying to make amends with me?

I turned my back on him and walked into the kitchen, a kitchen I would never share with his dumb ass. I took out a frying pan and opened the fridge and took out the eggs. When I was in pain I had to eat. I cracked them in a bowl. I sprayed Pam in the pan. I put on a small pot of water and turned the temperature knob on the back burner on high. I took out the grits.

He was standing behind me, watching me. He refused to say anything. When the water started boiling, I slowly poured in the grits, turning the heat down.

He looked at me with sadness and embarrassment in his eyes.

"I should have told you I was married. I don't have an excuse for cheating on you *or* my wife. I'm selfish. I've always been selfish. Watching my Daddy have it all when I grew up powered my greed. I wanted to be like him because he's my hero. He was one of the most successful, wealthiest pimps to come out of Portland, Oregon. I don't wanna lose you. I gotta have it all in my life."

"Have what?" I asked, frying the eggs. I added cheese in the grits. Sampson's lover was still in my fucking home, sitting at the table, fully clothed. He refused to leave. He thought I was going to kill Sampson.

"I gotta have it all," Sampson said, looking pathetic. "I'm *scared* of commitment. I didn't mean to hurt you."

I used the spatula to turn over my eggs.

"Go shower or something, man. I'm cool. We're over. Ain't no sense in fighting."

Sampson breathed a sigh of relief. But he still didn't run after his wife and child. Crummy asshole. Save the relationship with your son. "OK. I'll shower and then we'll talk."

"OK." I looked at his fling. "You can go, too. Obviously he ain't mine so why should I get mad over a man that ain't mine."

Both of them went to my room.

Eye waited until they were in the shower to eat my food. I kept looking at my grits and thinking evil thoughts. But logic overshadowed reason. I didn't want to go to jail for attempted murder. I didn't feel like pleading insanity in court. I was glad his wife and son were gone. I didn't mean to shit on her parade, but I wanted her to hurt the way I was hurt. We both lost a man tonight. The same man. I ate the food slowly and I wound up vomiting. I had too much on my mind. I was too hurt. I couldn't feel my arms or legs.

I went into my room and I heard them from the shower. Fucking. I had to see this. I had to see him taking dick. I had to validate that we were over. My real side came out. The Top I had suppressed to be submissive to a secret bottom male that had me fooled. I took off my clothes and walked in the bathroom. I might as well join in. He was a slut. I fucked sluts and pissed on them. When they saw me they stopped, looking me over. Sampson held up his hand and I took it. I grudge fucked both of them. I made sure I had on a condom. I fucked my ex and ole boy so good I made them both come.

I left them in the shower and dried off. I closed the door and raced downstairs and got the gallon of bleach. I poured bleach on their clothes and opened his side of the closet and knifed his entire wardrobe then bleached it. I closed the door and smiled. I wasn't done. Both of their cell phones were on the kitchen table. I boiled some water and threw them in there. He boiled all over my faithfulness so why not boil over his shit?

I then took their car keys and flushed them down the toilet. Bye, bye you *dangling* sonsofbitches.

I then used a key and let air out of their tires, with a note that says, "All the videos of us fucking I'm sending to your wife so she can wipe you out in court. And, oh yea I'm loading them on Nubian101.com and Xtube."

I bit my lip until I drew blood. I walked to the front door and, sucking in air, slammed my hand in it. It started to swell. I then head butted the wall a few times until my forehead was raw.

But then I had another thought and this one made me smile in vengeance. I poured bleach on their cars, lit a match and lit them on fire, walking to the security booth and reporting that my house had been burglarized. They snapped to attention.

My boyfriend had another man in the house, and they attacked me. Look at my face. He slammed my hand in the door. Please help me. They tried to throw a pot of grits on me and he pulled a Berretta on me."

While the guards called the police, I stood there, beaming.

My masterpiece was complete.

I had the liberty of the fire department putting out the flames on Sampson and his lover's cars. I couldn't wait for the cops to tell the *Cheaters* to go stand by the squad car so they could have their Miranda rights read. I was waiting on that part. They hadn't come outside yet. They had no idea cops had my place surrounded with a chopper overhead, shining a bright light on me. I felt good but something inside me *wasn't* satisfied. I didn't know what it was but I knew I wouldn't be the same. Neighbors filed out of the house and they walked over to us. A few asked me what happened and I kept a tight lip.

When Sampson came out of the house and saw his car he ran at me and his friend had punched me in the face and I grabbed a huge branch from the ground and opened the Post Office in their skulls by going postal on their asses.

The police grabbed us all and I swung the branch at a few of them. I was so upset I couldn't think straight. Sampson promised to kill me and they took that into account and said it would be used against him in a court of law. They apprehended him and his fuck buddy and put plastic handcuffs on them. One of the female cops got me to calm down and I hugged her and cried so hard I couldn't breathe.

"You're safe," said one of the Pinecrest cops. I broke down to my knees because vengeance hadn't been as sweet as I thought.

I felt I could have done more.

Maybe I should have killed him.

A few months later. I was thinking, "Fuck love." Yea. I said it. FUCK LOVE! Shall I *spell* it for you? F-U-C-K. L-O-V-E. I should have kept my legs closed, my pants up and my heart under lock and key because black men were so full of shit. Who needed shit from bulls? I couldn't believe this has happened to me. Months have passed and I was still not over what he'd done. It was making me bitter. I didn't want to forgive him. Why should I? He humiliated me. Why did I give my heart to a man who wasn't capable of loving his own wife and son? I was so blind that I couldn't see that his two plus two equaled ten. What was I thinking? Why was I so dumb? I should have listened to my mother. She told me to let love find me so long ago and I didn't listen because I tried to be cute. I figured that I was a grown man and Mama was old fashioned, everything from her style of music to her style of dress was stuck in the 1960's. She told me God would bring my soul mate along. God chose our mates, not the other way around. She said if I searched for it Satan would play me and my life like a tennis game. And that's exactly what he did.

Now I couldn't stop crying or clutching the phone, hoping he'd call. The man and his fuck buddy were doing five years in prison for assaulting me. My set up and ruining my hand and face got him convicted and I didn't feel a twinge of regret.

This was shallow because I knew he wouldn't call. How could he? He was incarcerated. They could only call collect. And why did I want him to call anyway? He cheated on me, left me out to dry in a rare type of sunlight unknown to faithful men like myself. I was slowly chocking, needing a drink and some bud but I knew well enough to know that I really didn't need mood and mind altering substances. I felt anger surging inside me to the point of throwing the phone across the room. I staggered to stand up and I stood in a living room me and my ex fucked in three times a day. I loved giving up the booty to his Royal Dickness. He was everything and more, my Kodak Moments trapped inside the boroughs of life, love and liberty. And all that was shattered when I read his emails. When a man I didn't know existed shattered Sampson's lies. When his wife showed up at the door claiming she wanted her husband. When his son wanted to see Daddy!

My heart couldn't stand the hurricane. I felt like China right now, lost everything and all hope.

I remembered calling one of my friends on the phone when I found out that my dude was with two other men during our entire relationship. I mean what the fuck?

He was the typical friend, had his Oprah Winfrey answer on stand by.

"By letting this man who hurt you make you shut yourself off from love; you're giving him way too much power."

I was drinking booze. "Um…whatever."

"I'm serious. The best revenge is living well and showing him that by his inability to love you the way you deserve, he hasn't beaten you. Plus he's a state number now…"

I had lit a cigarette and sat on the sofa, clutching the phone. I frowned. "Man, I don't want to hear that. Love will *never* live here. You just don't get it, do you?"

"Yes, I do. I have been there. But being hurt equips you to find your soul mate."

"*Bullshit. Fuck* love. My heart is shut down for repairs. It needs maintenance and the maintenance crew is on goddamn strike."

223 DAPHAROAH69

"This to shall pass."

"I am not a Bible scripture."

"Maybe you should try reading the Word, bruh. God heals all wounds."

I pulled on the cigarette, letting it fumigate my lungs. "OK, Moses, I hear you. I guess you're going up into the mountains with your stone tables to write some commandments, huh?"

"Well I didn't know he was cheating on you. If I did..."

"Yea, yea. Been around the world same song."

"Damn. He hurt you really bad. And I really thought he was the one for you."

"I know, right. Everyone knew he was cheating on me but *me* and everyone came over to my crib smiling in my face and eating my food and laughing in my face and didn't utter a word."

"You feel like that now..." he assured me. I knew he was being meaningful. But I wasn't ready to accept it. "But give yourself a while to defoliate yourself and to heal. You'll be alright. You're a good guy with a lot to offer. Just take your time and in the meantime, continue to do you and be the best YOU can be."

"This isn't the Army, man. What's up with these damn infomercial answers?"

"Man. I have been there. I was the same way when me and my ex broke up...We were together for 8 years. I've been single for 2 years now. Trust me, Papa. It gets better!

"Well, I don't feel the same way. Honestly, man. Why even try? With Sampson I have done EVERYTHING in my power to prove my love. When I say EVERYTHING I mean EVERYTHING! I did things I didn't want to. I am a Top man and I became a Bottom for him. Just to have him and it backfired on me because he was truly a Bottom and I got fucked by a Bottom. I feel like a dyke. I've sacrificed so much and what do I have now to show for it?

Not a thing.

If I sat here and told you everything I did for Sampson you would say I was a fool in love. I'm a Cancer. When I love I love hard."

"We all have gone through changes in our lives, Man. With two of my ex's … I worked and took care of them. I got one a job and he didn't work at all. He was a thug who refused employment just to run the streets. With one ex I told him to quit working and he could go to school to be a barber. He was really good at cutting hair. I would take care of us until he finished. That went to hell quickly. With the other ex he believed everybody but me. Fags wanted to break us up because they wanted him and it worked.  I did not cheat on him so he listened to his friends and cheated on me and let some dude fuck him. He then smiled in my face and told me he was glad he did it. I almost went to jail that night for aggravated assault."

I was getting depressed. "Damn, Boy."

"I have moved from my residence a total of three times to be with dudes out of state. One moved a new lover in and moved me out and I had no where to go. I had to live in a shelter for eight months until I saved enough money to move on and get my life back on track. The other man I met and fell in love with was so jealous and possessive he pushed me out. He said he loved me unconditionally yet he didn't. I've proven myself and have nothing left to give."

"I feel the same goddamn way. I'm emotionally drained. I just feel like you get more respect from a man when you talk shit to him, treat him like leftover chicken bones and dog him. Maybe Mama was right. When you look for love Satan play you and your life like a game of tennis."

"Homie. When I was a playboy I had more dudes trying to settle down with me than I do now that I am mature enough to handle a relationship."

"Why is that?"

"Simple. Niggahs want what they think they can't have. They go all out until they get it and once they do they use it, talk about you and switch and take your friends."

"I don't want to talk about this anymore. I gotta go."

"Man. *Cry*. Yell. Break plates. Vent. And move on."

"I loved him so much."

"Don't let it make you a bitter person. If you do then Sampson won. "

I hung up and burst into tears.

My father's a 1970s Mack from Macon, Georgia. I thought of him as I picked up the phone. I thought about calling him. He was too busy for me. Let's be real. When I came out the closet and told him I was gay three years ago he was suddenly too busy when I called him. We haven't had a real conversation in years. I hung up, shaking my head. Calling him would be a mistake. I logged onto the computer and I had gotten an email from a friend I hadn't talked to in a while. I smiled when I saw his name. I should call him but I decided not to because I had to get through this on my own, without my friends as safety nets. Plus their advice was starting to sound more like a campaign.

I got a call from my boy in Iraq. I wasn't sure how he got to a phone but he did. The connection was really horrible. A lot of static in the ear piece. I told him what was going on with me.

"I heard it already," he said. "I heard about Sampson. I am all the way in Iraq and I heard about it from a friend back home. Damn, Homie. Love doesn't like you much. But hey, listen. I am not going to preach to you but give it to God."

"You say that like you know what you're talking about. It isn't that easy."

"It's as easy as 1-2-3."

I was defiant. "Well 4-5-6 is a bitch."

"Let it be and let it go fuck with someone else. You have to keep in mind that being an attractive gay man is a blessing and a curse especially in the area you live in. Miami, Florida is a brutal city. While it seems that everyone desires you, not everyone is prepared for all that comes with you. Some only want you for sex. Let's be real. You are eye candy wrapped and delivered to the Tootsie Pop commercial set. You have to work so much harder to find a decent guy and you do that by not looking. You gotta be antsy, pro-active and selective in those you let into your world. For your protection. When you meet a potential mate or date ask them above-the-rim questions. Questions they can't reach by jumping. When they approach you start your Journalism antics. What is it that attracted you to me? What was your initial impression of me? Ask unbootable questions that they can't give you a baited answer to. For example. It's like when you ask someone if they are a Top or Bottom and they ask 'What are you?'"

I lowered my head for a minute. I had done that with Sampson. When he asked me was I a Top or Bottom. "What are you?" I asked. I didn't want to risk losing the potential lay.

He said he was a Top and I lied and said I was a Bottom when I had never been fucked in my life. So where did the true lie start? I was just as much to blame as he was. But I wasn't ready to accept that. I was still faithful to him. But what's faith when our foundation was built on small lies?

My homeboy went on. "You already know their answer is going to be whatever they can say to win you over...when you ask more interesting things, the truth will pop out. Give it time. You will heal. I love you. I'm being deported back home in a few weeks. Been over here for a year plus, now. I am in the closet 'cause I'm in the military but I'm tired of fucking Iraqi-sand-clad-military Niggahs over here in my platoon. Booty is good but I need American ass. Say a prayer for me."

"I will." I hung up the phone and closed my eyes, thinking about catching Bible Study tonight.

If I was going to get over Sampson and get my life together I knew I couldn't do it alone.

Or could I?

# Girl, You're Harping!

Girl! You're harping! You're harping *hard*! Over people and their bullshit. *Giirlll* lemme tell *you* one goddamn thang. You weren't put here to live up to nobody's expectations but your own. Look at yourself like a well-produced movie, the sequel to Friday. Everyone expected actor Chris Tucker to reprise his role as "Smoky, the Weed Head." Everybody and their Mama, daughter and dogs had all these expectations. Ah, Smoky going to do this and Ice Cube is going to do that and this and that will ensue to this and that and Thelma from *Amen* was going to kick Ice Cube out of her house because every time John Witherspoon went in the kitchen he was in the kitchen eating up all the pig feet and hog moss and chitterlings, Chile…grown men *shouldn't* be living at home with their Mamas and Miss Parker finally let Smoky knock the dust off her puss-say and when the movie came out and none of the aforementioned things happened then people, women, children and their dogs were like fuck this movie it sucked!

229 Dapharoah69

Don't put expectations on anything. Take it for what it's worth. Trust me.

Girl, Jesus *died* on time and one time for the sins of man, a One Night Only Event, girl, spread around the world in a matter of seconds…and you weren't put here to die for none of these dumb ass people so get your mind off nails and crosses and find your Jordan River to cross, God hath not forsaken your stupid self as of yet…

Chile, and cross it well.

If you got to bare your cross then float on that muthafuckah across your Jordan River and when you reach dry land make sure it's not a deserted island, where you'll be stranded in more bullshit.

Live your life. The hell with society! We weren't made to be economically and socially equal to whites, if you don't believe me believe the white man's document, the Emancipation Proclamation, not the Emancipation of Mimi, we aren't talking about air headed Mariah Carey, Chile…History, we talking history, you hear me? The Emancipation Proclamation, coined by crummy Abraham Lincoln, clearly did not free us from slavery, but tricked us into *thinking* the shit was over. So people running around here celebrating Juneteenth can take that shit and shove it up Christopher Columbus's ass so deep I want it dangling out his goddamn nose! Niggahs tend to believe anything they hear 'cause we're ignorant, and so are you, Chile.

What? Why you staring at your self like that in the mirror, Chile. I'm trying to talk to you, trying to put you up on game! Fuck people. Yea, that's right. Yea, I said it. Fuck people! They don't give a rat's ass about you, they don't pay your car notes, even though you been walking and talking right on to that City Metro Bus for three years...they don't pay your rent, even though you live with your Grandma, and doesn't she have multiple sclerosis or some shit like that?

*Giirlll*, lemme tell you another goddamn thang. Fuck men. Yea, that's right. I said it. Men aren't shit and the anuses they push it out with. Yea, that's right. I'ma be frank with you, girl. They aren't shit. You running around the hood giving up the pussy like standard issue and when they done passing it around like red-tipped blunts snaking smoke into the air you want to come home and get all mad. Men treat women how they want to be treated. If they classy and dress classy they treat 'em classy. If you running around here with booty shorts all up your ass, your tits about to pop free from that snap-and-you'll-destroy-it halter top that looked like no top, if you run around here talking about dick, loving dick and telling men how many dicks you sucked before the third quarter paycheck went in, then they are going to try you. They are going to disrespect you because you don't respect yourself.

Men love insecure pussy.

Look at 50 Cent. You couldn't get a man because you let a man have sex with you hours after you met him without even knowing where his lips and dick been. And nine times outta ten he just left from fucking another ditzy bitch so you shoulda asked him what that smell *really* was before you gave him head. He was a little funky down there and he told you, "Yea, girl, I just got off work, it ain't no thang," and you sucking another woman's pussy off his dick 'cause you stupid as hell.

That's why you got a fever blister on your top lip. You better pray it ain't Herpes. Ain't a cure for that shit, Chile? Hell no, I'm trying to tell ya'. Ain't a damn cure!

You feel hopeless and helpless with his dried nut on your lips, titties and ass. You feel violated. So much so you loose you're damn mind and go to the parole office and you ask for the officer, and the receptionist ask you, "Well, ma'am, who is your reporting officer?" and you say, "Well, I don't know, who's the officer of the day?" and she, clad in her fancy get up that made you shut up, stands up and she says, "Well…uh, yea…wait right here..." and you realize,

"Hey, I'm not on parole." You just stuck! Goddamn stuck on stupid.

Elementary bullshit shoulda stayed put up on the shelves with the Legos, Dr. Suess books and He-man toys. Ain't nobody playing with Legos and He-Man toys anymore. I don't want no green eggs and goddamn ham! Ain't anybody making new episodes of the *Thundercats* or the goddamn *Smurfs* anymore? You're supposed to be old school, and you moping and crying and bitching about not having a man. Stop giving up your pussy to every smiling face and keep your legs closed like MC Hammer's business then you can chase the horses away who want to eat your goddamn apples. You got to learn how to make these men bob for thy apples. Make 'em work for it. Get to know them. Talk about the future. You weave the jerks away that way.

They don't want to talk, they want to stick and move so talk and move. If they stay chances are you got a winner? Make 'em wait two to three months for the pussy. If they can't wait then fuck 'em. Just tell yourself "Potential AIDS victim, exonerated!" You gotta look at all men like they infected with something. I don't care how much dick you had in your life, Dr. Ruth had plenty of sex but you see the bitch got rich and made it her profession. Only good experience yields such education on good and horrible dick.

All she was doing was selling her past experiences and making money off it.

You need to get a goddamn clue, Girl.

It doesn't matter how whorish you were, everybody got a past. Half of these old people running around here and through church like the black plague talk down to the younger generation like were promiscuous harlots when they must have forgotten the high heeled pumps and mini skirts they one wore rotting away on the Goodwill shelves. They thought by donating all their Hoochie Mama clothes, clothes they used to get fucked in, exonerates them, and vindicates them from their pasts. Nah. Some old women got so many miles on thy lips, thy asshole and thy pussy that they had no choice but to turn to God because they have been ruined for years. Men don't want ruined pussy. And the old men, they act all holier-than-thou but once upon a time in the 1930s, 40s, 50s and 60s they had anything but holier-than-thou-dicks. For real, Girl. Listen to me, I wouldn't tell you wrong!

If you didn't raise your children by setting the perfect example then you might as well say you handed us the perils of mother earth on a silver platter. You can't tell your sons not to beat women when he was raised watching his father doing the same exact thing. Parents are your first goddamn teachers, and you taught them well. You can't tell your child not to go out and have sex when he or she can hear you getting dicked down through the walls every night and the more you say, *"Yes, baby yes tear my pussy up, yes it feels sooo good yes baby damn you got some good dick!"* What makes you think your son or daughter doesn't want to feel that good, you dumb ass?

Look at Joseph Jackson, he fathered other children so it don't matter what nobody say. Just do *you*. And *do* you well. In fact do you so goddamn well pennies won't vie for your wishes when you're...well off?

So now you're alone. You are walking around your Grandma's house complaining. How the house ain't never clean, when it's just you and your Grandma living there. You cook, clean and sow. You leave dishes here and there. You bringing men in and out of a house your Grandma had build from the turf up with her late husband's money. A home she reared, raising your mother, a home that reared your aunties and uncles who couldn't *stand* your ass.

Yea, I said it. I'ma ya' friend, ya' only friend and I ain't g'on say what you want to hear, I'ma say what cha need to hear. Yea, what, why ya' laugh? Why you looking at me in that fashion? If I wanted to be sized up I'd King Size my goddamn Burger King and Super size my McDonald's clad in a tutu singing Food, Folks and Fun.

But I ain't singing.

I don't care for music that hot. But, girl. You are harping! You harping something terrible!

You're complaining about how the bills are falling behind, yet you won't get off your ass and work. You talk about President George Oil Driven Bush, yet you don't even pay taxes and you didn't even vote so you are basically bitching without a goddamn reason to. Your Grandma has given you the world and her prayers and blessings, yet when they connected with your stank ass you come off as being edgy, ungrateful, egging the borderline of insecurity.

You give up ass but you can't get *off* your ass to get a real 9 to 5. If Dolly Parton could make a movie about it back in the 80s then you can *do* something with it in the 2000's, Chile.

Hell if push comes to shove and if shove comes to a tug-o-war match with you on both sides pulling your ass into a defunct hot mess, sell some ass. Yea, that's right. Sell it.

The pornography business was at an all time high; quite *frankly* it's a multi-billion dollar business. Never forget Bill Clinton didn't inhale and he got his dick sucked by slutty Monica in the Oval Office. She even saved the garment with his dried semen on it that lead her to millions and the selling of Monica's hand bags. Sex sells! Everybody selling body parts these days, enough to make *Hostel part 3*, Chile, some movie where American body parts make the Dow Jones in another country.

I know this is all confusing for you. I know you looking at me all crazy. Apply yourself, dress yourself up like Madonna and sell yourself. World War I started the moralistic, sexual decline. Fucked people up, girl. The Great Depression, Niggahs lost everything, migrating to the South, all they had was dick and pussy to console them. They fucked so much babies were being born haphazardly into poverty and times were so hard the men left, leaving the women to tend to the nappy-headed, snot-nosed brats. Then World War 2 claimed lives, Chile. Some 50 million women, men and children. Japan lay in ruins. The world was just reduced to a moralistic mess that has affected even us as a new generation because of what the environment shaped us to be.

Men can't walk past pussy without quivering.

They can't sniff pussy without getting hard-ons. They are like the Modern Day Sodom. If Grace Jones came off her pussy men would fuck it, and she ain't the most attractive bitch in the world!

Make those men come off those leather wallets, girl. The thicker the *slicker* is my motto, Chile. Get that Monay! Not money but monaaay, Chile! Yeeeah, ya hear me bitch? We live in the projects, we are ghetto, "get-toe" its pronounced, Chile. We Get in where we Fit in and never come up Too Short of anything once we apply ourselves. We are a jealous breed. We get advice from musicians who don't even write their own songs, who didn't even live that life. We go to church and say we love God but we lie, steal, cheat, sleep with married men and jump up and down in the clubs every Friday and Saturday night knowing we gotta go to church on Sunday. We love our weave and we still press on nails and we still got three and four baby daddies and we still have faith in our black men despite how we are degraded in the media. Janet's titty popping out at the Super bowl proved that. But Madonna tonguing Britney made for polite table talk the world over, and didn't she kiss Christina, too?

Niggahs talk about the white man, what they do, how they smell, how much money does Donald Racist Trump really have, I wanna be like Bill Gates and we get stupid. We don't wanna be like Martin Luther King or Malcolm X, they

239 DAPHAROAH69

weren't "rich" enough according to blacks; but if you look closely the world will talk about Martin and Malcolm longer than they talk about Donald and Bill. Knowledge is power, yet your dumb ass dropped out of school in the 12th grade, I mean bitch how do you figure?

You pass by Now Hiring signs everyday and your stuck up ass won't go inside and apply. You justify and make excuses. You tell yourself, "Hey, Lady I don't know about computers," as an excuse not to sit your ass down and see what kinda benefits and pensions they offer. But as long as you got a man with benefits you're good to go.

Now do me a huge favor girl, while you harping about being alone. Look at yourself again in the mirror.

Yea, there you go.

Like that. I'm alone, I'm alone God almighty I'm alone.
Nobody wants me I'm worthless, selfish and crazy and
deranged. I can't afford two quarters to rub together to call
"common sense" well girl I love being alone in front of my
TV because, no matter what you're going through I get the
chance to watch people more fucked up than me, worse off
than me and suddenly my problems aren't so big and while I
sit here watching Paris Hilton's tart ass being led back to jail,
thank the Lord…they been doing Niggahs like this for
centuries, throwing the books at our asses like were classes. I
smiled through my tears, turning back towards the mirror. I
am done with my self-talk, cussing my own ass out, and now
my Grandma comes out of her room, and I eyed the job
application on the table, I ignored the cell phone playing the
R. Kelly ring tone "Sex Me Baby," knowing that's a booty call
and it's time to stop making excuses for my behavior, it's
time to stop giving up my pussy for free, it's time to stop
playing with God when I go to church, it's time to grow up,
it's time for me to stop getting my advice from popular
music that aint' so popular a few months later; it's time to
stop blaming everybody but myself for my problems. And as

my Grandma picked up my application with "K-Mart" on the top, she smiled a toothy grin, her face lit up like Christmas trees and it's the middle of August and she says, "Baby, good luck. I happen to know the manager of K-Mart. And I'm proud of you for going back to school to get your G.E.D."

I sit in tears, shuddering.

I was about to fall apart.

I had to change my way of thinking, stop being the perpetrator and the victim.

"Grandma."

My voice cracked terribly. I felt like I was on fire.

She touched my shoulder. It was cool and uncomfortable in here.

The dishes in the sink were piled high. I had to wash them.

"You don't have to say it. And just because you were diagnosed with Herpes and HIV doesn't mean life is over, sometimes you have to go through something traumatic to open your eyes, to wake up and smell the coffee you might not even drink because you may want just a tall glass of cold water to cool yourself down."

Her tears fell into my hair.

I wrapped my arms around her legs, sobbing, letting it out. I knew one thing—

I was going to change my future.

First, with a phone call to my doctor.

So I could get the proper medication to start my rehabilitation, to start my treatment.

With no expectations.

Secondly, I was going back to church to et right with God. In him all things were possible so I had to get with it, walk my lazy butt to the front of the church when the Pastor does the part of church he trying to save souls.

And eye would take it one day at a time.

# Joints, Beer and the Cheating Lovers 2

In the heat of Passion, anything can happen. Cornelius Ryan, author, said The Longest Day in the world happened to be on June 6, 1944. He called it "D-Day."

I said *bullshit*. January 8, 2006 was actually The Longest Day of my life. It was "D-Day" in two ways.

*Doomsday* because my wife walked in on me after I fucked her best friend's husband.

And *Dick* Day because my boy got his first taste of dick.

Eye bet you Cornelius couldn't write this Classic Epic Story.

Dancing around in her surreal life, Beatrice hungrily hit the weed, feeling like she was snatched into the Twilight Zone.

But that was the furthest thing from the truth. I mean here I was, sitting in their living room, a living room that was once a teeming display of well-framed family portraits, paintings done up by their siblings, family gatherings, parties, and the whole nine.

I had many spade card games in this room. I had many victories in this room. I jacked off in this room to pornos when I used to housesit for them.

We lived in the ghetto. Even with Brinks security in our homes and bars on the windows it was still safe to have someone you trusted watching your home because Niggahs could get around anything these days and the police, like Flavor Flav said, were a joke.

They took ten years to answer your call, plus I never called the crackers anyway. I was a thug. I handled my *own* business.

I spent much time with my boy in this room. There used to be gorgeous red carpeting, very gorgeous vertical blinds, and soft pinks pouring into golden browns...African statues, tasteful shit. It wasn't over done. And my boy decorated it all.

Beatrice always admired his skills with interior design. And now we were in a War Zone. Gone were the pictures.

The carpet was snatched up. My boy snatched it up out of anger, when he learned his wife was sleeping with mine.

He broke every picture frame, and when he got to the wedding picture he couldn't touch it, like some unknown force beckoned him not to. Brandy's "Angel in Disguise" played that day.

She sang, "An angel in Disguise she was...but some how you fell for her...until she broke your heart that day...and left you in the rain...but...still I LOVE YOU!"

"SHUT UP, BRANDY!" He took the picture off the wall and attempted to slam it on the floor, a huge picture at that, but he froze.

He cracked open. He couldn't. I remember hugging him. "It'll be all right, pimp. I *know* how you feel."

Brandy didn't help matters.

"Yea, yea, yea...you fell for her...she broke your heart, yea...aww baby, baby, I waited for you baby...and left you in the rain..."

Brandy was right.

Huge brown boxes were all over the living room. He packed all his shit. And then on top of *that* my wife walked out on me, blamed me for sleeping with her best friend. Excuse me. I never knew I held a gun to her head and made her suck another woman's bloody pussy.

Suffice it to say, Beatrice smoked most of my weed.

We still nakedly sat on the couch. She was still in La La Land, trying to figure this all out.

My Niggah threw his wedding ring at his wedding picture, which was the only picture hanging up in the room, ironically.

It tore me apart to look at it. It really separated my feelings for my wife. She was my entire world.

There was nothing I wouldn't do for her. And now it all changed.

"So I'm listening," she said with a major chip on her shoulder, looking past me and at her husband.

She hated me. She hated my guts. How could she smoke my weed knowing she hated me? I felt...used.

It hurt him to look at her. And it took a lot for him to stop gazing into my eyes.

247 DAPHAROAH69

My Niggah got his first piece of dick and I gave him the whole pie.

Not a piece. I wasn't a peaceful Niggah, 'ya feel me?

The thug pranced around his mental zone.

"Beatrice, we're not talking. Why should we talk?"

"Because, good or bad, we're married."

"Married. That was before or after you slept with my best friend's wife?"

"I'm loyal to my boy now. I say that to you through clenched teeth. Call me a German General. Think of my boy as Nibelung loyalty. Think of us, you and me, as the German Alliance. We're at war. And I confess my loyalty through clenched teeth, like they did back in the early 1900s."

"Niggah, please. We're not talking about World War I, Austria-Hungary or Generals. This is real life. And you didn't cheat on me? Have ya'll always been screwing each other?"

"Nope. Never. Have you and my boy's wife always been licking pussy like it's the new line of Laffy Taffy's?"

"Fuck you, niggah!"

"Nah, my Daddy'll do that when you leave, cunt bitch!"

"So when did this all start, husband?" she asked sarcastically, hurt from him calling her a cunt bitch. But she didn't show it on her face, but her eyes waved it like red flags.

"...Tonight. We *needed* each other. I let him fuck me because I wanted an understanding. Why would my wife, who I gave everything, tip toe and cheat in the next room with my boy's wife? My boy's woman! Goddamn, Beatrice! Don't TURN THIS SHIT ON ME!"

He glared at her, putting on his Ecko jacket and I didn't want all that ass covered so I reached up, high and half drunk, and snatched it off, throwing it across the room. Beatrice's mouth fell open and so did mine, mocking her.

"I'm sorry," I told her, THUG all across my face. "This ass belongs to Big Pimpin' now; your husband is my bitch. I don't want his ass covered. I don't give a fuck if it's your house or not."

With sympathy on his face, my Niggah looked at me, sparkles in his eyes. He smiled. "Then baby boy I'll leave it uncovered." I slapped his ass, watching those cheeks jiggle and Beatrice jumped up to her feet and pointed at me.

"You ungrateful asshole! This is my husband! I love him."

"No you don't," my boy protested darkly. "You Ho's always speak of love. You want a Niggah with a car. Not just a car, but a Lexus, a BMW, a Rolls Fucking Royce. Not a brother who may be a hard working Niggah and happens to drive a beat-up Honda. You want a fairy tale Niggah: open my door! Cook my food! Help me clean up around the house! Your paycheck is peanuts! I want walnuts! And now, after you cheated on me, with my boy's wife, and we reciprocated the gesture, now I'm the bad guy?"

She was in tears. And it hurt me to see her cry; I mean I did love the woman. She was my boy's heart, his world, and we were best friends for a very long time. I loved anyone associated with him.

"Then it's settled." She felt defeated. "I guess I'll call my lawyer. No sense in going to a marriage counselor. Not with this Jerry Springer shit."

I just looked at him. I saw the hurt, the deception and the pleasure of the get back all on his face. He sat next to me, gave me some tongue and rubbed my dick.

He smiled, and I died. I was in love with this Niggah, at what point I fell in love was beyond me. I didn't understand it.

It's like the more he smiled the more in love I fell. I fell so hard eye couldn't think straight.

And with that in mind I still had to confront her, talk to her. Work on it. See how she felt. Hear what she had to say.

Yell.

Scream.

Blame.

Point fingers.

Justify.

Edit.

Censor.

Maybe I didn't. Want. To. See. Her. Maybe. I. Wanted. Her. To. Die. In. Her. Sleep!

Trifling bitch!

"*Leave*, Beatrice," I told her, kissing my bitch. I was rubbing that good ass, my dick standing up, and it was a killer. She died inside. "You motherfuckers! How could you—Baby, you gonna leave me—"

My boy looked at her maliciously. "You ain't left yet? I don't want you. It's over. I am moving on. And if you stay here I'ma start doing some shit that's gonna hurt you deeper. I'm trying to spare you."

She exploded. "THIS MY HOUSE!"

"Mine, too! I live here. You think I'm MOVING OUT?"

"Die in hell, Niggah!"

"OK, Lesbian City. I most certainly will, as soon...as...I—" He started sucking my dick in front of her and my mouth fell open in shock, but it felt so good.

And I opened my legs so he can watch my nuts play double dutch with the way they bounced up and down.

Devastated, she fell on the chair, holding her head. "She wants a show," my boy said, tonguing the head of my passion and trying to deep throat me.

I had too much dick.

No one could deep throat me. I fucked that mouth as slow as I could, holding his head. He was a cute little Niggah. He slurped my shit, pulled and moaned like a Niggah and I wanted him moaning like a bitch.

"Moan like a bitch! I want to hear dat shit. Whimper for this dick. Beg for me. To. Be. In. That. Ass!"

"Daddy I want that dick...baby boy goddamn. You're making a Niggah beg."

"You want me to fuck that asshole my Niggah?"

I pushed his bitch ass on the low-table and he looked at me with so much urgency and anticipation on his handsome face.

His skin was soft, beautiful skin tone under the chandelier lights.

So sensual and provocative. He smelled of Cool Water cologne.

Even around the parameters of his asshole he smelled of some body fragrance.

He smelled so loving. His lips slightly parted he opened his legs and started rubbing around his asshole, slow, his eyes narrowed; his lips were in the kiss formation.

He had sexy lips. Turned me on and made my heart skip a beat. And he was all mine. Finally. I found my soul mate.

He was next to me for years and I had no idea. He was at my wedding, standing with me when we married two lesbians.

And I never knew he was my rib, my chosen one, the one I wanted and needed and desired to spend the rest of my life with.

Flashes of my wedding exploded in my mind. I remembered my tux. It matched my boy's. We had on white top hats, angled over the left eye, like Gangsters.

Well, like Pimps. And once the real thugs got down on the dance floor, we cut a rug, dancing together.

We were so happy to be married. I think life was trying to show us then, because when he hugged me in front of cheering family members and our wives, wearing $7,000 wedding dresses, the type with the long trains, he accidentally touched my dick and he apologized, embarrassed, but he didn't look away from my heavenly eyes.

"No sweat," I had said, but my dick was hard as a rock and I couldn't stop looking at his ass when he walked off, but I played it off.

At that moment I knew I was in love with someone else.

I was in love with a man. My boy. I'd die for him! Now I had him. And I wasn't gonna let him go. He twirled that hot hole on his finger. Damn he was so sexy.

"Finger fuck yourself for Daddy. I'ma sit here on this couch and jack my shit and watch you fuck yourself."

He whined like a Ho. I loved it. "But Daddy, fuck me baby boy." He stuck his index finger in all that flesh, and he moaned in pleasure. "I never knew my hole would make me feel so hot!"

"Two fingers, bitch!"

He started fucking himself harder, faster. His legs started shaking; I could tell the pleasure was too much for his body to handle. I stood over him, slapping him in the face with my dick.

Tears ran down his face, I forgot Beatrice was in the room. She was sobbing. I fed off her grief. She hurt me. She fucked my wife.

"WHY ARE YALL DOING THIS?"

Tears ran from my eyes. I didn't want to hurt her. I *always* had her back. When she almost died from Cancer I was there, with my wife and my boy, three years ago.

253 DAPHAROAH69

I sat with her through her Chemo Therapy. She lost all her hair. She lost some weight. I was there, waiting on her hand a foot. So was my wife. So was my boy. I was there when she had a miscarriage. I kept her secret from my boy.

"Please don't tell him I was pregnant. I wanted to surprise him. I put this baby before God and God took my baby away."

I told my boy I didn't know what was wrong with her.

I was by her side when her Mama died.

Her mother was raped by some prisoner who escaped prison and she died from the shock of the entire event.

She died while a convict was beating up the pussy. I was by her side.

With my boy. I never made moves on her, even though she was fine, of Halle Berry proportions.

And she repaid me by fucking my wife?

So with that in mind I slapped my bitch with my dick, repeatedly. "Suck my dick and fuck that ass, bitch!" He started blowing me off, love in his eyes; he beat that asshole with three fingers now, all that ass jiggling.

"You don't want this dick. You don't want Daddy to nut. You playing Rainbow Bright with my dick, bitch! You are making me mad. I'ma beat your ass if you don't stop toying with my dick. Create a symphony with my Organ, bitch. Blow over the hole of my flute and pull that trombone. Let your fingers dance on the shaft like a Clarinet…blow that bitch like a saxophone! There ya go!" I leaned back, my dick falling from his pleasurable mouth and I snatched him up, bending him over the arm of the chair. "Didn't I say suck my dick, bitch?" I was slapping that booty. Those cheeks bounced. Damn. Hypnotized me. Fucking this Niggah was going to be the time of my life. And not that Patrick Swayze *Dirty Dancing* feeling, either.

"Yea, my Niggah."

"IT'S BIG DADDY! I'MA THUG NIGGAH I GET WHAT I WANT!"

"Fuck me, Daddy."

"You don't want this dick. Beg for it!"

I started eating that ass, tonguing that soft place, tongue fucking him. He moaned so sensually.

He started crying.

I smelled that ass, getting high off the scent.

So erotic.

Eye tasted my nut out his ass from our session when we got caught. I swallowed my own nut, I sucked out some more, snatched him by the head, turned him into my face, slid my dick up in that ass, started fucking him and spit my nut in his mouth, a long line of nut and he swallowed every drop.

"And you're a dirty bitch, I love dat shit!" I pulled out the pussy and watched his body slump.
Time to taunt the bitch.

"I don't wanna live without you."

"Spread this pussy, bitch! I don't care what state this asshole's in. I'ma clean this shit out with my tongue. OPEN DAT PUSY BITCH!" I slapped both ass cheeks so hard with my palms he jumped. I snatched him back down.

"Baby, you turning me out."

"Who does this pussy *belong* to?"

He was lost in my stroke game. "You, Daddy!"

I started finger fucking him, one hand on the ass, while he spread his cheeks apart. "Yea, bitch!"

"AW AW AW SHIT AW FUCK MY ASSHOLE NIGGH AW AW YOU FUCK BETTER THAN MY WIFE AW SHIT BITCH YOU SEE HOW YOU SHOULDA FUCKED YOUR HUSBAND GODAMN NIGGAH AWWWW SHIT THAT DICK AW SHIT YOU PUTTING THAT DICK IN MY ASS! AW SHIT GIVE IT ALL TO ME! AW DAMN NIGGAH!"

I had him doggy-style on the bare floor.

I stared at all that ass while it jiggled on my dick. I fucked the dog shit out the bitch!

I wasn't supposed to play around with the asshole, I was supposed to beat it up, boy or not.

Best friend or not, ass was ass, and my heart wasn't in my dick or in his ass and I loved him, that's why I turned the pussy out, I was molding this hole to my standards!

We were drenched with sweat.

TWO THUGS. Two ex gang bangers.

In the streets and with the Ho's we ran trains on. I gripped that ass and stuck my dick in his hole and pressed my groin against flesh and paused and he fell on his face, with the ass up.

"Get the fuck up. Are you *tired*? I'ma fuck this pussy times ten if you are, you tired?"

He tried to play it off, take back his word.

He tried to look so innocent, and it came off looking so hot. "I'm tired, daddy, I can't take no more." He started crying, really let go. "I can't take no more, I can't..."

I laid on top on him and fucked him as fast and hard as I could, I wanted this pussy moist, loose.

He wrapped his arms around mine, lying on his stomach, looking into my face with wide eyes, throwing that booty hole back.

"Damn bitch this some good pussy bitch I'll kill you if you give my shit away you my wifey now I want you Niggah you do what the fuck I say..."

"I love. You. Baby...."

Beatrice couldn't take it anymore. She ran from the room and opened her bedroom door, slamming it closed. Wham! Good for you, bitch. That was the thug talking. But the real me, I wanted to hug her and tell her I was sorry, that I wished I could take it all back.

After all a good friendship meant more than asshole.

His hole locked up and his body with it. "OH GOD IM BOUT TO NUT OH GOD YOU HITTING MY SPOT IM BOUT TO—"

"I'm 'bout to nut, Niggah!" I screamed out and I started letting go all my Trojan knights deep in this pussy while his asshole throbbed and opened and closed on my shaft. Goddamn what a feeling. I started screaming delightfully. "DAMN THIS FEELS BETTER THAN MY WIFE'S PUSSY!"

When I rolled over on my back Beatrice, with a loaded gun, shot me in the chest, and then shot me in the right knee cap.

The explosion of the gun deafened me and made my boy jump ten feet in the air.

My boy started screaming and all I could remember was the room turning black. The last image I had before I closed my eyes was an exhausted Niggah telling me, "Please, baby, don't leave me...YOU BITCH I'MA KILL YOU BITCH!"
And I was at peace.

I heard beeps. Pagers. Voices. Crying. Sobbing. I felt cold, then hot...then cold again...I was gasping for air. My eyes were closed. I was inhaling some weird-feeling air. Made my lungs expand. Made my heart race. I tried to open my eyes and I couldn't. I didn't know where I was. I didn't know who I was, or how I got here, where ever I was. Who was I? I felt pain in my arms and legs...a burning sensation tore me apart.

I tried to scream, but something was over my nose and mouth—

My eyes fluttered. So much light ran into them I was rendered speechless.

Lights came and went. There it was again. Light. Gone. Shit.

There it was again. Shit. Gone again. Another light. Gone. I blinked rapidly and the picture was coming into focus.

I felt myself turning while some men in white robes and holding tubes and a couple bags of water were over me as the lights came and went. Shit. I was in the hospital! I was looking at hospital lights.

How did I get here? What happened to me? Okay. Okay. Get a grip, niggah. Really think here. I weakly looked at a doctor. He looked concerned.

"You're gonna make it, Clive."

So my name was Clive. Make it from *what*? What exactly happened to me?

"You were shot. You were rushed to the hospital. Your vital signs are weakening, but you're stable. You're being rushed to surgery."

I tried to speak. I couldn't. Out of nowhere I heard a man scream my name.

"CLIVE! HOMEBOY! YOU'RE ALIVE!" He was standing over me, helping the doctors and nurses push my gurney. "I'm here with you, pimpin'! I'll be right by your side through this shit homeboy, don't think I'm gonna flex! I can't believe my wife shot you."

Once again I tried to speak. I couldn't. My mouth was glued shut. He had fresh tears falling from very gorgeously crafted brown eyes that sparkled vibrantly. Kevin. His name was Kevin. My baby, my lover and my best friend. I never loved him the way I loved him at this moment. He was by my side, clad in the red Ecko jacket I snatched off him—

Wait!

I was shot!

Beatrice had shot me!

Motherfucker!

Eye felt myself getting tense, rowdy.

"Beatrice shot you, my niggah."

I wished I could talk.

"She was taken into police custody."

As oxygen was being fed into my lungs, my mind screamed. Fuck the police! Let me kill the bitch.

"But don't worry about anything, homeboy," he said, his face going from soft and caring to dark and deceptive. He leaned up to me. And he whispered, "I gave her something to drink before the cops arrived."

And? What did that mean?

"She'll be dealt with. It's in the hands of the law now."

He wasn't telling me something. I knew this niggah like a book. He could never lie to me or fool me.

My body was getting a little stronger, the machine attached to my gurney beeped a little slower. I looked at my vitals. They looked stronger. That was a good sign. I'd survive this ordeal. I just had to.

I just looked at him, wanting to hug him. I didn't know how I felt. I cared and loved Beatrice like family. Did I want anything to happen to her? Did this make me feel any better? Should he have called the police on her? Did he break the code of the streets? I didn't want my boy labeled a snitch. I was in a thunderous Mecca of thoughts.

The doctor said, "Kevin, you can't go beyond this point. We'll take care of him. He's improving. He'll be just fine."

Kevin winked at me and patted my shoulder and I was wheeled into surgery.

"I gave her something to drink" never left my mind.

Without resistance or a fight, Beatrice was arrested for shooting Clive Sampson.

It was like pulling a nail out of a termite-infested board when it dawned on her she would never see the inside of her so-called happy home again.

The people at her job would surely laugh and poke fun at her when it came out she sucked pussy while she was married to a sexy, super ultra fine black man all the girls at her job wanted to suck, fuck and pacify into their dull lives.

When she crossed the threshold of the front door and out into the world,, heading for the awaiting squad car, she had flashbacks of Kevin, happy and giddy, carrying her across the threshold of their home after they were married.

She could remember they saved their Special Dance for a Special Occasion.

They didn't dance at the reception. Others did. They wanted to dance alone. They honeymooned in their living room.

Kevin spent $2,000 turning their living room into Jamaica, complete with catered Jamaican and Bahamian food (He was both), marijuana incense mixed with strawberry.

Twelve dozen red, green and pink roses. Jamaican music. He ate her pussy to some Patra.

She wanted a "Romantic Call."

She rode his big dick to some Shaggy "Mr. Bombastic."

He carefully licked her throbbing nipples when he turned her on her back. He didn't take off her wedding dress.

He made love to her in it. He just took off the panties and pulled out the titties. She had amazing tits. Mouth watering and very seductively mastered by the Good Lord.

*And they're all mine,* he thought to himself.

He was completely sexy in his Timberland boots and birthday suit.

Low-cut Caesar haircut.

Light brown eyes.

Caramel complexion with sexy lips to match.

Bedroom eyes.

Fabulous ass.

Nice and tight.

Her dress was so soak and wet with sweat it clung to her.

He tapped the pussy from the back, all that ass jiggling all over the dick like waves over a frolicking shore line.

He had never made love to any woman the way he loved his wife, his heart, his passion and the very air he breathed.

She remembered, with bitter-sweet bliss, he pulled out of her and wanted her to give him head and taste her pussy juices off his dick.

She did so.

"Stick your finger deep in my ass, baby," he told her matter-of-factly. "It helps me come harder."

She smiled. She obliged, sticking her finger so deep in his asshole tears escaped his eyes. She pounded his hole while she slurped and pulled on his amazingly beautiful dick, running her tongue across the head like a snake chasing a rat and trailed a long line of saliva down to his nuts, which bounced like the Heat played the Pacers.

And when he was about to come he locked up, his toes curling, and he shoved her head down on his dick as fast as he could.

"Fuck that hole baby, yea, yea, yea, yea, bitch, goddamn baby..."

He was riding her finger, playing with his nipples, his nuts just jumping all over the place.

"...I'm COMIN'! AWW SHIT BITCH SWALLOW DAT SHIT HOE GODDAMN!"

And she swallowed every drop as his dick throbbed and pumped his seeds down her throat. She got hornier just watching his reaction. She felt his hole throbbing on her finger.

It turned her on. And when he went in the bathroom, damn near staggering, to wash up, she took out her cell phone and called Liana.

She was on her honeymoon at their home.

"Where is Clive?"

"In the restroom, showering."

"Meet me at Rebecca's down the street."

"Why?"

She smiled deceptively.

"I wanna know what that pussy tastes like after your man nutted in it. Let me suck Clive's juices down my throat, now bitch get there before they get out the bathroom."

"I'm on my way. And girl hurry up. Cause he sucked my pussy like some free Mountain Dew and he hates Mountain Dew."

She hung up, creeping out of the room.

And now she was distraught, fidgety and despite the new media swarming around the crime scene she kept her head high. Spectators and neighborhood citizens piled out of their homes, taking in the horrific scene.

Inside her home, a home that used to be her safe haven with the man she pretended to love, Coroners snapped pictures. Blood was all over the bare floors and walls.

Picture frames were shattered. They snapped pictures of the $4,000 wedding ring lying under the cracked picture casing housing the memorable wedding photo.

"They looked so happy. They made a cute couple, Beatrice and Kevin," Officer Gaines, a five foot seven inch beauty, said, shaking her head in disbelief. "Why would he cheat on his wife?"

Officer Roberto said, "Rumor has it that she cheated on him with Clive's wife during the duration of their marriage. And he slept with Clive out of revenge."

"Yea. Okay. But he didn't deserve to be shot."

"Crimes of passion. The worst kind. Complicated."

Officer Gaines lit a cigarette, and closed her eyes. Sucking in the smoke.

Relieving her and the resounding stress that followed.

"Where's Kevin?" she asked.

"He rode away in the ambulance with his boyfriend. Clive's in pretty bad shape. He has a chance to survive, even though he lost a lot of blood. They'd probably rush him to surgery and give him a blood transfusion in the process. I don't agree with what he did, but..."

"It's not about you," Officer Gaines corrected. "Keep it professional. Don't personalize it. This is a very heart-breaking case."

He sucked his teeth, stared at her for a minute and when she spun on her heel to take in the rest of the scene he stopped his dick from getting hard, looking at her amazing ass.

Wow!

What an ass! And she was wearing those goddamn tight black jeans; the front of them seemed to get sucked up in her pussy.

The V-shape drove him mad. He had to wipe his face.

The City of Miami had mighty fine police officers, and they combed through her home like white on rice. She gave a smile for the cameras as flashes popped in her face and reporters raced up to her, extending microphones.

She felt like a star of her own production. She looked at the palm trees differently. She gazed at the fading blue sky differently. Her freedom was slowly being taken away and she didn't care. No man made a fool of her.

And if she had half a brain she'd realize she was really angry because the joke was played on her.

How would Liana feel about the shooting of her husband?

"Ma'am, did you murder your husband's lover in cold blood?"

"Yes," she said, smiling so hard, even the police were mystified.

"Why did you shoot him?"

"Because he cheated on me."

"But you cheated on him with his wife Liana, is that true?"

"No it's not."

Why didn't they just leave and go home? My house used to be a home.

Now it was just a house holding painful memories. My marriage!

Why did I throw it away? Why did I lead my husband on?

Why was I getting sleepy?

Like I was losing all of my energy. Even my high was going away.

I wanted some more to drink. At least Kevin was nice enough to pour me my last drink as a free woman. Hypnotiq Ice. Even though it tasted tangy and different. I still loved it...my eyes were getting heavy. *What's* wrong with me? And yet I couldn't get my mind off shooting Clive.

Boom.

Boom.

I shot him in the chest and I forget where else.

No one crossed me! Fucking my man in front of me?

What the fuck! *Yes*, eventually I wanted marriage, kids and the white picket fence but I wasn't ready for it when I married Kevin. I was in love with Clive's wife.

Liana. My heart. My love. My sweet lady. She was a young-looking Lyotine Price, Opera Singer with Della Reese's eyes and Nancy Wilson's class and decorum.

I wouldn't dare compare her to Beyawnsay Knowles, Halle Berry Crystal Light, Lil Barbie Kim or Vivica A. Fox.

Only when in Make-up. Liana had that Old School flair. We have been through thick and thin.

We grew up together in Watts, California, moved away together when we were twelve years old, becoming prostitutes to make some money.

We were raped, burned and used by men, grew up in the streets.

We dressed like Hoochies, but we made a vow: we would always be together.

We used to hold each other at night when we slept in hotel after hotel, and had to do unspeakable things to keep a roof over our heads.

We had fake ID's made and we became call-girls, and strippers when we were fifteen.

We moved from Watts to Miami, Florida in search of a new beginning and happiness.

We weren't always lesbians, but our love stemmed from a burning passion to be heard, to be loved, to be appreciated.

Our parents wrote us off like taxes. And actually did it before April 15th when I was thirteen.

We were outcast; everybody in the family abandoned us.

So we abandoned them. Despite our lives we stayed in school.

We knew education was the way to go. But that go hard as hell when it came time to make the money.

I got us the clients, Liana was the book keeper.

But things got crazy between us. Liana and I. I was aggressive. I wanted my way all day and all night. This had always been my frame of mind, ever since I was five years old.

When I could never afford that doll. When Mama told me, "No, baby, I can't afford that easy bake over set."

When my father said, "No, baby. You can't go outside and play. Too many thugs on the block and too much gun violence."

When Grand ma bluntly told me, "Take you pissy looking ass in the room and find a book to read. You can't wear dresses. Boys like to stare at cha pussy all day, hot little bitch! You ain't as smart as you might think."

So I became aggressive, getting the things I wanted when I wanted how I wanted all the goddamn time.

I knew a woman's lower part of her body was her true breadwinner when all else failed.

Men loved twat and I made sure they got it. They had to work for it.

Give me money up front for it. No strings.

And now I was going to jail.

Because I shot my husband's man. I couldn't believe what was going on. This was all so surreal to me.

How I threw my life away because my husband decided to give me a freak show in my house in front of me.

How fucked up could he be? What was I supposed to do? Leave? Meditate?

I didn't know how I was supposed to feel. I had to do something.

And now I had mixed emotions. I cheated on my husband with Liana.

Liana was my world. I was so in love with her, she made me whole, complete.

But we weren't ready to be out the closet. I didn't wanna deal with the hurt, the shame. The finger pointing.

My family disowning me. I wasn't ready, despite the things they did to me in the past. I loved being with a woman.

A woman was soft, sensual, understanding, didn't stick a dick in me and pound me like drums.

Liana ate my pussy better than any man ever had. Truth be told, one thing occurred to me when my husband had gave me something to drink, after I shot his man.

I never loved him. I only married him to cover my feelings for Liana.

And now it affected everyone's life. At least that's how she felt.

It was just after 6 p.m., and the sun was setting, along with her feelings for Clive.

Clive was her bread and butter, there for her when she beat Cancer.

She owed so much to Clive, who was like her brother. And now he may be dead. And she was glad. Glad as hell.

She was forced into the squad car. She made Instant News across the country.

"Terry Macmillan let her man get away with being gay. I shot mine. Even though what I did makes me a hypocrite. That's what you call the Interruption of Everything," she whispered bitterly, crying and letting go as the squad car pulled off, heading for I-95.

She was going to the Downtown Police Precinct.

When Officer Gaines and Officer Roberto pulled up in the police station, Officer Gaines opened the back door and said, "All right, Beatrice. Time to get out and get booked. Let's go."

She took Beatrice by the arm, leading her into the precinct.

She felt woozy.

"Damn, I'm tired."

After she was fingerprinted, she was given a jumpsuit and a bunk.

When she lay down, covering her face, she couldn't control her breathing.

She began to sweat. Her eyes rolled to the back of her head.

She would never see daylight again.

I have been seeing Ms. Simone for two months. I feel nothing.

I feel helpless, hopeless and I fear that I may say something she might not like. Before I went out a few days ago, I was watching the news.

Some guy was shot by another man's wife. The lady was charged and booked. She was found dead the next day in jail. I didn't care. I didn't know those people.

I already called Simone a "Black tar bitch!" the other day when she showed up at my boy's Bachelor Party, knocked on the door like the police, and when my boy Shimmy answered, she waltzed in, wearing Prada this, Prada that, throwing her blonde hair all over the well-decorated apartment like Brooke Shields and she snapped.

"Niggah, you told me you were going to get your clothes outta the cleaners." Three Tupac posters hung on the black walls behind her. You could smell cologne, booze and weed and pussy in the air.

I ducked behind the bar. I made a mistake and spilled Hennessy all over my white Sean John pants suit and my Cool Water cologne was wearing the fuck off because I was sweating bullets. I didn't need this shit. I couldn't believe this was actually happening.

Caught up in her own sick world, she cautiously walked up to the counter, eyeing everybody with a very disquieting look.

Everyone was laughing, the music stopping.

She said, "Stand up, Niggah."

I did. Pissed. I averted my face, and bit my tongue.

"I like *these* Cleaners. How much do they charge to clean a shirt?" she asked sarcastically.

"Simone. Chill. OK? I'm a grown. Man. I am. Not. Married!"

"We're going home."

"I'm not. And we don't live together." I got the right temperature to knock this bitch in the mouth if she doesn't shut the hell up.

One of the sexy, tall, Amazonian strippers, with her titties and ass out walked up behind her and said, "Baby, you uptight. For fifty dollars I can suck that pussy and make you nut out all that pent up feminist shit."

Simone faced her. Next thing I know Stripper Woman was knocked the hell out, laying cold on the floor. All the niggahs started waving twenties in the air.

Leonard said, enticing Simone, "I got fifty dollars on the small black stripper with mosquito bites for tits!"

She faced me. "Ready?"

I was fuming. My face twitched so badly I had to burp.

"How dare you come here and treat me like this. I'm grown. We have known each other for two months."

"You're a wimp. Lying to your woman."

"Alight, you black tar bitch!"

Her mouth fell open. And my mouth closed, as I snatched her by her weave and kicked her ass out the apartment.

My boy Harold, who I've known forever, pulled me to the side, clad in Scarface everything, from his pants to his shirt; and said, as the music pulsated again, "Niggah, cancel that ugly bitch."

"I can't."

"Why?"

"She's a cop. Plus she makes good money."

"I ain't saying you a gold digger."

"But I ain't messing with no broke bitch," I joked, hugging my boy. I felt electricity. I felt a stirring in my loins and I felt the blood rushing the head of my dick. He hugged me a little too long and I pushed away from him just a little bit and looked him over. "Man. Sup with you?"

Harold was a sexy man. But I never brought myself to think about it.

He had a tight little ass, a tight little body and was about five feet nine.

He was always clean shaven, always dressed nicely, even though he always had somebody on his clothes.

Yesterday it was Biggie Smalls. He drove a souped up Chevy with $10,000 rims bought with drug money.

He ran his own cartel. Very low key. Very discreet. Three kids.

Bitches threw pussy at his dick like a Frisbee. That's what I liked about him. He got shit done.

"I'm straight," he said, his voice shaky. "Man, come in the room. I need to holla at you."

I became suspicious. But I followed him to the room and when he closed the door he kissed me and I cringed inside.

I didn't know what to do. Yell. Kick his ass. Or shoot him.

But I decided to let him finish and the more our tongues danced the hornier I became. He locked the door, looking so goddamn good, and he unbuttoned my pants. They slid down my slender legs.

He got on his knees and took my chocolate stick into his hot mouth. I melted. A man never sucked my dick before.

And I loved it.

The way he locked his jaws and put that sensual suction all over my dick.

I humped his mouth, holding the back of his head. He worked that tongue until I became weak in the knees.

There was a knock on the door and my dick deflated so fast I didn't even remember how I pulled up my pants, had them buttoned and told my boy, "I'll catch you later."

I was gone.

But Miss Simone. She acts white, talks white and smells white despite having skin blacker than four crayons. I don't love her. I don't trust her. She doesn't trust me. She is a controlling asshole. She isn't compassionate. She drinks too much. She listens to Elton John a little too goddamn much and she takes advice from Barbara Walters.

Go figure. My name is Donnie. I'm 5 feet 8 inches above God's green earth, caramel complexion, light brown eyes, a buck fifty. I have a toned body. I am not guided by insecurity and I wanna get married, despite having five kids from five different bitches who I loathe and hate.

I work for an elementary school. I am a janitor, cleaning behind bad ass little kids eight hours a day, five days a week. I drive a Buick. On Wal-Mart spinners. Hell, they're clean so that's good enough for me.

I met some woman today. She was entering the movies when I was leaving. I bumped into her purposely.

"I'm sorry," I told her, eying her up and down. "I apologize."

"No problem," she said, extending her hand. "I'm Liana. And I'm in a bad mood. My husband cheated on me. With another man."

My mouth fell open. "Well damn, Ma. I know I'm leaving the movies, but, hell, do you need some company?"

She seemed so vulnerable. And I suddenly wanted to protect her. "Yea. But I'm warning you. I'm a lesbian. And I'm in love with a woman who just killed my husband."

I suddenly remembered what I seen on the news. Every television show was interrupted to talk about some guy named Clive being shot. That he was in a gay love triangle.

The wife was screwing the other wife and the husband screwed the husband, or some shit like that. *Liana was involved in that?*

"What movie do you wanna see, Liana? My treat."

*I didn't know where this would lead.*

*But I wanted to find out.*

# Reality TV

Sitting in my Buick, I sighed, looking over the sparkling stars. They seemed to hang like ornaments in the Savannah sky. Deeply withdrawn into myself, I looked at my life and wondered how I got here. I didn't know what to feel. I didn't even want my heart beating life into my lungs, brain and my dick.

My dick, ha. Let's not even bring up that worthless vessel.

My hard on has been the source of my…lack of judgment. I let my dick decide everything, and now look where it got me…

I lit a joint and pulled on it for dear life. My job did random piss tests, but I didn't care, because I don't even know if I want to go on. I mean, why should I? Everything that mattered to me I have lost. I love my Dad. I lost Elroy.

I lost my cousins. And Mama doesn't even want to talk to me because I wouldn't put Daddy in jail. So why should I waste God's time and draw another breath? Why shouldn't this Glock sit on my lap, beckoning me to use it? To dispose of my brain, because it was a terrible thing to waste and it has become waste, since I lost my family for…

## Σ

Ten months ago...I surveyed my parent's front yard. The same raggedy, broken down Cadillac sat on top of cinder blocks and bushes were growing all around it. The Brownsville projects were directly behind my parents' home. Looking as depressed as ever. Thank God I chose to go to college and try to make something of my life. For what good that did. Because I was back in town, looking at something that I have tried to forget. These projects looked like jail cells.

Sitting in my Buick, I looked at Jaden. The love of my life. "We're here."

Looking at the engagement ring on my finger, Jaden said, "I know. Are you sure you're ready for this?"

"Yes, I am," I answered, taking Jaden's soft hand and kissing it like it was a wounded bird. "I hope you are. My family can be some imbeciles when they want to be."

"Let's get it over with."

"I can't wait for you to be my wife..."

We kissed passionately, my tongue dancing with my fiancé's.

"And I can't wait to be your everything..."

Opening the car door, my Stacy Adam-clad foot inherited the pavement, and I pulled my dress shirt over my 11 inch cut dick. Being back home wasn't the homecoming I imagined, because so much has happened in this little four bedroom/one bath home. Mama told me my room looked the same. I didn't want to *think* about my room. I couldn't bring myself to remember the ruffled sheets I clung to when I was a teenager, because I was scared of the dark. The darkness, that had eyes, a mouth and a life-force that saw more devastation than my heart could ever muster, forever branded my soul. How could I remember Mama's perfume that drifted through the AC vents when I cried myself to sleep? When the darkness loomed over me, redirecting my thought process to a weak version of what I thought I should be.

My mind ran parallel with the memories, I was headed for my parents' front door.

Losing my erection.

A little out of it, I walked into my parents' home on Easter. "Hey, ya'll," I told my folks. *Here we go,* I thought bitterly, trying to fake a smile. *I'm back in the house for the first time since I left home after graduating high school.* We just got home from a long, grueling day of church, preaching and speculating. I didn't want to go to church earlier, but I had because Mama insisted. Jaden didn't care for organized religion, so my baby stayed in the hotel room until church was over…

Mama, clad in a gorgeous red satin dress with floral bust, stood up, extending her hands. I took them, kissing each one. She beamed with pleasure.

"Hey, baby." Her eyes glittering happily, she kissed my cheek, her lipstick getting on my skin. I didn't mind. She was Mama, and Mama could do what she wanted.

"Hey, Ma." We embraced.

"I raised a polite gentleman," she began. "I see you know how to treat the ladies. I know they're falling head over heels for you up in Georgia."

"Yea. They are. That's why I keep a broomstick handy."

My little brother Elroy sauntered by, patting my shoulder. He leaned up to my ear and whispered, "Yea, your…stick, and I'm not talking about a broom."

Blushing, I playfully punched his upper arm.

"Behave, horny boy."

Daddy was behind her, waiting for his turn to show me love. Standing a mere 6 feet 5 inches, he was a very volatile man who loved sports and detested politics, and just because Obama was running for president didn't spark his interest in the Road to the Whitehouse. I loved my father more than anything in this world.

"I thought you were going home after church?" she inquired, sitting at the table. My cousin Bucky set up the plates and my kleptomaniac cousin Bruce Bruce, with his dumb ass, lay out the silverware. He kept looking at me, rolling his eyes and I wanted to snatch them out.

Daddy firmly shook my hand. "I'm glad he didn't go home. It's been four years since I've seen you."

"A life time, huh, Pa?" We were patting each other's shoulders in unison, clearly happy to see one another. *Keep it together. I look at Daddy and I see something I don't care to ever remember. But it's all good. I forgive you, Pa.* He grabbed my face and kissed my forehead. I cringed inside, but I willed my muscles to relax. He had huge tears in his eyes, but he refused to let them fall.

"You've ignored my calls, boy," he said, taking my hand and pulling me to the table. I nodded at Bruce Bruce and he grunted, tugging on his jacket. Those questioning eyes again befell my body and I felt like the Swamp Thing.

*I've been ignoring your calls, Pa, for a goddamn reason. See, I need to chill. I am with family. And this is Easter. And Jesus didn't rise for this bullshit.*

"No, Pa. I haven't. I have been busy with graduation and everything in between."

Dad pulled out my chair and I sat down, eyeing Bruce Bruce. He started to perspire. I knew his ass like the back of my hand. He was up to something.

"So, my son is a Morehouse graduate," Mama said, holding up my degree. I beamed with pride. My family clapped and whistled happily. Daddy, sitting next to me, embraced me again.

"Ah, it's nothing."

"But it is," said my cousin Bucky, kissing me on the cheek. I thought she looked absolutely stunning in a skirt and rose-colored blouse with hanging chandelier earrings bringing out her doe-shaped eyes. "I'm proud of you."

"Thanks."

"My son made it out of the projects…I tell you this," Daddy went on, grabbing the bowl of mashed potatoes. "I don't want you staying in these here slums. Brownsville isn't the place to be. Your Mama and I been living here for twenty plus years. We want you to be better than us, Son."

"I look up to you, Daddy."

"I know you do."

Bruce Bruce sat next to my father, barely putting salad on his plate.

Mama set my degree next to her. She took it the minute I earned it, since her money paid for my schooling. She and Daddy worked numerous jobs to supply everything I needed, from the lap top I used to do my term papers to the cost of tuition and books.

Mama said, "So, how does it feel to be the first in the family to be a college graduate?"

"Feels good, not to mention I'm glad all my loans and stuff are paid off. I want to thank you Mom and Dad for helping me get through a rough four years."

"You're my Booker T. Washington," Dad said. He handed me a book by Booker T. Called *Up From Slavery*. I looked it over, setting it by my keys and wallet. I was tired, shit.

"Well, let's eat," Mama said. "I'm glad we prayed for our food on the way home. Damn, I'm hungry."

Daddy kissed her. "Your greedy ass is always hungry."

Elroy hugged me from behind. "How many girlfriends do you have?" he asked me. He was 16 years old and going through puberty, so his hormones rages mightier than the seven seas.

*Oh, Boy. This is going to be harder than I anticipated.*

"One."

Mama and Daddy looked at me, beaming.

"What's her name?" Mama asked, being nosey. She never met my lovers. Mainly because I fucked them and left them in the same breath.

"Jaden Francis…"

"Jaden Francis," Daddy uttered, listening to the way it filtered into his ears. "Ah. That's a nice name. Where is she from?"

Everyone looked me in the face for my answer.

I felt a little uneasy. "Have you heard of a town called Lane in South Carolina?"

"Yes," said Mama. "I have been there. I don't even think it's on the map."

"It's not," said Daddy, patting my hand with *Atta Boy!* dancing in his gorgeous light brown eyes.

*Let's get on with it.* "She's here," I told him, and my parents gawked at me with disgust.

"And you didn't invite her in?" Mama asked, standing up from the table. She dabbed her lips with a napkin.

"I bet you she's fine," Bruce Bruce said, not giving a damn. "You always…chose pretty girls." He nearly snickered.

I shook my head, warning him he was getting dangerously close to an ass whipping.

"It's hot outside, boy," said Bucky, leaning back in the chair. She eyed me evilly. "You don't treat women like growing crops. Invite that girl inside. Offer her some food."

"Mind your business."

"What kind of man are you? You're seated at the table, eating and that girl is inside your hot ass car, burning up. You're going to hell."

*In more ways than one.*

Daddy wiped his mouth, sipped some tea and stood up. I looked down at the table, silently praying to God.

Elroy said, "I'll open the door for her."

Mama was already headed for the door.

Daddy told me to stand up and I did. Smiling, he looked me over.

"My boy has a woman in his life. Is she pregnant?"

"Hell no, Daddy. You're rushing…"

He punched me so hard in the chest I flew back into my chair.

"If you ever invite a woman to my house and you leave her outside burning up in your car I will offer her room and board and beat your ass with the boards in your fucking room! GOT THAT?"

The house shook when he yelled. Like a scared child I said, "Sure, Pop. Sorry."

Mama was fixing her hair in the mirror by the door. Dad was walking behind her. Bruce Bruce found it all funny. He walked past me and said. "Jaden Francis…sounds like a hot looking bitch." I smelled alcohol on his breath.

"Watch your mouth, Bruce Bruce." I stood up, gathered myself and made my way over to my family.

*Shit is about to hit the fan.*

Mama opened the door and Jaden Francis smiled, shaking Mama's trembling, liver spotted hand.

"I'm Jaden. Nice to meet you."

Daddy lowered his eyes and my brother was so stunned into silence he ran to his room. I heard the door slam.

Bruce Bruce said, "I told you she's probably a hot little thang. Oh, my bad," Bruce Bruce said, pushing me out the way and shaking Jaden's hand. Laughing, he said, "Jaden is a man."

"Oh, Jesus," Mama said, disappointed.

We were cryptically seated at the table. Daddy sat by Mama and he refused to look at me. Even when I tried to meet his eyes he refused to meet mine. Mama kept everyone cordial and Jaden was eating meat loaf, trying to relax. I could tell he was an ice cube just plucked from the tray. Only he didn't float in a glass of water or even a glass of tea or lemonade. It was on the table, thawing to room temperature and he would soon be a puddle of water, evaporating into whatever vapor God wanted him to be. I loved him.

The way he carried himself took my breath away. I remembered when I first met him. We were registering for classes at Morehouse. He looked lonely and he had tears in his eyes. His mother had just died and he was telling me about her warm smile and her gorgeous face.

We were strangers; two Negros trying to build our Hampton Institute like Booker T. did back in the 1880's. His grief brought us together.

We graduated together. Hell, we shared the same room for four years. Making love to him was by accident.

I was homesick and reliving a family tragedy that happened in my teenage years, one I didn't reveal to Mama and he held me and he showered my face with warm kisses

289 DAPHAROAH69

and told me it wasn't my fault, that I shouldn't blame myself. And then our lips met by surprise and our tongues became the transitional center, booking quickening heart rates and laying out floor plans for our sexually awakening bodies.

I fucked him so good he was calling me Daddy by the time I came. He pulled me out of him and sucked himself down his throat, kissing my feet and making invisible shapes on my nuts with his tongue.

He said I was beautiful. I came on his face, rubbing it in like lotion and told him he was really beautiful.

Looking and talking to him, one would never guess he's my boyfriend. We were engaged to be married in three weeks.

After four years of a fledgling relationship, going through the typical highs and lows of love, I was ready to be his husband in Holy Matrimony.

"So where are you from?" Mama asked, wiping tears from her eyes. Her voice cracked. She was trying to be courteous, and I appreciated that.

Jaden was uncomfortable. He wiped his mouth and said, "I am from Flint, Michigan."

"My parents were born there," Daddy implored, nearly whispering. His lips trembled and anger seeped all over his abstract face.

*Thanks, Dad for trying to hold a conversation. Even if your lips and true feelings have become useless elastic and the seams were breaking away.*

"Really?" Jaden said. "The food taste so good. Thank you for having me."

Jaden reached for the biscuits and Bruce Bruce pulled the huge bowl back, placing it by Daddy.

I said, "Bruce…" I shook my head. He nodded. He passed the biscuits.

"Never mind, I'm not hungry," Jaden said, clearly offended. He wiped his mouth and cleaned his hands.

"So how long has this been going on?" Daddy asked, his blunt side coming out.

"James," Mama warned, touching his hand. "Not here, not now. It's Easter."

"Jesus didn't rise from the dead to see my son fucking somebody in the ass. What the fuck is wrong with you, Son?"

I stood up. Jaden stood behind me, petrified.

"Dad. Please. Don't disrespect him."

*"This is my house!"*

I was getting pissed. "Right. Slap in the middle of the fucking projects. Whoopie! This rundown piece of shit with the burgeoning rat problem. You can keep this garbage! We can always leave your fucking house! My bags are in the trunk, maybe I should tell those big ass roaches in the guest bathroom to go get them."

Deeply offended, Mama stood up and back slapped me so hard I held my mouth.

"How dare you insult my home! We raised you in this house. It was all we could afford, Mr. So what you got a degree. That don't make you better than us, motherfucker! You better fucking cool it!"

*Mama I didn't mean to insult you. But Daddy is treading on thin ice and he better shut up before I crack into a pissy damn!*

"I know you're not going to trip," I spat icily, taking my degree from by her plate. The hell if her disrespectful ass will keep my goddamn hard work.

Daddy made one last desperate attempt.

"Son…"

"Daddy, you can't talk. All of your brothers are gay. And *you* were a bisexual man years ago, remember? Mama walked in on you fucking a man and you got the fucking gall to stand here, because you've been married for decades, and insult my lover. Because Mama forgave you don't mean shit to me!"

Daddy was defeated.

He walked around me and took Jaden by the arm. He pushed him so hard Jaden flew into the living room.

"Get your faggot ass outta my house!"

I went to my lover's aid. Mama held Daddy back and Bucky was reading scriptures aloud from the Bible.

"A family that prays together stays together doesn't work for this family," I told her, telling my man we were leaving.

"A Morehouse Faggot is in my house. Get the fuck out, you little bitch before I kill you," he warned and I rushed up to Daddy and punched him so hard in the face he fell back on the chair.

Mama grabbed me and I pushed her into the wall. I was pissed.

"You wanna insult my lover?" I asked, snatching him by the dress shirt. He was getting with me. Throwing a series of blows that failed to connect with my body.

"GET OUT! NOW!"

Elroy stamped down the hall, jumping on my back. "Get off my Daddy! We don't want that faggot in here!"

Mama was sobbing, falling to her knees. She hated any kind of drama.

"You raped me when I was thirteen, Daddy! How soon we forget! All of you know this shit! And now you throw stones!"

"SON! I didn't rape you!"

I released him. Jaden took me by the arm. Mama refused to look up.

Bruce Bruce was quiet and Bucky looked at my father.

"Yea, you did. Remember you got drunk. You and Mom had a fight. You wanted someone to talk to. You gripped the E&J bottle for dear life. I told you I was too young to fully understand grown up matters. You called me a pussy and you slapped me. You then pulled down my pants and you raped me on my fucking bed!"

Mama lashed out at Daddy. "You sick sonofabitch! And you have the nerve to jump on my child for being gay! YOU DID THIS TO MY SON! DIE!"

Mama ran past Daddy and he was behind her, calling me a compulsive liar.

"Jaden. Let's go," I said, Bucky grabbing my arm.

"Bucky. Let me go. Please. None of you will ever see me again!"

"You can't leave your family like this."

"Yes I can. Watch me."

"Baby," Jaden said and I held up my hand. He remained quiet. He was my bitch. I was the aggressor. What I say went at the moment when it came to my family.

If he didn't like it then he could fuck off too!

Bucky pleaded, gripping the Bible. "We are blood. Don't you turn your back on your family? Did you think you could waltz in here and lay 'I'm gay, my lover is here' on your family and not expect repercussions?"

Jaden said, "Baby. Bucky is right. I even warned you that now *wasn't* a good time, but you insisted and I love you so I went on with it…"

"I know…Damn, what have I started?"

"A war," Bruce Bruce said.

I hugged Bucky. "Take care. We're leaving for Georgia tonight."

"Call me. I'll keep you updated with what's going on here…Did your Dad really rape you?"

"Yes. Twice. And it wasn't a good feeling at all."

"Why didn't you say anything?"

"I did. I went to a lot of people in the family. But they didn't believe me so I let it go."

Bucky was shaking her head. "I hate him!"

I heard screaming from the kitchen and crashing sounds.

Frantically, I rushed past Bucky and my brother was on my trail. Bruce Bruce sprinted past me and I saw the knife plunging into Dad's arm. Mama was a beast.

"You raped my son? Your own son? Die, you evil bitch DIE! GO TO HELL YOU PERVERTED MOTHERFUCKKER!"

Before the knife plunged into his abdomen, Bruce Bruce grabbed Mama's hands and I wrapped my arms around Mama and she held me tight, openly sobbing, her snot soaking in my shirt.

"I'm so sorry, Baby! I didn't know he raped you! My own husband! I can't believe this is happening on Easter! Of all days! I'm so sorry! I failed you as a mother..."

"No, Ma. You didn't. It wasn't your fault."

"I could have protected you! I hate him! I want your father out of my fucking house tonight! Or I will shoot that bitch straight to Satan..."

Daddy, wrapping a towel around his upper arm, said, "I'll leave right now."

Mama snatched away from me and slapped him repeatedly. "You don't talk to me! You don't talk to my son! You are banned from ever coming around this family."

Daddy was angry. "OK, get over it. It was years ago. And we're married..."

"Ha! Get out!" She picked up another knife and ran at him and I grabbed her. She was trying to break free. I didn't realize how strong Mama was.

"If you show your face I will tell everybody in the continental U.S. you raped your own goddamn son you sour booty bitch! GET OUT!"

Dad left without another word.

I tell ya'. Life could be a challenging piece of shit. And the people benefiting from life's pot of air has become so goddamn predictable that one hadn't a choice but to have an alternative lifestyle.

I hated my other life. I couldn't stand it. If it had tits and a dick I would snatch the wig of that tranny and give it something valuable to use but I wasn't a creator.

In fact I couldn't create shit. The massive hell hole my life has spiraled into has since been expunged, but I haven't been vindicated because my heart holds me hostage inside a lifestyle that wasn't designed to benefit love and happiness. Just brief sexual encounters and the framework to playhouse with another man for a limited time only.

Let's be real. Being gay or bisexual or a transgendered individual or a Try-sexual (willing to try anything) has become so overrated no wonder reality TV has been on the constant up rise. The world tune in and watch grown up act worse than children for a million dollar prize, and by the time the I.R.S. take their cut you're lucky to have enough to buy a house.

To tell it bluntly, people were full of shit. Backstabbers comprised American families. I lost my father and brother when they found out I was gay.

They translated my outing as me wanting to be a "faggot," and that was not it.

Faggots were flamboyant little bitches who wanted to be women, yet couldn't stand the feel, look or scent of a woman.

I didn't care. Mama called the police on my father and reported that he raped me. And when they contacted me I denounced it, because it served no purpose.

What's done was done. I didn't have the desire to see my father going to prison. I would feel bad and guilty. He was drunk, and I knew I was making excuses for him but overall he was a good man and he did his best to raise me. I should have kept my big mouth closed. I shouldn't have allowed him to get under my skin. We all fell short of God's glory. Yet some of us would like to think we were closer to the sun than the rest of the world.

I should tell that to Mama. She was so distraught from me telling the police to back off that she drove up to Georgia unannounced, bammed on my door and when I answered she slapped me hard she started to sob again. It really ate her up that Daddy would rape me under the same roof she shared with him for 20 plus years.

With that being said, my asshole has gone through an evaluation then a stark devaluation. Jaden and I were married now and I regretted it. It wasn't the bells and whistles that I thought it was. We had a private ceremony at our apartment, in Savannah. Close friends supported us and Bucky drove up and offered her love. The instant we got our lives on track and I was enjoying coming home to fine ass Jaden I catch him sucking another man's dick in his office.

I stopped by to surprise him with his favorite Subway sandwich (with the cheese and meat balls), and I was the one who was surprised. Quietly I tip toed back to the main lobby, and drove home, crushed.

Men wanted me for one thing and, back when I was the Whore of Babylon's brother (in high school), I used to give them exactly what they wanted. I used to validate my life through sex. If I didn't get it how I wanted it then I figured he didn't want, desire of love me.

But being blinded by what you wanted and shunning what you needed have gotten me nothing but sleepless nights, expensive eating habits, a disruptive rise in my booze consumption, being intoxicated in the board room and pushing away the very people who have become my back bone.

With my rising grocery bill comes the rise in toilet paper because I have been friends with the Kohler commode for God knows how long.

I was on it now, trying to push myself to confront Jaden and make his ass move out.

I tried reading *Ebony* magazine while taking number 2 to number 19, but I couldn't focus. Leaving the termite-infested door open, I found myself eyeing my bed. I love my man, God I do. He has always given the best that he had, in ways Anita Baker wished she had. But her defunct ass was just that: defunct, and my man was my present and my future.

*Well, he used to be. But he cheated on me. How can I overlook his infidelity?*

If only I could look past my flaws we would be the happiest couple in the world. If only I could erase the image of him sucking his boss's dick we would be fine.

If only I could have shown up thirty minutes earlier to Jaden's office, I wouldn't have walked in on the biggest surprise of my life.
It took a few minutes for me to clean myself up, flushing the toilet. Spraying the bathroom with air freshener, I looked at Jaden as he walked into the room.

The same phony smile, like he didn't do anything.

His eyes sparkling, he walked up to me and said, "You've been on the toilet a lot, baby."

I washed my hands.

"Yea, appears so." I refused to look at my reflection.

"What's wrong?"

I hugged him. I cringed the instant his body touched mine.

And I lost my family over an unfaithful man. Big mistake.

"Nothing. How about a drink. I want to make you your famous strawberry daiquiri."

"Cool."

I was in the kitchen, using the blender to crush the ice and blend in the strawberry daiquiri mix. I poured in two glasses of Vodka, just what he liked, amongst other little treats.

When it was well blended, I turned off the blender and grabbed two fancy flute glasses. Pouring in the contents, I walked back to my bedroom, my dick swinging. I never wore clothes in the house.

Jaden was on the phone, laughing when I walked in the room. He looked at me and said, "All right, bruh. I gotta flex. Yea, whatever…Bye," and hung up the phone.

I was jealous. "Who was that?"

Jaden accepted the drink, staring at me quizzically. "You never questioned me."

"So answer it." I sat next to him, toying with the glass. I picked up the remote and turned on the TV.

"I was talking to Kevin."

"Who is that?"

"My boss."

"Your *boss*?" My brows rose. *He's talking to the man right in my goddamn face.*

"Yea. We were going over some…reports."

I was skeptical as hell. "Dealing with?"

"Nothing special, Baby. Anyways…" He drank some of the drink. "Yummy. It tastes good."

He leaned over and pinched my nipple. I stood up and sat on the sofa by the closet.

He sipped the drink again.

"What is it? You never got up and sat away from me. I can hardly keep your hands off me."

I rolled my eyes. "*That's* going to change."

He was confused. "Why?"

I took off my wedding ring and tossed it in the trash.

"WHY DID YOU DO THAT?" he exploded, jumping up to his feet.

I sat there nonchalantly.

I refused to lose my cool because if I did I would beat the bitch under the bed like he was a box of unworn shoes.

"I'm filing for a annulment."

"Why?"

"I need to get out of this relationship." I faked a yawn. He was getting angrier. Pacing the room like he wanted my head on a platter. After nine months of giving him head on the bed, the platter didn't seem like a bad idea.

"You're…" He held his stomach, sitting on the bed. "What is wrong with me?"

I smiled at him, grabbing my cigarettes from the little table in front of me. I extracted one, lighting it. Pulling on it hungrily, I could care less.

"What's wrong?"

"My stomach hurts."

"From what?"

"I don't know. Ow! It's getting worse."

"I know it is, baby," I said, tears falling down my face. "It's going to start burning…"

His face contorted, he lashed out at me, his hands gripping my neck.

He squeezed and squeezed but I didn't put up a fight because he was slowly dying.

The poison I put in the daiquiri worked faster than I thought.

For better or for worse, for richer or for poorer.

I meant those vows.

301 DAPHAROAH69

I have forsaken all others, even my family to love Jaden and to provide us a home.

I worked my ass off for it. Sometimes when I came home I didn't even have the energy to take a shower.

And 'til death does us part became a reality when I saw his boss's dick in his mouth. I imagined it now, as his grip on my neck dissipated. His eyes became devoid little creatures, mourning the ailment of dissolving pupils.

Eye stood up, sobbing into the air when his dead, lifeless body fell to the floor. I cringed with fear when I poured the gas throughout my house, the nauseating fumes engulfing my nose. I wouldn't go to jail for murdering the cheating, loose booty fucker. I splashed gas on memorable photos. Memories I would never see again. Memories I didn't want because he touched them and tarnished them with his whorish hands.

I put on a pair on basketball shorts and slides. I didn't desire to wear a shirt.

Dead inside, I lit my joint and tossed the match. Flames exploded from the floor behind me, snaking its way to the cut off stop at the front door. My gut instinct told me flames were devouring a body I used to enjoy, a body that was my wonderland, my loving playground. I would miss tagging that ass like monkey bars. Blowing smoke in the air I refused to look back at the aftermath.

Getting in my car, I turned the key in the ignition as flames started to tear through the roof. They were hungry, and they would feast on my college degree and the dead flesh of a man who wore my ring and promised to love me above all others.

He did not keep his word. He broke his vow. He signed that vow in blood when he signed his John Hancock on the marriage license.

The cost was his life.

Little bitch. Die.

After arriving at 14045 Abercorn Street, I parked in the Savannah Mall Parking Lot, cutting the engine. It was crowded on this Friday night. I let down the windows, the cool air blowing over my bare chest. I shook with fear, fear of being alone, fear of the unknown.

I didn't want to live without Jaden. But he made his choice, the day he sucked up his boss and came home and tried to hide it all. Why didn't I give him a chance to explain things? Why didn't I confront him with what I knew?

Was I afraid of the answer? Was I man enough to weather the response?

I would never know those answers. As I miserably sit in my Buick, watching a few patrons prance by, I told myself I didn't want to know the answers, either. Knowing them would defeat the purpose of life. My life. The reality show. The ones I say on TV. Only there wouldn't be any prize money for the I.R.S. to tap into.

*Oh, Jaden. I love you. I always will.*

Gun in my lap, tears staining my face like stained windows in the very church I enjoyed with my family last Easter. My hands trembled, puffing the last of the joint. I was high. Looking in the rear view mirror my eyes were redder than the love I had for Jaden. I love you, Baby. You were my search party. You found my heart and showed me a gorgeous man who wanted to be loved. And then you destroyed me when you gained your position.

*Daddy I love you…I forgive you…I really do.*

*Elroy, you will become a mighty fine guy when you get older. You can have all the girls, because I always wanted all the men.*

I picked up my cell and phoned Ma. She answered on the first ring.

I held in my grief. Didn't want to give away anything. It would spoil the surprise.

"Why are you calling? Are you ready to turn your father in?"

"I *love* you, Mama."

"That isn't what I asked you."

My pulse quickened. "I will always love you."

She was really quiet. "Baby…what's wrong?"

"I forgive Daddy. I forgive you, Mama. I forgive you for stabbing him when I told you he raped me. But there is something else I didn't tell you."

"What, baby. *Tell* me. You're scaring me. You don't sound like yourself."

"Your conscious must have failed you, because you forgot about something very important. And this is why I can't turn Daddy in to the authorities."

"What was that?"

"You told him to rape me…"

I heard her gasp through the phone.

I went on. "You told him. I remember very clearly. I heard you through the wall before he got drunk and came to my room. You were having a discussion. You told him you think I was gay and that he needed to come in my room and show me what it felt like to have a man. You wanted him to scare me away from the lifestyle, have you forgotten?"

"SHUT UP! I NEVER SAID THAT!"

"You were *adamant*. You told him to do that, Ma. You knew he was a gay male and you married him with conflicts a marriage and warm pussy could never alleviate. But you tried and you failed. Because of your instigating and speculations, that man raped me and you listened through the walls. I know you did. Because I smelled your perfume coming through the AC vents…"

"YOU ARE A LYING…"

*'Till death do us part.*

I raised the gun. And pulled the trigger. The explosive boom and the sparks ignited death through my body as the bullet sliced through my temple, and blood splattered all over the car.

I heard beeps. I heard soothing classical music. I felt relaxed. I couldn't feel anything. Was this heaven? Was this the white light? I couldn't see that light, though. But I was trapped in the darkness.

I slowly opened my eyes. I had on a gown. The room was padded. I was sitting in a wheel chair. I was thirsty, so I tried to stand up but nothing moved.

What was happening? A nurse came in the room. Her hair was blonde and her hair was swept away from her angelic face. She had devilish blue eyes.

"Hey. You're up. Time to take your pills."

She put them to my mouth.

*I don't wanna take any pills!*

I tried to tell her but gurgling sounds escaped my lips and I was stunned, trapped. I couldn't talk. Oh, God!

"Baby, what are you trying to say? You know you're paralyzed from your left arm down. You can't even talk. But I commend you on wanting to talk to me." She put the pills in my mouth. She held the cup of water up to my lips and I drank ferociously, water spilling into my gown.

"I meant to tell you something. Your parents are on their way to prison."

I was gurgling again.

"You tried to commit suicide. You wrote a note. Maybe you don't remember. In the note you talked about being raped. That your Mom initiated it. That you didn't mean to kill your lover for cheating on you. You have a court date. Your layer said you will plead guilty to insanity. You'll most likely get it and die in this mental institution."

She sat in a chair, turning on the TV. It was a porno tape. She locked the door.

"Now don't gurgle, young man. I work too much and my husband isn't hear to beat my pussy so I guess I gotta do it."

I was gurgling out of control. I couldn't feel anything, a prisoner of my mind.

"You shot yourself in the head and lived. Let's see if I live after I shoot this come."

She worked her pretty pussy and I wanted to puke. I hated the smell of a woman. I was gay. Get a clue, bitch. Those devilish eyes reminded me of Satan. God's most beautiful angel rebelling.

She stood up, looking at me. She was rubbing my lips, manipulating her clit. Her pretty titties were bouncing behind her Mickey Mouse uniform scrubs.

307 DAPHAROAH69

"Oh, shit. Damn. I'm about to come."

She raised her skirt, and used her hand to spread her pussy. She came in my face, the gooey liquid trailing my face like tears.

I was trying my best to move. I couldn't. Oh, God! Help me! Free me!

She licked her come from my face.

She gave a killer smile.

"You know what the punishment is for suicide? Hell. Burning for an eternity. You're burning now. Trapped in a paralyzed body. This is your hell in eternity." She kissed my lips. "And I get the pleasure of rubbing my pussy in your face four nights a week. I'm not worrying about you telling anyone. No one has time for your…psycho babbling!"

She laughed like a witch, grabbing the Bible from my nightstand.

She opened it and set it in my lap. She rubbed my head, leaving the room. The door closed behind her.

My eyes cast down to the highlighted biblical pages.

*The Epistle of Paul the Apostle to the*

# Galatians

*Verse 10. For as many as are the works of the law are under the curse: for it is written, Cursed is every one that continueth not in all things which are written in the book of the law to do them.*

# *Acronyms*

My daughter called the police on me. She had an attitude when they got there and being that I was her mother didn't move mountains with me because she was a grown little slut and I wasn't going to tolerate her sneaking guys in and out of my house when I was at work. I was a career woman and I didn't care what people had to say about me. But what she did just upset me.

I came home early because I was going through menopause and I was tired. My body wasn't what it used to be. I was 49 years old, paid my taxes and stayed to myself.

I noticed a car parked next to hers I had never seen before. She had a lot of women who came over to see her. She was very popular, considering she did hair so I figured she was hooking them up.

I come in the house and put my purse and keys on the dining table. Taking the bills from the wicker basket on the counter, I flipped through them. Light bill. Water bill. Chase Manhattan Mortgage bill.

I set the envelopes on the table and started for my room. I looked in on my daughter and my heart stopped. She was spread-eagled on the bed with a pretty young woman eating her pussy. I was disgusted. I couldn't stand lesbians and my daughter knew this. I was in shock. On the floor were two other girls. One got on her knees, bending over and the other put a dildo in her pussy and the other girl back backed up on the double ended thing and they slapped asses with the dildo in the middle. In both their pussies.

I stifled a scream. I held my neck, silently praying to God to save my child. I didn't raise a lesbian, and I had never molested my child. She had never been raped or anything. As a growing girl I kept my own child and sometimes took her to work with me. I didn't trust anyone around my daughter.

And now this. "WHAT THE FUCK IS GOING ON?" Was all I could say. Everyone froze. My daughter looked at me with her mouth open.

She didn't know what to say. She covered her body and her lover hid under the blanket. I saw her shaking.

"Oh my God! Ma!"

I ran at the girls on the floor. I snatched the short blonde one and pulled her up the hallway. My daughter was on my ass, trying to pull me off. I pushed her on the floor, ran to the back door and opened it. I screamed so loud, alarming my two pit bulls and they came running.

When my dogs thundered past me they ran at the sluts of Babylon. They ran out of the house in a screaming panic. My daughter stood in front of them and they whimpered, sitting on the floor.

"GET HER!" I screamed at them, slapping both their asses and they snapped at her, trying to tear her ass apart.

She told them, "Donna. Velma! SIT!"

They sat. Looking confused.

"GET HER!" I said.

They jumped at her, biting at her feet. She didn't flinch.

"SIT!"

They sat. Whimpering again. About to cry.

"GET HER!"

Again, the two bitches jumped at my daughter.

"SIT!" They sat. "OUT!" They ran out the back door and she closed it. She held up her hands, approaching me. "Ma, let me explain."

I was so hurt. I couldn't even look at her. She took her clothes from my couch and got dressed. I saw two skirts and a pair of pants and some blouses, which told me they started in my fucking living room and made their nasty, sick asses to her bedroom.

NOT IN MY HOUSE! I feel defiled in my own home.

She looked at me and I turned my back on her.

"Ma. It's not what you think. I was experimenting."

"With girls?"

"Men are creeps."

"Baby, that's not the way to go. Sleeping with women is not appeasing to God. I know men can be jerks. I've been married to one for years. He's on the way home now."

"Will you look at me, Ma?"

"No."

"Ma."

I faced her with tears falling down my face. She looked so beautiful I had paid $90 for her sow-in hair. It was long, curly with hints of red.

"How could you do this in my house? You could have gotten a hotel room. But you were in my home and you invited those whores in here."

"I apologize."

"That's not enough, darling. You broke my heart. I am disappointed in you."

She hugged me and I hugged her close. I inhaled her and I smelled hints of those other girls. I was angered all over again.

I pushed her off me and she pointed at me. "Ma, be for real. This started a long time ago. When I was young. I always loved girls. I hid it because you told me it was wrong so I had to pretend to like men. I tried to be with men as I got older but all they want is sex. They don't want emotions;

311 DAPHAROAH69

they don't know how to nurture a woman. Who better to understand a woman but a woman?"

"I'm about to kick your ass. You came in my house with filth and you must pay."

"You can't touch me."

I snatched her by the weave and was yanking it out. She was swinging at me and I kicked her in the shin. She was jumping up and down and I took the pillow off the couch and slammed it into her face. She flew over the chair.

She picked up the phone and called the police on me.

I looked at her and said, "When you hang up pack your shit you lesbian whore and get the fuck outta my house."

When they arrived it was a woman cop named Officer Dame and a short white male cop in plain clothes named Officer Droid.

"We got a call about an attack on a Rita Sanchez," said Officer Dame, looking at me and my daughter, her hair messed up, said, "That's her! She attacked me."

Officer Droid said, "Ma'am, and who are you in relation to Rita?"

"I'm her mother."

They seemed to back away. Yea, Rita. Mama was always right.

"She was having sex with women in my house and I came home and found them, naked, doing unspeakable things and I jumped on her dumb ass for disrespecting me!" The tears flowed and Officer Droid took my hand and told me to sit down. Officer Dame glared at my daughter and Rita said, "I called you. She hit me."

"I pay the bills here. You don't even have a job. Grow up. That's my hair in your head. I can snatch it all I want!"

"No you can't!"

"Yes I can! Officers, I still got the receipt. How can she press charges on me for ripping my hair out of her scalp? I didn't want her to have it anymore."

Officer Dame had a smirk on her face and she walked outside she stop herself from laughing.

Rita was heartbroken. Didn't turn out like she thought. She gotta remember that she was in my house. Rita said, "You can have your hair. And yes, I'll move out."

I looked at Officer Droid. "Escort her out of my house. She isn't to take anything out of here. I bought the bedroom suit, the clothes and her shoes. I bought her cell phone and her car in the driveway is in my name. I am reclaiming it."

"You can't do that!" she whined.

"Get out! Now! Or I will have you thrown out by the authorities. Go move with those whores and suck pussy until you burp bullshit."

I spun on my heel and went to my room, slamming the door closed.

I meant what I said.


When my husband came home he called Rita's name, like he always did.

I had cooked a meatloaf and some white rice and black beans. I opened the fridge and took out the pitcher of lemonade.

"Where is Rita?" he asked me. He set his brief case on the table. He was a lawyer and a damn good one.

"She moved out."

He smiled. "Finally? We can walk around naked and make love all over the place?"

He hugged me and I kissed him. I had to fix his plate. I couldn't bring myself to tell him that I kicked her out.

"Yes, it means that."

He said, "Yes!"

"Freedom!"

"Why is her car still here?"

"She said she wanted to try to do things on her own, without her parents. She said she won't be calling much, that she wants to discover America and find out what hard work is like."

He was pleased. "That's my girl."

I hugged him again and said, "Sit down. I'm about to fix your dinner."

"I bet it's good."

"You know my cooking is the best."

"Yes it is. That's why I love you."

"Because I can cook?"

"No. Because you helped me raise a mighty fine girl."

"I guess we did, huh?"

*I can never tell him that his little girl loves to eat pussy as much as he did.*

*I'll take it to my grave.*

I went down to the police station to see Officer Dame.

It took her a moment to come out to the front desk.

"How are you?"

I set my purse on the counter. "I'm fine. I need something."

"What is it?"

"I wanna put a restraining order out on my daughter Rita. I don't want her contacting me or her father, period. At least not right now."

"Come into my office."

When I got in there she said, "Why?"

"She's spoiled. And I guess that's my fault. Always doing things for her. But I don't tolerate lesbianism. I love all people, but I don't support it. Its time to show her tough love. She wants to be grown its time to show her that playing pretend grown up doesn't pay the bills."

"So this is a scare tactic?"

"Yes."

"I'll have it drawn up and served to her through the courts no later than Friday."

I shook her hand.

*One way or the other she will see things my way.*

That's what she thought. When she was trying to teach me a lesson. Come on, Mama. Eye was a hustler. Next time be careful who you tell your plans too, because the cop she told came and told me. Eye was secretly eating the cop's pussy on the low, since eye was a secret lesbian and let Mama think she was getting over on me.

Ok.

Eye guess she thought she had all the sense.

My name was Rita. I was 19 years old and I was ahead of my years. When I was nine Mama said I was a smart little bitch who was about buying candy just to sell it in school. She was just jealous.

While she begged a man for money I made money and was driving a Benz by the time I got in the tenth grade. A bitch always rode solo because I sucked dick solo to earn the funds.

Bitches talked. Yes. "She sucked dick to buy that car." Um, yea. Yet you sucked the same said dick for free and is still catching public transportation. Chile, Boo. Move on. Hmm. Real men stand up and the undercover punks sit the hell down. Because I'm tired of all these playah playah Niggahs running around with their fancy cars and drug money thinking they made the world go round. These niggahs ain't Obama, shit. A man that gets all the pussy ain't a secure man, he's an insecure, scared little bitch.

He always need a Ho in his face telling him he's the man, he's the shit and he has to test new pussy to see if his dick can do what it did to the previous cunt.

A secure man can get a bitch and keep a bitch long enough to fuck the hooker/cooker into a hooker in the sheets and a cooker when she washes them. He will buy her roses and massage her feet after a long day at work.

Good dick will tame any bitch.

There are geometric measurements to a woman's psyche when it comes to good dick.

From three to five inches she will make you stick to eating pussy. For 6-7 inches she will call over her lesbian lover and send your ass packing after you pay some bills.

From 8 to 9 inches a tight pussy, always-feel-it-in-her-gut bitch will praise the ground you walk on. Ten to 12 inches will make a bitch call you once, maybe twice a week.

She doesn't want shredded wheat for a pussy. Anything bigger than that reminds them of horses and bitches ain't having it. A thirteen inch dick is good to suck, not to fuck.

A secure man knows sex alone doesn't keep a bitch. And just as quickly as she transitioned from hooker/cooker to prominent wife she can divorce your ass and turn back into a hooker/cooker. Simple.

He will keep her nails done and those Asians dissecting the toes in hot water and sponge rubdowns. It kills me to think a man judges his worth by how wet he gets a pussy. Dumb motherfuckers.

Wake up, get up and stand up. Score cards don't equal intelligence.

But I'ma leave that alone because I'm sure I just pissed a Niggah off. If the shoe fit wear it. First off, if a bitch didn't like me don't speak to me.

317 DAPHAROAH69

I am not a phony bitch. If I know you don't like me and you speak I will snatch the wig outta your ass. I'ma real bitch.

I don't have fake nails and hair or get Botox injections. Bitches, sluts, dykes, married women and Ho's.

I got something to say.

You bitches work too much. I'm serious. Don't overwork yourselves. There's a way to get money and keep money without money making you strip at the clubs and clean your pussy juices off the silver poles.

I got some advice for all you bitches. Let's turn the word into an acronym and give it a meaning. Tupac said Never Ignorant Getting Goals Accomplished and I say B.I.T.C.H.E.S mean  Bitches Initiate The Cash Ho's Eat Shit! Yea, I said it. What, you Ho's can't whip my ass and you can't hold a candle to my wax, bitch.

And you don't have to listen to me if you don't want to. I don't know what makes author Zane thinks she has all the game. Bitch doesn't got it all. Some chicks think they got all the goddamn sense.

All the sense doesn't make dollars. All money isn't good money but what you do with it and how you earn it says a goddamn lot. That "Dear G-Spot" shit wasn't as spunky as "Addicted."

I am a real bitch. I wear my rings and flea market jewelry, I got about five different baby daddies with long dicks and good tongue and love fucking other Ho's while making me think (and telling me) I'm the only woman they needed.

They suck pussy like it's a dick and make my clit feel like a dick. There's nothing like a drunk man dropping it like its hot while eating your ass into remission.

I couldn't commit to these men because they loved Fingers in their assholes when I jacked them off and sucked them up.

Any man of mine taking an enema, finger or dick up the ass didn't have me as a woman, no Sir. My men had to be men.

I wanted them throwing a tantrum just to take a shit. Real men don't like anything in their assholes.

Not a finger stroke, not a tongue and damn sure no penetration.

I live in the heart of the ghetto and ghetto bitches know these things.

We have been getting over for years.

Get pregnant from a dumb ass man, have another kid and collect a check. Hey, definite money. And sometimes you can just ask the niggah for loot.

Men were irresponsible with money. They spent it on Playstation 3 and Madden 90 whatever seasonal games. They gave their money away, always looking for things to spend it on.

But if you want to improve your game and earn some cash then turn off the Home Shopping Network, this shit can't be bought.

Turn off Beyonce, she's about a dumb bitch, and listen to a real bitch.

You can't find this in a self-help book and you can't play a Whitney tune and lyrically sing it. No.

Fuck Ilyana Vanzant and turn off Oprah.

These bitches don't give a fuck about you, they just want a book sale and a rating.

Look at me.

There you go.

Damn it, turn off the *Lifetime Channel* also.

You don't have to watch Wife Swap to get knowledge about these brain dead men.

If you wanna dress in Chanel and Prada, spray Gucci perfume on your pussy and shower with the best body wash then you will follow my plan to the hilt and hope to cross the fucking T.

This type of game Adam and Eve has never heard of. Attention Attention, bitches listen up!

Never get a man's money *before* you suck his dick because if you don't suck it right, put your teeth all up and down the shaft, don't make him come soon he will ask for the money back.

Get the money after you make a man come because when you make him sing and pull your goddamn hair that motherfucker will give you his damn wallet.

Let's be real.

I examine the penis before the lips to dick contact. I check for bumps and scrapes. If I see a bump I call it a night. Take your ass home and don't return.

Make these men put a deposit down on conversation. Talking is money and hustlers and liars do it day in and day out, rain sleet or snow so get him to pay your phone bill and give you some cash just so you can look good. Tell him, "You want me to look cute don't you? You like that push up bra I wear? You like that Janet Feedback ponytail I wear, the one you be pulling on? Well, that shit cost money and my money is funnier than Katt Williams so help a bitch out."

I suck dick to pay my bills, pay my rent, pay my car note and to pay for my mama's day care.

That's all I wanna do and if a niggah got the medical plan part of the friends with benefits that's even better. My name is on seventeen different men's medical plans. I got my dental plans paid ten fold.

It's so bad I don't have to pay a co dependant fee. If I cancel, well, I don't have to pay that either. My body is my temple, my tits is the goddamn roof and my pussy is the basement and if you really wanna get jiggy with it my asshole is the drive way.

My lips are the sidewalk outlining the fortress and if a Niggah gets rowdy I would release my pits, meaning eat some beans before he gets there and fart in his face if he eats the pussy wrong and I'll call it a Blockbuster night.

# The
# P
# A
# I
# L
# Man:

**Taken from PHΛROΛH**
**The KING of Erotica's Autobiography**
**Doomsday: 6.26.20.10**
**Dapharoah69's 33rd Birthday**

Eye remember one day, when eye was a teenager, eye had just got off the school bus, going over to Chad's house. Eye was going to Southwood Middle School and hated it. Chad lived with Tanka, his auntie. He didn't come to school and eye was going to take him his homework.

Eye was walking through Perrine (wasn't far, about a ten minute walk) and eye passed a tall, burly man with a weather-beaten face. He was pulling up weeds in a rose garden. Eye knew he had to be a crack head. Crack heads were the only men digging up weeds on a flower garden, from what eye saw.

This man looked at me and said Psst…psst.

Eye looked at him like, "What?" with a look on my face like eye was breathing shit instead of air.

He raised a finger mid air, dropping the Hoe on the ground. Black ants scattered onto the sidewalk, and the smell of trees and grass gave me a slight head ache.

He had some dirty, filthy nails. My grandfather taught me to never befriend anyone with dirty nails and clean hands because they just dug outta some shit.

"Come here, Boy! And hand me that there pail with the rocks."

It was filled to the rim with rocks. Eye was tired, didn't feel like being another adult's goddamn slave. Shit, bad enough eye gotta go home and clean up.

Despite my inner voice screaming NOOOO eye got the pail. Eye was taught to never talk to strangers, but that was contradicted when mama said respect my elders.

And he gave me a direct order to get the pail of rocks. So eye had to respect the stranger and do what he said.

After putting my other book bag strap on my shoulder eye picked up the pail of rocks by the thin metal hook. Wasn't that heavy, thank God.

Eye looked up at him and he kept licking his lips all weird. His eyes narrowing momentarily.

"Something wrong with your tongue?" eye asked.

He grinned. "Naw, Son, Just that my lips are chapped. And dry."

"But its 95 degrees. Hot as hell. And you're sweating, it's all over your face."

"Eye'll pay you $5 to bring that pail to the house over yonder."

Eye looked at it. It was abandoned, and the windows were boarded up. All eye thought about was the money. Five dollars, shit eye could buy some stuff from the store and eat it in class.

Suddenly carrying the pail was a cinch.

Eye started to perspire. Eye was clad in a long sleeved gold and black shirt, business pants and shiny loafers grandpa ordered for me out of the JCPenny mag, since he claimed me on his income taxes. Eye always dressed nice for school. Eye was always a step ahead of my opponents by my style of dress while getting in education. Learning was serious business. That was real grown man shit, reading and writing and comprehending, and eye had to dress the part.

My friends and other students were too busy buying a gazillion pair of Nikes, in various colors and wearing flea market shit.

White man already wanted to reduce me to a state number back then, police always bothered the neighborhood kids, accusing us of peddling drugs for our parents so eye didn't need them in my face so eye stayed in school.

While eye was walking up to him he licking his "chapped" lips again, and he said, "Go on over to the house. Eye gotta build another garden for the people who are about to move in that house. Eye'll follow you, carrying my garden tools."

He's giving me directions while he walked behind me. Turn here, open the door. Sit the pail down.

I set it down, wanting my money. Eye opened the front door, sweating.

A huge spider web was across the top of the door.

"Take the pail to the back room. Its down the hall. The last door on the right."

It was kinda dark, the cracks in the board provided little light. Eye was cool with it. Eye would take the pail to the room, get money and go home.

Eye started walking down the hall and eye heard him closing the door.

325 DAPHAROAH69

It creaked as it closed. The house wasn't abandoned, but it was being built. From the looks of the installation and framed walls, it was in the final stages of being built.

So it wasn't abandoned.

When eye walked into the last room, it was very dark. Eye couldn't see my hands. Eye set the pail down and eye heard footsteps. Where did he want me to put the rocks? Its dark in here eye can't see. "Where's the lights?" Eye picked up the pail.

"Man eye want my money!" eye said, as something occurred to me.

He said he wanted me to carry the pail of rocks because he was going to carry his garden tools.

He never came to the house with anything in his hands.

Eye turned to face him. He was digging in his pocket. Good.

"Where is my five dollars?" eye asked, and he said, "RIGHT HERE!" and he punched me so hard in the face eye flew back on my ass.

Dropping the pail. Rocks everywhere.

Eye got up on my knees, attempting to stand up but eye was so scared and so nervous. "No! Oh, God no! Noo! No! Not again! God, no not again!" Eye screamed at the top of my lungs, my hands fists, adrenaline rushing to my head.

He pushed me further in the dark room.

Closing the door.

He grabbed me by the shirt, beating me in the back. He punched me. Over and over. It was so dark eye couldn't see. But eye felt and smelled him. Worse smell of my life.

He pulled down my pants…

To be continued.

Thank you for
Supporting The King of Erotica 6
Battle Plans


The King of Erotica book 7:
PHAROAH
My autobiography
Coming 6.26.2010
My 33rd Birthday